Don't Quit The Day Job

J. S. Cooper

Copyright © 2024 by J. S. Cooper

All rights reserved.

No part of this book may be reproduced in any form or by any electronic or mechanical means, including information storage and retrieval systems, without written permission from the author, except for the use of brief quotations in a book review.

This one is for the girls who wish they had a hot boss they could handcuff to a chair...

Blurb

Dear Grumpy Horrible Boss,

You suck as a lawyer. I don't even know how you passed the bar. Or how you sleep at night taking clients like Jack Whittington.

Just in case you didn't know, you can't fire me just because I have a part-time job working bachelor parties. What I do on the weekend is none of your business and not a part of my employment contract. If I want to go back to wearing coconut bikinis and popping out of cakes, I can.

As soon as I get my big break as an actress, I will be leaving your employ. I am literally counting down the days. You must be dreaming if you think I'm going to be working from 6 am to 9 pm for the next month just so you won't report me to HR. Go ahead and report me.

See if I care Mr. Wannabe hotshot playboy lawyer. You're not that hot and I do not want you.

Also, stop emailing me at night with lists of to-dos.
Your not very well paid assistant,
Lila Haversham
Lila,

I hope you can count to infinity because that's how many more days you're going to be working for me. If your acting is as good as your dancing, you're not going to be making it anytime soon.

Five words of advice: Don't quit your day job.

Your very well paid and handsome boss,

Max Spector

P.S. You've been given a new phone so we can communicate via text instead of email. Or, if you'd rather, we can communicate from my bed. I rather not christen that blowup mattress again.

P.P.S. I think your actions in the shower at the gym tell another story about how much you do or do not want me...care to drop the soap again?

Chapter One

Max

"We have two drink specials tonight, sir." The sultry blonde stares at me as she pushes her perky breasts toward me. She almost purrs as her green eyes attempt to seduce me. "Would you like to hear what they are?" She's leaning down so low that I can see she's not wearing a bra under her silver sequined top. The sight of her jiggling, glittery breasts should arouse me, but I'm frankly not interested in what she has to offer. Which is why I think that, of the three of us men sitting at the table, she's spent the last five minutes trying to garner my attention.

"Not particularly." I shake my head and stare back down at my phone. The blonde is attractive, but I'm not interested in any dalliances tonight. "I'd like a whiskey on the rocks."

"I wouldn't mind hearing." My law firm partner and friend, Remington Parker, leans forward with a flirtatious smile and the blonde turns her attention to him. I watch as she takes in his handsome face, tailored dark gray suit, black Italian leather shoes, and the $150,000 Patek Philippe watch that hangs nonchalantly on his wrist as if it were a five dollar shell bracelet he'd picked up on a beach in Bali.

"So the first drink is a special that I helped to name," she says proudly as she perches on the edge of the seat. Her eyes are bright as my other partner Kingston Chase also leans in as if she's about to impart the secrets of the world upon our trio. I tap my fingers impatiently against my phone screen as I wait for her to leave. The three of us are here to discuss business over drinks, not flirt up a storm with a sexy waitress that looks like she'd be happy to go home with any one of us.

"And the names are?" My tone is blunt, and I watch as Kingston and Remy exchange smirks. "We don't have all night, Ms...?"

"My name is Kitty." She throws her head back and runs her fingers across her lips in an attempt to be sexy. I try not to roll my eyes at her obvious attempts to bed one of us. "But I let my friends call me Pussy Cat."

"I bet you do," Remy chuckles and loosens his silky red tie. "I wouldn't mind calling you—"

"Remy, really?" I raise an eyebrow at him. "We have some cases to discuss," I remind him. As partners at one of the preeminent law firms in New York City, we always have work to discuss, but tonight is more important than most because I've been given notice that the Governor himself is paying close attention to the work that we did. Which can only mean one thing: he's eyeing one of us to be nominated for a judgeship. And if I have anything to say about it, it's going to be me.

"'The cases aren't going anywhere, Max." He shrugs and beams at Kitty. "Don't mind my partner, here. We're lawyers at a firm and he's eager to get back to work. You know what they say, you can take the lawyer out of the courtroom, but you can't take the law out of a lawyer's head."

Don't Quit The Day Job

"Ooh, lawyers." Kitty's eyes look like she just won the jackpot and I watch as she shifts onto Remy's lap. "I love lawyers."

"The name of the drink specials?" I clear my throat and remind her.

"Oh, yes." She giggles, running her hand up and down his thigh, and then, because she didn't seem to get the hint, she uses her other hand to rub my thigh. "The first special is called a cockwarmer."

"A what?" Kingston sputters on the water he's drinking and I can't help but smirk. Neither can Kitty. She knows what she's doing.

"A cockwarmer." She grins. "It's named after one of my most favorite activities as a submissive." She giggles and bats her eyelids. I have no idea what she's talking about, and while I'm curious to know the answer, I don't want to get into a discussion with her about it. I have no patience for inane banter and I certainly don't want to give her the impression that I'm interested in continuing the conversation. "It has tequila, and let's just say when you've had two of them, all you can think about is having your—"

"Three whiskeys on the rocks," I say firmly as I remove her hand from my thigh. My phone beeps and I see it's a message from my assistant. "Gentlemen, we really need to get down to business."

"You work too hard..." Kitty turns all of her attention to me. "You're too handsome to spend so much time focused on work. You need a lil pussy...cat to help relax you."

"And I'm guessing that pussy cat is you?" I lean back and look her over. The pouting red lips, the long blonde hair that screams of extensions, the green eyes with the heavy mascara, the glitter all over her cleavage. She was practically begging me to take her home for the night. And maybe if I were younger and less focused on the job, I'd give her everything I had for one night, but I'm just not interested. I've had enough meaningless sex to last me a lifetime. Not to say that I'm a monk or anything. I have three or four women on rotation that I call up if I'm feeling particularly horny, but I haven't actually gotten laid in three months. Not since Vanessa, an accountant I slept with a handful of times, told me she loved me and burst out crying when I told her that I wasn't going to fuck her without a condom. That incident had made me take a step back from casual sex. I really didn't need the drama.

"Let's just say that my mouth and my kitty make great warmers." She winks at me and I feel her hand moving up my thigh toward my crotch. She frowns as I grab her hand, push it away and jump up.

"I'm headed for a piss. Be a dear and grab the whiskeys." I turn around and head to the restroom, opening the text message from my assistant on the way. I've been waiting on her to get back to me for over two hours. She hadn't come in to work today and I'm in need of some memos being typed up and some discovery sent to opposing counsel for a case. I stop outside the door and lean against the wall, ignoring the sounds of people laughing and talking. I normally enjoy hanging out at The Owl and the Pussycat, but tonight I'm stressed out. A part of me wonders if I should bang Kitty just to release some pent-up energy, but I don't want to spend half the night listening to her talk before I get some. My hand can do just as good a job as her mouth in about a quarter of the time.

"**I quit. Effective immediately.**"

"Fucking stupid," I mumble under my breath as I see my assistant's text of resignation. "How unprofessional." I grip the phone and let out a deep sigh. I'm tense and I can feel the anxiety rolling down my back. I run my fingers through my silky hair and close my eyes for a few moments. I cannot believe that yet another assistant of mine has quit. I know I'm a difficult boss, but it's because I have goals. Though, sometimes I wonder if my goals are dictating my life. My eighteen-year-old younger sister, Marie, sure seems to think so and loves to tell me so at every opportunity. She thinks that I'm boring and wasting my life away and she wants to go to college in New York so she can live with me and try to set me up. She loves to boss me around like she's the sibling that is seventeen years older than the other.

I take a deep breath and head back to the table. I'm glad to see that Kitty has left the group, but the knowing glances on my partners' faces as I approach the table has me steeling my spine.

"Before you say a word, just know that my latest assistant just quit and I'm not in the mood."

"Shit, another one? Already?" Kingston raises a dark eyebrow. "What's that now? Five assistants in six months?"

"Something like that." I growl as I sit down. "Your last assistant quit as well, so it's not like you're batting any better."

"Mine quit because her husband got a job offer in Iceland." He smirks. "Yours quit because why?"

"Who knows?" I shrug, annoyed as I look around. "Where the hell is my drink?"

"You scared the poor kitty cat away." Remy chuckles as he pulls out his phone. "That's why you both need to get an assistant like mine. Dowdy and only interested in her dogs, or cats, or rabbits or whatever."

"He scares them away because he—" Kingston starts and I glare at him.

"I don't scare anyone away. I'm a great boss. It's not me,

it's them. I didn't realize I had to nurture these assistants like they were plants. But now that I do, I can guarantee that I will never have another assistant quit. It doesn't matter who they are. I can take anyone and teach them to be an amazing assistant and ensure that another one never quits."

"Never?" Remington laughs loudly, slapping his hand down onto his thigh. "Wait until I tell Gabriel." Gabriel is the fourth partner at the firm. Even though he isn't a named partner, he still has full equity.

"If HR had informed me they were hiring snowflakes, I would have—"

"Let's make a bet." Kingston grins as he opens up his cognac-brown leather wallet and pulls out a stack of hundred dollar bills and places them on the table. "I bet you a thousand dollars that your next assistant quits within one month."

"Oh, you're on..." I smirk.

"Wait, I'm not done." He grins. "You say you can take anyone and teach them to be an amazing assistant, right?"

"Yeah, don't you know who I am?" I nod slowly, wondering what I'm getting myself into. Kingston loves to bet about everything. If he were anyone else, I'd be worried he had a gambling problem, but I've known Kingston Chase since the first year of law school and the only issue he has is with commitment to anything other than work. In fact, all of us partners are dedicated to the law. That's why we all came together to start a firm a few years after we graduated law school and that's why now, seven years later, we have one of the most successful firms in the city. The law is our life and very little comes before our jobs.

I know none of us have great work-life balance, which Marie says will lead to an early grave, but right now, all that matters to each of us is becoming the *best* law firm. Forget

Don't Quit The Day Job

Skadden, forget Latham, Chase, Parker, and Spector are here to dominate.

"You're *the* Max Spector." Kingston winks at me. "Valedictorian of his high school class, graduated with a 4.2 GPA from Vanderbilt University, editor in chief of the Harvard Law Review, order of the coif, top ten sexiest single lawyer in New York City..."

"I'd say top three." I can't help but laugh.

"Perhaps, behind me and Remy..." He chuckles while flexing his biceps in a way that would make most people think he's a douche. "And I'd say Gabe comes before you as well."

"So I'm fourth then." I shrug. "I'll take it."

"So, Mr. Hot Shot, I say you have to hire the first person you meet tomorrow that comes to the job fair HR is holding tomorrow." He grins. "You can't look at age, gender, or experience. If you're so brilliant, any one of them will do."

"Is that it?" I shrug. "Anyone coming to a job fair at a law firm will have the requisite experience. And yes, I can turn any of them into the best assistant the firm has ever seen." I hold my hand out. "You're on. You may as well give me that grand now."

"I think not." He smirks. "They have to last at least a month before you see this cash."

"Are you going to hire the first person you see as well to be your new assistant?"

"No, I'm not crazy or full of myself." He smirks and his smile widens as he looks ahead of us. I turn to see Kitty sashaying back to us with a small tray filled with three glasses of whiskey. There's a thin smile on her lips as she makes eye contact with me and I can see that she's pulled her top down to expose even more cleavage. I can practically see her nipples. If she thinks that's going to make me want her, she really has never dealt with a man like me. I like the chase. The easier they come, the less I want them.

"So we're on?" Kingston offers his hand and we shake on it. "First applicant you see tomorrow is your new assistant."

"You're on." I lean back into the chair and try not to think of all the work I have to do later tonight. "You'll all be begging me to train your assistants next. Once you see how I can churn out the best assistants in the world."

"From the worst to the best." Remy shakes his head. "Now this I gotta see."

"Trust me when I say, my new assistant will be the envy of the legal community." I take my glass of whiskey and nod my thanks to Kitty before taking a long gulp.

I watch as a group of women to my right start singing and dancing to the pop song that is blasting out of the speaker behind them. They look as if they haven't got a care in the world as they shimmy their behinds and giggle. For a moment, I think about jumping up to go and dance with them, but I stay seated. As I always do.

Unbeknownst to everyone in my life, even Marie, there is a part of me that wants to be a bit more carefree, but that part never comes out. I don't have time to throw caution to the wind. I have a carefully planned trajectory for my life and I cannot let anything upend it.

Chapter Two

Lila

"You'll never have my heart, Rodrigo Alejandro Suarez." I clasp my hand to my chest and look to the right dramatically, my lips trembling in tortured emotion as my shoulder-length blonde hair bounces against my back. "I will never forgive you for sleeping with my sister." My voice catches and I blink rapidly, desperately trying to get tears to fall.

Zero tears fall. My eyes are drier than the Sahara Desert.

I pinch myself with my newly manicured pink nails and start again. "You'll never have my heart, Rodrigo Alejandro Suarez. I will never forgive you for sleeping with my sister. Just because I am a paralegal doesn't—."

"Your man slept with your sister?" The older lady sitting next to me on the train looks up from her phone. She speaks with a slight Southern twang, and I try to ignore how disgusted I feel as she chews her gum loudly and droplets of spit go flying everywhere. There's a look of pity in her blue eyes and I quickly shake my head.

"No, not at all." I smile to show her I'm not genuinely sad. "I don't even have a sister." I hold up the stack of half-crumpled pages in my hand. "I'm trying to memorize lines for my audition. It's for a TV show." I try to keep the excitement out of my voice. "It's a small role, but if it goes well, it could lead to more bookings at Telemundo." I sit back, trying to make myself comfortable on the cold plastic as it presses into my thighs. I knew I should have worn a longer skirt. There's also a distinct and unpleasant body odor in the carriage that I'm trying to ignore.

Riding the subway is not for the faint of heart. I stare down at my short navy shirt and bare skin and squeeze my thighs together. There's a man standing to the left of me, holding onto the pole, and he appears to be licking his lips as he stares at me.

"Oh..." The older woman scratches her nose and I look away as she digs into her nostril. "I was going to tell you to light his shit on fire. Burn it all to the ground." She's getting agitated now. "Don't let him get away with it!"

"It's not real." I say quickly as I glance back at her. Maybe it had been a mistake to rehearse on the train. "I think you misunderstood me. I'm an actress." I pause to wait for her to ask if I've been in anything she'd know or possibly mistake me for someone famous, but she just stares at me, no excitement or recognition in her eyes. "I'm just reciting my lines. See they're here on the page." I push the page toward her. "I'm not burning anything down. I don't even know a Rodrigo Alejandro Suarez."

"Aha..." She nods and offers me a huge wink. "And I don't know a Danny Johnson that lives in Florence, South Carolina. And officer, I sure don't know how his car got all them scratches on it after he fucked around on me at the strip bar."

"Uh, okay." I push my papers back into my handbag and look around the train. The blue-haired skateboard hippie on the other side of us appears to be listening to music on his phone, but I can see his lips twitch as he keeps glancing at us. He's eavesdropping.

Unless he's glancing at my handbag. It's a real Chanel bag that my best friend, Zara, got for me when I moved into my own place a couple weeks ago. I stand up and head to the doors so I can get off at the next exit. I'm not taking any chances that I'm about to be robbed. Or molested.

The man who was holding the pole is now closer to me and trying to look down my shirt. It's professional in that it's a shirt, but the top two buttons are undone and I know boobage is showing. But the outfit is for the role: Maria Conchita Violeta Estella Diaz. Maria is a professional, but she likes to appear sexy. I am neither a professional, nor naturally sexy. I wish I had the sassiness that permeates the character on the page. Though, I don't really like pervy men looking at me like I'm a piece of meat.

I really need to stop taking the 1 train, but it's not like I can afford cabs and my hopefully-soon-to-be skinny ass has no interest in walking the four miles from 121st Street and Amsterdam to 9th Ave and 31st Street, where the audition is being held, in the hot sun. It's an hour-and-a-half walk. In heels. Not going to happen. The next stop is Lincoln Center. I hesitate as the doors open. I'm supposed to get off at the Cathedral exit. I don't really want to walk any farther than I have to, but as I look around the train, I see both the sketchy perverted man adjusting himself as he stares at me and the skater kid who is *definitely* eyeing my bag and hurry off and onto the platform.

I'll just have to walk. And try not to die of exhaustion.

My phone rings as I head up the stairs and I smile when

I see it's Zara. I answer immediately. She'll know how to calm my nerves.

"Hey girl," I answer and take a deep breath as I get to the top of the stairs. "What's up?"

"Why do you sound so out of breath? Did you go running?"

"Did I get a lobotomy? No, of course I didn't go running." I join the throngs of people leaving the subway and make my way to the street. "Though, maybe I should start running so I can get into better shape." I take another deep breath. "I had to get off the train early and now I have to walk a billion blocks in those black heels I got on sale from Neiman Marcus and my feet are already killing me."

"Where are you off to?"

"My audition, remember?"

"Oh yeah, where you have to sing Ale-Ale-jandro to your cheating ex?" Zara's tone is light, but I know she wasn't impressed by the script.

"Zara, look, I'm telling you that even though the show isn't Shakespeare, it could lead me to getting a TV deal with Telemundo."

"But you don't speak any Spanish, Lila," she reminds me. "Why on Earth would they want you?" She stops abruptly. "Wait, that came out meaner than I intended. I just meant that..." Her voice trails off and I let her stew in her contrition for a few seconds before I burst out laughing.

"It's fine. I don't actually think I'll get the job. There's a job fair in the building next to the audition, so I'm going to hit that up as well. Find me a way to pay the rent on my gorgeous new place in Morningside Heights." I beam as I think of my 300 square-foot studio apartment. I only have an inflatable mattress so far, but I don't mind.

"Lila, you know that Jackson is more than willing to hire

you at his company..." she starts, but doesn't continue. She knows that I don't want any handouts from her new billionaire fiancé, Jackson Pruitt. He's hot and I love him for her, but I want to make my way on my own. Or at least try for more than three weeks before I give up and go running home with my tail between my legs.

"No thank you." I keep my tone pleasant because, even though I'm not willing, I'm still grateful for the offer. "I appreciate it, but—"

"But you don't like to take handouts and you want to make it on your own." Zara sounds like she's reciting lines from the Lila Haversham handbook. "I get it, so I won't offer again, but if you need anything, you better come to me."

"I will. I promise." I continue my way down the street and avert my eyes from the pastries enticing me from the French bakery I'm passing. What I wouldn't give for a *pain au raisin* and a double shot of espresso right now. However, I have neither the money to waste nor the time to give, as now that I'm walking to the audition, I will arrive about three minutes before schedule.

"You'll never ever ever have my heart again, Rodrigo Alejandro Swore...ah shit, what was it again?" A young woman with long fiery red hair and green eyes curses under her breath as she passes me. I watch as she grabs a page from her handbag and reads what appears to be the same script that I've been memorizing all morning.

"Hey, Zara, can I call you back later?" I whisper into the phone. "I need to concentrate on getting there."

"Sure thing. Break a leg, Lila."

"Thanks." I hang up and hurry to catch up to the redhead, who has now passed me, which is an admirable feat because she's in heels even higher than mine.

"Hi," I say as I step into sync with her. "Are you also

auditioning for the part of Maria?" I ask with a warm smile, hoping she is friendly and not combative like some of the other actors I've auditioned against.

"Yes, I am." She looks at me and I notice that her green eyes are in their own way just as fiery as her red hair. She's striking and reminds me of some sort of Scotch-Irish warrior woman. She would have fit right in with the cast of *Braveheart*. "I doubt I'll get it," she says, giggling, and I'm immediately warmed by the sound. "I know I don't look like the stereotypical Maria Conchita, and I can't even remember the lines, but it's all practice right?"

"I'm in the same boat," I say as I play with my blonde hair. "But an audition is an audition."

"That's what I was thinking. Plus, I'd love to be flown to Miami and put up in a hotel." She grins. "I need a vacation."

"What?" I blink at her in confusion. "Are they flying the cast out on a vacation?"

"No, but Telemundo's studio is in Miami," she explains patiently. "Whoever gets the job will have to relocate there for filming."

"Oh, I didn't realize that." I wrinkle my nose as I think about leaving New York and my brand-new apartment. "I don't know that I can relocate right now."

"You don't want a free trip?"

"I'd love a free trip." I laugh and hold out my hand awkwardly. "I'm Lila by the way, broke-ass actress by day and even broker actress by night."

"Nice to meet you, Lila. I'm Skye Redding, and if I'm honest, I'm not really an actress. I just thought that a couple of weeks in Miami sounded fun, so when I saw the audition call notice in the paper, I decided to give it a shot." She grins. "I really need to find a real job though. I have bills to pay and trips to fund."

"Ooh, where are you going?" I ask because I'm hopeful that Skye and I will become friends. Now that Zara is all loved up and spends most of her time with Jackson, I need to find some new friends or I'm going to wind up bored out of my mind.

"I'd love to backpack around the world." Her eyes light up. "Australia, New Zealand, England, France, Kenya, Peru." She sounds wistful. "It's been a dream of mine since I was a little kid. I just need to make a billion dollars first."

"I feel that." I nod as I take a deep breath and try to ignore the knot in my stomach, the one that always shows up when my mind turns to personal finances. "I just moved into my own place and need to start bringing in a paycheck ASAP."

"You just break up with a boyfriend?" Skye asks me, and I shake my head.

"I was living with my best friend and her sister, but they've moved on," I say. "I had a bit part in a play, but it got canceled."

"That sucks." She shoots me an apologetic smile. "Hopefully you get the role today."

"Aw, you're too sweet, but I doubt I will. There's a small hiring event at a law firm next door that I'm going to swing by, too. Always good to have a backup plan, right?" I play with my hair for a few moments. "I think the building houses several law firms as well, so maybe more than one is hiring."

"Ooh, maybe I'll go with you." Skye grins. "I need to make more money. The weekend work isn't paying as great as I hoped."

"What do you do on the weekend?" I ask. It's probably a nosy question, but Skye seems open, so what the heck.

"I work bachelor parties and other events." She looks me up and down. "I can get you in, if you want."

"Oh, no thanks." I say quickly. "I'm not—"

"We're not strippers or anything." She giggles. "We don't get naked. We just dance around and blindfold the groom or birthday boy. One of the girls also jumps out of a cake. The men love it. Some of them try to touch, but they know we're not for sale. I mean, some of the girls will give lap dances. But you don't have to and no one does anything more than that." She pauses and leans forward. "Well, aside from Louisa. I heard she gives blowjobs for five bucks."

My jaw drops as she giggles. "She's a hoe though. Buy her a drink and she'll be giving you a blowjob before the bartender's filled the glass. That's what they say at least." Skye shrugs as if to say, *you didn't hear it from me.*

"Oh, wow," I say, surprised at the turn in the conversation.

"She doesn't work with us anymore," Skye continues. "If you're interested, you can come to the bachelor party I'm working this weekend. We always need more girls."

"I don't think so." I shake my head. "I don't have the confidence for that kind of work."

"Can you dance?"

"I'm an okay dancer." I nod. "I took some classes for stage work. Ballet and tap though, not pole dancing." I make a face, then quickly backtrack. "Not that I'm judging you or anything," I say quickly. "I *wish* I had those skills."

"Oh, honey, I can't climb a pole to save my life." She grins. "The job isn't seedy like that. I think you might even enjoy the attention. Why don't you see how the audition goes and then let me know."

"Sounds good." I nod and sigh gratefully when I see we are only two blocks away from our destination. My heart starts racing as we get closer. I always get nervous about auditions. I know the odds of being cast are awful, but there's always a small hope in my heart that the next audition will be my breakout role. I've been acting since elementary school and have known since age ten that this is what I want to do with my life.

And it has nothing to do with becoming rich and famous. I just truly enjoy embodying the personality and emotions of fictional characters. I love interacting with my fellow actors and creating stories that audiences love. And while I'm still a long way from my first Oscar, I've already memorized my acceptance speech.

"We're here." Skye stops suddenly and makes a face, an expression halfway between disbelief and shock. I look to see what's gotten to her and my jaw drops as I see the line of women outside the tall gray building. There has to be at least a hundred different girls there, all lambasting Rodrigo Alejandro Suarez. Shit! I look at Skye, who is twirling a long curly red lock of hair around her finger and looking as nervous as I feel.

"I don't know about you," she says, frowning. "But I don't really want to wait hours to audition and not even get the part."

"Me either." My heart thuds as I survey the long line again. I'm no statistician, but I know my odds of beating out hundreds of other actresses are slim to none. Plus, the role called for waterworks and I couldn't cry on cue if my life depended on it. "Job fair?" I ask Skye and glance over at the tall skyscraper next door. The façade is made up of mirrors, and I have to admit, the way it reflects the buildings across the street looks cool, like it's calling to us. There's a large brass sign that reads Chase, Parker & Spector right at the top. "That's them." I say, pointing to the sign.

"Count me in," Skye says with a shrug.

"Hopefully they're the type of law firm that hires people that don't know the law," I offer.

"In the mail room, perhaps." Skye gives me a look. "They don't pay much in the mail room, but I heard attorneys make bank."

"I don't think I can get a job as an attorney," I giggle. "I didn't go to law school and I'm not Mike Ross. I don't have a photographic memory. I can't recite every case known to man."

"I loved *Suits*," Skye says excitedly. "But yeah, it would be hard to fake being an attorney long enough to start collecting the paychecks."

"I heard they are looking for paralegals and legal secretaries." I shrug. "I can type."

"But can you do legal research?"

"I can research. That's what Google is for." I wink at her. "Who's going to know if I go onto Reddit for some advice?"

"Hmm." Skye looks at her watch. "Wanna grab a coffee or should we go to the job fair first?"

"Let's go put in some applications, then grab something after." I beam at her. "I'm so glad I met you this morning."

"Me too. You have such good energy." She rubs her hands together. "I hope we both get amazing jobs. And hey, we're actresses-*ish*. If anyone can fake it 'til they make it, it's us."

"You got that right. If Maria Conchita Violeta Estella Diaz could get a prize for being the best paralegal at Ramos, Ramos & Ramos, even after her boyfriend was cheating, I can land a job with no boyfriend and no heartache." I laugh.

"I am most probably the best paralegal The City has never known."

"Yes, girl!" Skye lifts up her hand for a high-five and giggles when my hand comically misses the mark, glancing of her palm with a dull thud. "To being the best paralegals in The City," she says, still giggling.

We step toward the law firm and away from the audition and I plaster on the best smile I can muster to mask the disappointment that I feel at knowing that I've failed once again as an actress.

Chapter Three

Max

I am running late and the long crowd of young women lined up at the building next to mine threatens to make my bad mood even worse. I'm more irritated than is reasonable. Not that I care if I'm reasonable or not. I cannot believe my latest assistant quit and left me with unfinished work. She was totally unprofessional and I refuse to acknowledge that maybe I'm part of the reason she quit.

I've got two depositions and a new client meeting today and I don't have time to worry about the files making it to the opposition on time.

"Yes," I snap into my ringing phone as I pull it out of my pocket.

"Max, don't forget our bet." Kingston's smug voice grates on my nerves as I continue on my way. "First person you meet that tells you they are looking for a job with the firm."

"Yes," I say, annoyed that I'd made the bet. "How could I forget?" I listen to the sound of Kingston laughing and try not to roll my eyes. I sure hope there will be some good candidates.

"I am most probably the best paralegal this city has ever known." A sweet laugh catches my attention and I pause before walking through the doors of Chase, Parker & Spector. I watch as two women head my way, a blonde and a redhead, and smirk as I think about the last time I saw a blonde and a redhead. One was on her knees while the other one massaged my back. Good times.

"You are the best paralegal in the city." The redhead states to the blonde and my eyes narrow as I give the blonde a once over. She must notice my eyes on her because she glances at me, offers me a sweet smile, then looks away. Her blue eyes meet mine once again and I take in her pretty face and bright red lips. Her hair hangs around her shoulders and she's wearing an extremely short skirt and top. She may think she's the best paralegal in the city, but she's certainly not the most professional. She's most probably looking to find a husband.

I hold the door open for the women because, even though I'm judging them, I have manners. I'm a good Southern boy and my parents raised me to treat women with respect. You don't grow up in Aiken, South Carolina without becoming a gentleman.

"Thank you," the blonde says, smiling at me as I nod. The redhead says nothing, but she's too busy typing something on her phone to pay attention to me. "I'm not sure where we're going...let's ask at the front desk." The cute blonde says just before she drops a stack of white papers on the ground, sighs, then bends down to pick them up. My eyes follow her movement and take in her shapely ass and long, bare legs. She's hot, but dressed utterly unprofessionally for a law office.

"A quick word." I step forward and look the blonde over as she straightens up and stumbles slightly in her bright-red "fuck me" high heels.

"Yes?" She looks at me questioningly, her blue eyes are clear as the sky on a cloudless day and I watch as she looks me up and down. She seems to appreciate what she's seeing, if the slight curl to her lips is any indication.

"The best paralegal in the city would know better than to wear a skirt shorter than my little finger." I wiggle my right pinkly in front of her and her jaw drops in shock.

"What?" She gapes and blinks at the same time and I want to laugh. My comment is completely uncalled for, but I operate by an honesty policy, whether or not my opinions are asked for.

"Just saying." I shrug and smirk, and I think she's about to say something else, but she mumbles something indecipherable under her breath instead and presses her lips together. She glares at me, the slight flirtation in her gaze gone, does an about turn with her friend, and I watch as they walk to the receptionist.

I head to the elevator, my mind going to my first meeting of the day. It's with the CEO of a Fortune 500 company. He's recently been let go and wants me to negotiate a golden parachute deal so that he stays comfortable as they kick him out of the hatch door. I press the brass button of the elevator and look over at the blonde's legs again. I'm surprised to notice that she's turned back to look at me, and the hostility in her eyes makes me want to chuckle. She's still mad at my comment.

"Hey, Max." Kingston sounds amused. "Did I just hear someone in the background saying she's the best paralegal in the world?"

"Yeah, and?"

Don't Quit The Day Job

"Is she coming to our firm for a job?"

"I have no idea." I look over and stare at the two ladies, who are laughing about something. I'm surprised that neither one of them are looking back at me, checking me out.

"You should check. Because she may be your new assistant."

"I have no clue if she's even looking for a job." I purse my lips, very much doubting she'd make a good assistant, though I'm not going to tell him that.

"Then you should check..." He pauses. "Unless you don't think she'll last a month."

"I'll call you back." I hang up and take a deep breath. "What am I doing?" I mutter under my breath as I put my phone back into my pocket.

The elevator dings its arrival, but instead of going up to my office, I find myself walking over to the reception desk, curious as to where the two ladies are going. And if I'm honest, I really only care about the blonde. Maybe if she's lucky, I'll ask her out for a drink and let her sit her sweet little ass on my face for a night. Maybe. There's no way she's coming to get a job at my firm. No way I have to hire her. But she's the first woman that has stirred something in me in a long time. I'd take her out for a nice dinner before taking her back to my place.

"Hi, can you tell us how to get to Chase, Parker & Spector please?" The blonde asks the receptionist, and I freeze. She's coming to my office? Shit. This is not good. Not good at all.

"You can ask Mr. Spector." The receptionist gazes at me with pouted lips. Carmen has been trying to fuck me for the last six months, but I don't shit where I sleep. She's hot, but I'm not interested in having a stalker working in the lobby of my office. And I have a feeling that Carmen wouldn't be able to accept one night with me and move on with her life.

"Mr. Spector?" the redhead asks and looks back at me. Her green eyes widen in surprise, then change to a look of warmth. "Are you holding the job fair?"

"Oh, hell no," the blonde mumbles. She obviously doesn't intend for me to hear it, but I do. It looks like our World's Greatest Paralegal isn't so hot at keeping things confidential is she? Her eyes are spitting daggers at me as she turns around. Instead of acknowledging she's still upset with me, I offer them both a warm, wide smile. The blonde rolls her eyes and I give her a quick wink, because I know that will annoy her all the more.

"How can I help you both? Is there a reason you two legal superstars are coming to my office?" I signal them to the side of the large lobby and listen to the clackety clack of the blonde's heels against the white marble floor. They exchange "oh no" glances and I press my lips together. "Is there a—"

"We're going to the job fair." The blonde pushes her shoulders back, tilting her chin up at me, and I wait for the tongue lashing. She readjusts her black handbag and pats her hair back as I slowly nod. Something about her comment rings a bell in my brain. Fuck it, I'm in trouble. If I am honorable to the bet with Kingston, I should hire her, but everything in me screams that all she will do is make my life hell.

"To grace my law firm with the best paralegals in the land?" I tease, and the blonde's lips twitch. I quite like staring at her lips.

"I'll have you know that I, Maria Conchita Violeta Estella Diaz, was the best paralegal in all of Mexico City and now have taken the City of Angels by storm. Don't judge me by the heartache that Rodrigo Alejandro Suarez caused. Judge me by the work that I produce. Judge me by the cases I close. Judge me by the settlements I win. Judge me by the lawsuits I threaten..." She pauses and my jaw goes slack as tears form in her eyes. "You'll never have my heart, but—"

"What the hell?" I interrupt her as the redhead starts clapping. Had these two escaped from a facility recently? My heart starts racing. I cannot hire this nutcase. Even my small head thinks she's off. She's hot and there's something about her that glows, but I couldn't imagine working with her. I will have to lie and tell Kingston that I couldn't find the woman in the background that he heard because there is no way I'm hiring this nutcase.

"Oh, you need to go next door right now." The redhead sounds excited. "You're good. You're really good. You even have tears in your eyes."

"What is going on here?" I cross my arms in front of me. "Am I being punked?"

"No!" The blonde grasps her hand to her chest and throws her head up. A single tear falls down her cheek. "We're actresses by day, paralegals by nigh..." Her voice trails off and she makes a face. "Okay, I can't lie. I'm not a paralegal, never have been." She shrugs. "We were going to the auditions next door. You must have seen the lines of women?"

I nod and she continues.

"We both wanted to audition for the part of Maria, but the job fair only lasts for three hours and I really need to make some money and I couldn't even cry on the train, so I figured I wasn't going to get the role. Plus, I'm blonde." She holds up her hair and makes a face. "Not that Mexicans can't be blonde as well, but I just felt like maybe making sure I got a job was more important." She finally stops and takes a deep breath and offers me a warm smile. "Hope that makes sense."

I blink as I slowly shake my head. This overly talkative lady is crazy.

"So, let me start again. I was on the train practicing my lines and—"

"Lady, I don't care." I hold my hand up. "I think I get it. You are not really a paralegal. You were reciting lines to an audition you bailed on, so you're here at my firm, looking for a job."

"I mean, I don't even know who you are." She has the gall to roll her eyes at me, as if *I'm* the annoying one. As if she didn't just hear my name a minute ago. I stare at her with a supercilious tilt of my head. I want her to know that I know she's lying. When she blushes, I try to stop the smug grin from spreading across my face.

"I'm Max Spector, named partner of Chase, Parker & Spector. The law firm you're trying to get a job at." I look down at my Rolex. "And I have a meeting in thirty minutes I need to get ready for. You can follow me up in the elevator and I'll show you to HR." I head toward the elevators. "Also, if I were you, I would only apply for assistant positions. Paralegals don't win settlements and they sure as hell are not threatening to bring lawsuits...unless you are filing pro se."

She looks confused and I sigh loudly, wondering why I'm allowing this lady to distract me from my day. She has no business applying to work at a law firm. Especially not *my* law firm. There is no way I'm going to make her my new assistant.

"Unless you decide to bring the lawsuit for yourself," I clarify.

"Well, you don't have to worry about that," the blonde shoots back as the two women follow me to the elevator. "I'm only looking to be a part-time assistant so I can still continue to audition for roles." I wonder if she realizes she's not making herself sound like an ideal candidate.

"Sounds like you're our ideal candidate," I say with a straight face as we walk into the elevator. "Who doesn't love an employee that only cares about the job between auditions? I mean, imagine if you make it big, you can help promote the firm."

"What?" The blonde blinks at me suspiciously and presses her lips together. "I'll have you know that I'm a consummate professional."

"Oh, I don't doubt it." My phone beeps and I pull it out. It's from my former employee telling me she forgot to send me a memo about discovery on a multi-million dollar case. "If you hadn't quit, I would have fired you." I mutter under my breath. I am absolutely fed up with everything right now.

"Everything okay?" The blonde steps forward and lightly touches my shoulder. I glance into her wide, clear blue eyes and nod. She really is pretty. She has the looks to make it as an actress, that's for sure. "Anything I can do to help?" I stare at her for a few seconds. I'm about to make a crude comment, but I stop myself. There's something about the genuine warmth and concern in her face. She reminds me of a puppy, innocent and sweet. And then I picture Kingston's face and the bet we made. If I were an honorable man, I would hire the blonde. That was the deal I made. The first person I came into contact with looking for a job with the firm was to be my new assistant. Could I make her the envy of the legal community?

"How good are you at scheduling meetings, going

through documents with a fine-tooth comb, and thwarting the mechinations of eager women?" I ask, half-joking, wondering if I am really considering hiring this woman as my new assistant. She's goofy in a way I know will irritate me on a daily basis if I'm around her. I don't come to work to joke around. I come to work to win cases and make money. I'm trying to make a name for myself. I need to win big cases if I want to make it to the Supreme Court one day. My dad won't be able to say I walked away from the family business for nothing if I become a Supreme Court Justice. One of only nine. Clubs don't get more exclusive than that.

"I am great at scheduling meetings, I have an eagle-eye for detail in documents, and no eager women will ever find their way into your presence, other than me." She giggles and offers me an exaggerated wink as she flutters her hand back and forth in front of her face as if she needs air. Is this lady flirting with me? Seriously? I just basically offered her a job and she's flirting with me? My lips twitch as I watch her. Her friend is standing in the corner of the elevator gaping. Even she looks shocked that her friend is coming on so strong.

"Are you hitting on me, Ms. I'm-the-best-paralegal-in-the-world-but-really-a-wanna-be-actress?" I still have time to change my mind and walk away. Kingston will never know.

"Oh, you misunderstood me." She's blushing heavily now. "I didn't mean I'm an eager woman that wants to be in your presence, I just meant I'm a woman that would be in your presence. And also I'd be eager. To work you. I mean to work *for* you. I mean, yes, you're hot, but that doesn't mean I want to bed you. Can I say that here? Bed you? I mean, I have standards. Not that you're not up to the standard, but you'd have to admit you were a bit rude back there and I prefer my men to be romantic and sweet and woo me with flowers and chocolates and you rather seem like the sort of man that thinks handcuffs equal romance and while I'll admit that sometimes I'm up for some role-play, which is neither here nor there, by the way, it's not exactly the fantasy for most women. Not that I think you want to take me on a first date or care about my fantasies..." She stops and goes a bright red. "I mean, you got me. I do think role-playing as cop and criminal would be kinda hot, but..." She slaps her hand over her mouth and looks over at her friend, whose eyes are bulging now. I stare at the two women and laughter escapes me because this is the most ridiculous thing I've ever seen. And I don't hate it. This blonde is definitely never going to be paralegal of the year. She likely wouldn't even make a good assistant, but I've had the best assistants in the world assigned to me and *they* didn't last. What do I have to lose by hiring this woman? And maybe this is a good test to see if I really do have the skills to make anyone great at their job. I do love a challenge.

"You're hired," I say as the elevator dings and stops on my floor. "Follow me," I say, walking out and leading the two women down the corridor. I may have lost my mind, but the blonde is making me laugh harder than I've laughed in years and it feels good. Everyone needs some comic relief now and again. Maybe she won't be half bad. And if she is, I'll fire her. After a month. The bet was that she wouldn't quit, not that I wouldn't fire her. I won't be able to sleep with her though...as disappointing as that is. I don't cross that line with assistants.

I stop outside the HR office and nod toward the redhead. "You can fill out an application here, tell Wendy that Max Spector said you were to be hired today." I then turn toward the blonde. "Now you, come with me." I pause as I realize that I still don't know her name.

"Lila," she says, as if reading my mind. "Lila Haversham." She looks slightly shocked as she swallows hard. Her throat is long and slender and she's wearing a gold necklace with some sort of charm that I can't make out.

"Nice to meet you, Lila," I say, shaking her outstretched hand. "Just so you know, this is a full-time job and you won't be taking off for any auditions." I look her up and down, my eyes lingering on her cleavage as I take a visual photograph of her. "Unless we're doing some sort of role-play in my office, comprendo?" I grin at her. She frowns in confusion and I watch her freeze as her mind wonders if I'm saying what she thinks I'm saying. I want to snicker, but I pull out my phone instead and send Kingston a text message. **"I hired my new assistant and she's going to be absolutely amazing."** I hit send before I can stop myself. I don't often lie, but I'm not going to tell him that I think I may have hired the worst possible person for the job.

Chapter Four

Lila

A billion thoughts race through my mind. Is this hottie lawyer really flirting with me? And did he really just hire me? Am I now gainfully employed? Do I want to be gainfully employed by *him*?

Max Spector looks like bad news with his big, teasing blue eyes, dark hair, and navy-blue power suit. The man is the sort of handsome that has your panties off before you can say panties. The kind of handsome that gets you out of those practical Hanes numbers and straight into a slinky thong so you could make him rip it off with only his teeth. The very thought of Max's mouth against my ass is turning me on, far more than it should be.

"Sorry, what did you say?" I blink as I gaze at his expectant expression. I've completely forgotten what he just said because my mind was in the gutter. Working for him is definitely not a good idea.

"Shall I show you to my office so we can get ready for today's meetings?" His voice is smooth as whiskey and I shiver slightly at the knowing look in his eyes as he slowly bites down on his lip. Is this man a mind reader? Does he know that just a moment ago I was imagining his teeth in my asscheeks. "Lila?" he prompts, and I nod quickly.

Get your mind straight, Lila Haversham!

"Of course. I'd love to get straight to work, but don't I have to fill out some paperwork first?" I peer up at him, a sweet, innocent smile on my face. I am not going to let this guy know I'm taking mental snapshots to think about tonight when I go to bed.

"You can do it on your lunch break. I'll have HR bring the requisite forms to my office."

"Doesn't seem like much of a lunch break if I'm filling out W2s." I tilt my head to the side. "Also, I don't even know my salary."

"You didn't come to my office today to eat lunch. You came for a job." He folds his arms and looks like a stern teacher. "If you want this job, you have to understand that you're to work *all* hours. You can take the breaks you need, but this job may require you to work all hours."

"I don't know if I want it now." I step back and look into the HR office. "I might try my chances for another position."

"Then go ahead." He shrugs. "Go and join your friend and see what you qualify for." He turns around and my heart sinks. He takes two steps he turns and looks back at me. "The salary for this position is $150,000 a year, plus full health care, a ten percent match to your 401K, $25,000 a year allowance for education, and twenty-one days paid vacation." He smirks. "Or you can see what's behind door number two."

"One second," I say as I rush into the HR office. I can see that Max looks shocked. He probably thinks I'm a fool, but I'm not actually checking out other jobs. I need Skye's phone number. I don't often meet cool women in The City and I'm not going to let a potential new friend disappear out of my life. Skye is standing in a line behind two other women and I let out a huge sigh of relief. "Can I get your number?" I ask her as I hand her my phone. "We should hang out soon."

"Of course. You have to work these weekend parties with me too." She grins as she types in her number. "What's up with you and Max?" She looks at me with curious green eyes. "Do you know him?"

"Never met the man before in my life." I giggle. "But if he wants to offer me a job, I'm not going to say no."

"I thought he was going to ask you on a date. Or at least to a hotel for an hour or two."

"Skye!"

"*Sorry...*" She makes a face. "I didn't mean to offend you."

"Oh, I'm totally not offended." I lean in and lower my voice. "To be honest, if he asked me to go to a hotel for an hour or two, I may have said yes. Especially if he included room service and guaranteed me the time of my life." I press my lips together. "But it's probably better that he didn't, because I'd rather have a six-figure income than a one minute orgasm."

"He looks like he can give you five minutes at least." She giggles and I know at that moment that we will be friends for life. It's rare to meet someone that has your same sense of humor. "Here's your phone," she says as she hands it back to me. "Also, don't look now, but your new boss is standing at the door glaring at you."

"Good." I wink at her. "He's seeing who the real boss is." I laugh at her shocked expression. "Yeah, I might be getting fired before I even get my first paycheck." I give her a quick hug. "Nice meeting you, Skye, and good luck. Maybe we can grab a drink or dinner later this week?"

"Perfect." She nods and beams at me as she brushes back her long, red hair. There's an impish look on her face and I realize that she's even more stunning than I originally thought. "Oops, looks like your new boss getting impatient." She nods toward the entrance and I turn to see Max Spector standing there, glaring at me. Our eyes meet and I feel a frisson of excitement as I head toward him. I've barely known this man an hour and yet somehow feel like I've always known him.

"What are you doing, Ms. Haversham?" There's snark to his voice as I stop in front of him. "This is your first and last warning. While you're working for me, you're not to cavort with your friends."

"Uhm, I don't technically work for you yet. I didn't say whether I'm taking door number two yet. Also, I wasn't cavorting with friends. I literally only met Skye this morning as we were walking to the audition and I wanted to get her phone number because she seems like a cool person, unlike..." I let my voice trail off as I look him up and down. He raises a single eyebrow as his long silky lashes blink slowly. He's too handsome for his own good and I'm almost certain he knows what he does to women when he makes that smoldering face. His blue eyes are distracting me from being annoyed at his grumpy attitude. I can already tell that he's going to be a hard boss, but I'm a glutton for punishment. I love taking on hard tasks. In fact, the harder he is the better. I giggle at my dirty thought and his eyes narrow at me.

"What's so funny?" he asks, staring at me in a way that stops my breath for a few moments. He reminds me of an old-school movie star: distinguished and untouchable to the likes of me. Though, I could get lost in his ocean-blue eyes. I don't even love swimming, but I'd definitely take a dive into his waters. I have a feeling that even his stormy moods would find a way to carry me far away.

"Nothing. I'm ready to see my office now." I walk past him into the corridor and pointedly look at my watch, like I've been waiting on him the entire time. I look back, expecting him to tell me to get out of the building, but there's an amused expression in his eyes instead.

"You just met the redhead?" he asks in surprise, and I blink at him in confusion. For a brief moment, I wonder if he's asking about Skye because he's interested in her. Maybe he noticed how beautiful she is. Maybe he didn't hire her because he wanted to date her, and he thought it was unprofessional to date his assistant. Not that I would ever date someone like him.

I'm into hot, funny, goofy guys that like to run in the park and recite moonlit monologues to statues. I like men that like to eat ice cream for dinner and fries for breakfast.

Max Spector doesn't fit any of my wants—except that he is hot. Blazingly, smokingly hot. Okay, so he fits *one* of my wants. But just one.

And sure, I don't know him, but I can tell from the way his pinstriped, navy-blue suit fits him that he is a man that doesn't know the meaning of the word fun.

Plus, he's a lawyer. Lawyers are dull, boring, and full of themselves. And they never appreciate my sense of humor or respect the fact that I am fine making minimum wage so long as I can chase my thespian dreams.

"Yes, like I just said, we were walking to the audit—"

"You seemed like old friends." He cuts me off as he walks past me, and I follow him to a large office. He stands to the side and ushers me in. On the right side of the room are four large bookshelves with red and black books. "Law treatises." He smirks. "No Shakespeare here."

"I have my own Shakespeare books, I don't need yours." I tilt my head to the side. "And besides, I'm more of an Arthur Miller girl anyway."

"I speak my own sins: I cannot judge another. I have no tongue for it," he says smoothly, and my jaw drops.

"You know *The Crucible*?"

"I'm not just a pretty face." He winks and there's a twinkle in his eyes as he makes his way to his large oak desk. There's barely an empty space on the surface. Files and stacks of tabbed papers are spread everywhere. There's a desktop computer in the middle of the desk and an open laptop next to it. Max walks over to his black leather chair, takes a seat, picks up a folder, and starts reading. I stand there awkwardly wondering if I'm expected to grab a pad and pen and say I'm ready to take notes. Or maybe I should push all the folders onto the ground, delicately make my way to the top of the desk, undo a few buttons on my blouse, and say, "Take me." Max Spector does seem like the sort of man to get a joke, but then again, I don't want him to think I'm actually offering up the goods.

Which I might be.

But not really because I don't even know him and I'm a good girl.

Though I've been wanting to be bad for a long time.

A long time equaling the forty-five or so minutes I've known Max.

"Is there something I should—"

"So you're really not the best paralegal in the city," he says, sighing and sitting back. "If you were, you would know that I don't like being disturbed when I'm reading case files." His tone is full of judgment, and while I want to keep my mouth shut, I just can't. I hate condescending pricks. And just because he's offering me the largest salary I've ever earned, I'm not going to put up with his crap.

My dad always said, "Start as you intend to continue." I'm definitely not going to let Max Spector think he can talk down to me.

"You can't expect me to know the ins and outs of this office and how you like to work in one minute," I say. "I'm not a mind reader." I shoot him my best Lady-of-the-Manor stare. I know I'm in no position to take this tone, but I don't care. "I don't know what you expect of me. I don't even know the details of the job. You can either explain it to me, like a good boss would do, or I'm going back to HR to apply for a different job so I can work with someone that's not so much of an a..." My voice trails off as I silently reprimand myself. Calling my new boss an ass feels like a bridge too far, even for me.

"What were you just about to call me?" He puts his folder down and raises a single eyebrow. His lips appear to be twitching but I'm not sure if it's because he's pissed or amused.

"I was just saying that..." I pause again and cross my arms. "Are you going to tell me what you want me to do or are we just going to sit here chatting all day?"

"I think that—"

"Max, you busy? I need to talk to you about the Fabricant case." A gorgeous man with dark hair and vibrant blue eyes walks into the office as if he owns it. My heart thuds as I stare at him in his dark suit and crisp white shirt. He doesn't seem to notice me as he continues to the desk. "Sheila fucked up the settlement. I swear to God I'm going to fire her." He slams his hand on the desk and pauses when he sees the smirk on Max's face.

"And you thought *I* was bad." There's a pointed tone to Max's voice as he looks at me. "Kingston, have you met my new assistant, Lila? Lila, this is one of my partners, Kingston Chase." I watch as Kingston turns his perfectly sculpted face toward me and gives me a curt nod. His blue eyes are keen and they narrow as his gaze settles on me. I'm sure he's wondering how I got the job and it makes me blush.

"Nice to make your acquaintance." He steps forward and offers me a very warm and solid hand. "I missed your name in the stack of résumés I was handed earlier today." He looks toward Max. "I thought we were both going to—"

"I've already made my choice," Max cuts him off. "You can choose from the others. There are a lot of candidates in HR." He sits down again. "Trust me when I say I don't think you would have hired Lila."

"Excuse me?" I step toward him. "What does that mean? I'm highly capable and—"

"I didn't say you weren't. I just know that Kingston values experience, whereas I value more..." He pauses for a second and shoots me a look that I find hard to read. "Unconventional skills." I blush again and he continues. "What I'm saying is, I'm willing to give you a chance. God knows, my last few assistants have been shit, and they had years of previous experience in the legal field." He grins at me, looks me dead in the eye, and for some reason my heart feels like it has officially stopped. Shit, Max Spector is not only devastatingly handsome, he's legit approaching gorgeous. "So let's see what you have, eh, Maria?"

"I thought you said her name was Lila?" Kingston frowns slightly and Max just chortles in response. "I'm going to leave you both to get acquainted, but Max, please come and see me within the next hour. I have a call with opposing counsel early this afternoon and I think we might want to settle." He nods, then looks me over. He looks like he wants to start laughing and I'm not sure why.

"Sure," Max agrees. "Should we let Remy know as well? Wasn't Fabricant his client?"

"Yeah." Kingston strides out of office. "Tell him, will you? I'm headed to HR. Hopefully they've got some competent applicants this time."

"See? It could have been worse." Max chuckles as he steps toward me, his blue eyes bright with laughter. "I don't seem that bad now, do I?"

"Do you want the truth? Or would you rather I lie to you?" The words are out of my mouth before I can stop them. I swallow as he pauses in the doorway, leans back, and licks his lips slowly. His eyes narrow and he leans forward to whisper softly, "I don't think you want to know what I really want, Ms. Haversham. The thoughts in my mind are not suitable for innocent young actresses." He smirks and straightens up before reaching over to brush something off of my cheek. "Eyelash," he explains before turning and walking into the office.

I stand there in absolute shock. I am going to faint.

He touched me and that one brush of his fingertips made my heart explode and awakened sexual feelings in me that I didn't think could be awakened by a brief touch of a finger.

Max Spector is going to be trouble and I'm not sure I'm the smartest woman in the world for walking into his office, but then again, I never claimed to be Marie Curie.

I look around the office. Aside from the desk, it's pretty tidy. Plus, I don't see another desk, so at least that means I don't have to work in the same office as the man. Which is probably good because my body is giving me some seriously conflicting vibes about being around this guy.

And I need the paycheck more than I need hot sex on a desk.

Cause I have no doubt that the sex would be hot and that I would be so embarrassed that I wouldn't be able to go back into work again.

I debate running out of the office and going to the audition next door. I still have time. If I run out of money, I can swallow my pride and ask Zara and her billionaire fiancé for a loan. She'd give it to me in a heartbeat. Or I could ask my parents. They'd love that too much though. "Ready to grow up and give up that silly little dream, Lila?" That's what my dad would say. As if acting isn't my life. As if being on the stage isn't my everything.

"You're thinking about something." Max's voice is soft and I realize that he's standing right in front of me. I wonder if he thinks I'm fantasizing about him.

"Not you," I say quickly. "I'm dating someone. His name is Hank. He's an actor. He's amazing. We starred in a play together." My voice trails off as Max smirks. I don't know what possessed me to lie. It's not like Max is interested in me. And I'm for sure not interested in him. I do not do corporate men. No men in suits for me, unless I'm seeing them as research for an acting gig. Which this is not. Though the suit certainly fits him well. Really well. I wonder if he has a six-pack.

"As much as I'd like to know more about your love life, I'm a lawyer, not a therapist, and I have a call to take. A work call, just in case you get the idea that you can make personal calls to Wank while on the job."

"His name is Hank."

"Whatever. I don't care about your personal life, Ms. Haversham. I think you'll find that having a real job is nothing like the life of leisure you and Wank have been leading."

"I haven't been leading a life of leisure. I've been acting." I ignore his new name for Hank. This man is not going to make me lose my cool.

He stares at me with a blank expression. "Why don't you go and get me a black coffee and an everything bagel with lox and cream cheese from the deli on the corner?" He glides back to his seat and picks up a black phone on his desk. "I should be done with the call by the time you're back, and then we can go over your duties."

The sneer and disdain on his face make me want to ask him why he hired me in the first place, but I don't want to push my luck. Besides, I don't even care. The pay sounds amazing, and right now, money is all that matters.

As soon as I get my big break, I'll be able to tell Max Spector where he can stuff his everything bagel. I bet his eyes won't be so sparkling then.

"Yes, sir," I say in my best Cockney accent while giving him a small curtsey. "Is there anything else, sir? Shall I clean your shoes before I go as well? Or perhaps you would like a massage?" I rush over to the desk and stand behind him and squeeze his broad, firm shoulders. He tilts his head to look at me and the expression on his face makes me swallow hard. Max Spector doesn't look upset, like I'd expected. In fact, he looks amused and, if I am reading his face correctly, he also looks turned on.

Shit! I'm in trouble.

Chapter Five

Max

Lila is babbling about something in her fake English accent and the sane part of me knows that I should tell her I've made a mistake. She's far too impertinent and mouthy and I don't have time to make her the assistant that I need. I don't like those qualities in my assistants *or* my women; not that she will never be my woman. I need to get my mind and pants out of the gutter. I don't know why I'm so attracted to her. She is not my type, whatsoever.

A little birdy sounding just like Marie whispers in my brain that maybe what I need in my life is someone who isn't "my type," but I ignore the voice just like I ignore Marie when she talks her nonsense to me in person.

Even though every brain cell in my head harkens to be heard, I ignore the doubts. I'm normally a smart man who thinks out his every move, but this decision had been impetuous. Hiring Lila may have been a mistake. Bet or no bet, she is far too distracting and the fact that we had flirtatious banter is not a good sign. I do not do flirting and I sure as shit do not do banter.

Especially not with beautiful capricious women that I just hired to be my new assistant.

"I'm not English," she says suddenly, flapping her hands around again. She is far too animated for my liking, but I can't seem to get angry at her. "I mean, I daresay I have a relative somewhere that's from Great Britain, but don't we all?" She grins. "Actually, I heard we're all descended from this one African lady named Alice, I think. Isn't that cool? Though kinda creepy as well. How can we date at all if we're all related. Incest much?" She giggles again and her hand flies to her mouth. "Okay, maybe that's not a funny joke, but—"

"Lila." I hold my hand up. I don't know whether to laugh or cry. I know Kingston is already counting on winning the bet based on their first interaction. "Take a seat and be quiet. I have a call." I watch as she obediently sits down. At least she listens well.

"But what about the coffee?" she whispers, then shrugs as I glare at her and make my call. I turn my back on her and head toward the window and look out. I stare down at the line of women that has now grown even longer. I wonder why Lila decided not to go through with the audition. Did she think she wasn't good enough? I turn around to study her again. This woman who has cascaded into my life like an impromptu typhoon is quite unlike anyone I've ever met. Women like Lila Haversham do not attend Harvard Law School.

I watch as Lila fiddles with her fingers as she sits stiffly in the leather chair. I can tell by the expression on her face that she's not quite sure what to do. She's looking down at her lap, most probably embarrassed from all the nonsense she'd been spilling at me. I listen to the phone ringing and withhold a deep sigh. I hate to be left waiting. The call goes to voicemail and I hang up.

"If you want to go and get that coffee and bagel now, you can," I say, almost casually, but I know there's a command in the stilted manner I speak. I need to be alone to think about the decision I've made. I need to decide whether or not this has been one of the worst mistakes of my life.

She looks up at me, her blue eyes filled with an expression I can't quite read. It's a mix of annoyance and worry. As if she's pissed off at me. The thought makes my lips twitch. Like she has reason to be annoyed with me.

"So you want me to go and get the bagel and coffee now after all?" There's an inflection to her tone that makes me want to spank her, but I don't think she's quite ready for that walk on the wild side. I don't even think *I'm* ready for it yet, though I know I could be easily convinced. "Is that what you're saying?" The exasperation in her voice is ridiculous, as if she doesn't understand that this is, in fact, a part of her job.

"I do," I say. "Unless you need to babble on about something else in a bad accent."

She bites down on her lower lip and I try not to notice how pink and juicy they are. Something stirs in me but I ignore it. I know part of the reason I hired her is because she's attractive, but I don't normally hire assistants just because they're attractive. In fact, I hate to hire assistants based on looks because I don't want there to ever be any reason other than they just couldn't cut it for them to quit. Most women of a certain age like to shoot their shot with me and I'm just not interested in mixing business with pleasure, but for some reason, Lila has intrigued me enough to dismiss that concern.

"Are you going now?" I ask her as she stands up slowly. I stare down at the ticking hand on my Rolex, then lean back and gaze at her. Her skirt has ridden up, and if she were to shake once or twice, I'm pretty sure I'd be staring at her shapely ass.

Unfortunately, she pulls down her way-too-short skirt and holds her hand out. "Yes. I guess so."

"You want to shake my hand before you leave or what?"

"The money," she says, staring at me with daggers in her eyes. "You're going to give me money to buy the coffee and the bagel, right?"

"You don't think I'm good for it?" I smirk, looking around the office, and tap my fingers against the solid wood desk. I can't comprehend why I am playing these games with Lila, but I find that I'm enjoying myself.

"Well, I don't really know you like that," she says, shrugging, and I can't stop from laughing at the face that she makes. "I've watched enough Judge Judy episodes to know that you don't go spending your own money without a contract."

"Really Lila Haversham? You don't think you can trust me for a five dollar coffee and bagel?"

"I don't know any bagels with lox and cream cheese that cost five dollars." She wrinkles her nose. "Or perhaps, this is an alternate reality and we're not in 2024 and this isn't New York City."

"What reality would you like us to be in?" I wonder if she'll say the Stone Age. I wouldn't mind picking her up over my shoulder and carrying her into my cave. She brings out the alpha male in me, that is for sure.

"Hmm, maybe in the future, like 2200, where we all fly in cars and men feed me all day." She giggles and I realize I quite like the sound. It's feminine and sweet and authentic.

Much like her. The thought baffles me. I've never been drawn to a woman like this before.

"So are you going to give me money?" She clears her throat. "Because you're an attorney whose name is on the door and I am an assistant. I don't even know if my official title is that of legal assistant or personal assistant," she says, blinking at me like the differentiation matters tremendously. "Which one am I?"

"If you keep this up, you're not going to be either. At least not for me." I give her a pointed glance and rub my stomach. "Do you want this job?"

"Please don't fire me," she mumbles. "It really wouldn't make me feel good to get fired on my first day. Especially as it hasn't even been ten minutes since I got the job." She pauses. "Well, maybe it's been twenty minutes. I don't know."

I continue staring at her without saying a word.

"You're going to fire me, aren't you?" She sighs deeply and rubs her forehead. "Look, I know. I'm not the ideal assistant or the best paralegal in the world, and I talk too much, but I am a quick learner and I really need this job."

"You're not the best paralegal or assistant in *Manhattan*. In fact, you're not the best assistant in this building. Maybe I made a mistake in hiring you so quickly." I will not tell her that I never would have hired her if it hadn't been for the bet.

"I get it," she says, taking a step closer to me. "But you're the one that hired me knowing that I'm an actress, or wannabe actress, and I'm guessing that was because you saw my potential." Her eyes are beseeching as she pleads with me.

"Potential for what?" I let out a long sigh. "I mean, if you were really serious about becoming an actress, wouldn't you have gone to the audition?"

"So you're judging me now. You're saying that I gave up before I even started?"

"I didn't say that."

"But that's what you're thinking."

"No, I think that's what *you're* thinking," I counter. "Why didn't you go to the audition? You came all this way across town for it. Right?"

She blinks and nods slowly. "I couldn't cry," she finally says.

"What?"

"I couldn't cry." She sighs. "One of the lines, you have to be really emotive and cry and I couldn't get the tears out. It was like I'd never experienced heartbreak or hurt in my life. And trust me when I say I *have* experienced heartbreak and hurt. In fact, I was dating this guy that..." She pauses. "I guess you don't really want to know about him."

"Unless you're going to tell me some exciting story about how you were dating a dominant and you were submissive and it's a scintillating story, then no, I don't care to hear about it."

"What?" she says loudly, her hand clasping over her mouth a moment later.

"Why are you looking shocked now, Lila?" My patience is leaving me.

"Did you just ask me if I'm a submissive? Are you a dom?" Her jaw drops as she paces back and forth. "Oh my gosh. Is this going to be one of those moments where you pull out a contract and then ask me to get into some dom-sub relationship with you? Is that why you're offering to pay me so much money? Oh my, I cannot believe this. I thought

J. S. Cooper

that was something that only happened in books and movies and on Tiktok." Her eyes look me up and down like she's considering an offer I never made. I am about to kick her out of my office when she runs her hands down the side of her body and looks me up and down like she's actually excited about the idea.

I should tell her to leave my office.

But she's so cute.

She will only bring drama to my life.

But I want to see her without her skirt on.

She will not make a good assistant.

But she will make you laugh.

She will put me behind in my work.

But watching her ride you in the mirror would be hot as hell.

Fuck it, I'm in trouble. I have been since the moment I looked at her.

I hold my hand up. "I don't know what books you are reading or what movies you're watching, but I'm not pulling out any contract or asking you to be my sub." I snort slightly. "Though, it would be interesting to see if you could play that role well." My mind wonders what it would be like to have Lila as my submissive. I'd love to have her lying on a bed, tied to the headboard with handcuffs, while running a long feather down her naked body. I wonder if she's ticklish.

"What's that supposed to mean?" she asks indignantly, interrupting my sexy thoughts.

"I mean you haven't shut up since I met you and a good sub wouldn't be as mouthy as you." Not that I've ever had one. Though, there is something quite exciting about the idea of taking Lila to the top of the mountain and making her wait for release.

Don't Quit The Day Job

"So you're saying that you're a dom and you don't want me because you think I talk too much?" Her hands are on her hips now.

"I'm saying that I'm not a dom. I don't know why on Earth you think I am. I'm saying that if I *was* a dom, you would not be the partner I would want as a sub. I don't think you'd make a good sub." I pause for a few moments. "But considering that I don't think you'll make a great assistant either, maybe I am not thinking with my head today, anyway." I smirk. "At least not the right one."

She licks her lips nervously. "Okay. So you're not going to offer me a million dollars to sleep with you or anything?" She giggles slightly at my shocked look. "I take it you don't read any kinky romance books."

"I don't read kinky or non-kinky romance books, and no, I'm not going to offer you a million dollars to sleep with you." I take a couple of steps forward and look down at her face. "And you know why?"

"Why?" she says, blinking up at me. "Don't tell me. You're not attracted to me."

"No, I think you're very attractive, Miss Haversham." I smirk as she blushes.

"Then why?"

"Because I don't think I'd have to give you even *one* dollar to sleep with me," I say softly.

Her jaw drops and her eyes widen. I can see her pulse beating quickly in her throat. She licks her lips nervously and I lean down and blow in her ear.

"Or are you saying that your panties aren't extremely wet right now?"

I hear her sharp intake of breath as she glances up at me.

"What did you just say to me?"

"Well, I could repeat it, but I think we both know what I just said. I'm not going to offer you a million dollars for kinky sex. I'm not going to give you a contract saying that you'll be my sub and I'll be your dom. I have no plans to bend you over my desk and spank you or whatever happens in those romance books that you read. But if you want to fantasize about me and everything that I could do to you, go ahead. I'm sure you don't really need my permission."

"I'm not interested in you whatsoever, and I certainly would not fantasize about you. I told you I have a boyfriend," she says, blinking quickly. Her face is bright red now. "And he would not like the nature of this conversation."

"But he'd like you to take a million dollars for sleeping with me?".

"I never said I would take the million dollars. I was just wondering if you were going to offer me a million dollars."

"I'm not offering you anything, sweetheart. And we both know that if I did, you would definitely be taking it."

"You really think so?" She shakes her head vehemently. "You must be out of your mind because—"

"Because what? You don't find me attractive?"

I place my finger at the side of her face and run it along her jawline toward her lips. My thumb brushes her lower lip for two seconds before I push it into her mouth. She sucks it gently for a couple of seconds, then I pull it out and suck it myself, my eyes never leaving hers.

Then I step back and lick my lips as I lightly run my fingers down the side of her body. Her entire body is shaking, but as much as I want her, I'm not going to play the game. My phone is vibrating in my pocket and I know it's business related. I've spent too much time allowing Lila to engage me with inane conversation and I need to be focused on work.

"Are you going to go and get my coffee and bagel now? I don't want to give your boyfriend any more reasons to be nervous about you working for me." I smirk as I lick my lips and she blushes a deep red, probably feeling guilty that her panties are wet for another man. Because I can almost bet that she's drenched. I mean, I'm harder than I've been in months, so I know she has to be at least as affected as I am.

She blinks at me for a couple of seconds. I can tell she's in shock. I can tell she's probably wondering if she should even come back to the office. I grab my wallet and pull out a fifty dollar bill and hand it to her. "Feel free to get whatever you want as well and you can keep the change."

She nods without saying anything and heads toward the door. "Oh, and Lila," I call out after her.

She pauses and looks back at me. She still looks absolutely stunned. "Yes, Mr.," she mumbles. "Um."

"Don't tell me you forgot my name already."

"Of course not. You're Mr..." She looks frazzled.

"Spector," I remind her.

"Yes. Max Spector. I will go and get your coffee and your bagel right now." She stares at me for a couple of seconds and I can see she is completely dazed. "Were you going to say something else, Mr. Spector?"

"Ocean or faucet?" I ask her, and she frowns, not understanding my question. I decide not to push it and instead turn around. The morning has already reached the pinnacle of inappropriateness and I need to stop.

I don't know why some sort of horny college boy has taken over my brain. It must be that short skirt, those long legs, and that innocent, sexy smile that she gives me every couple of seconds.

"Nothing," I say with a shrug. "Just hurry because there's a meeting for all the new hires later today and I don't want you to miss it." I tap my fingers against the desk. "I need to ensure you're the best assistant this law firm has ever seen."

Chapter Six

Lila

My heart is racing as I take the elevator down to the lobby. Had Max Spector really just stuck his thumb in my mouth and then sucked it? It was the most sensual non-explicit interaction I've ever had in my life and I cannot wait to tell someone. I also can't believe I lied and told him I have a boyfriend. I'm not sure if it was to protect myself from him or to stop myself from dropping to my knees and telling him I wanted to see if he was as big as his attitude said he should be.

I wait until I leave the building before I pull my phone out and call Zara. She answers on the second ring. Thank God for good friends.

"How did it go?" Her voice is soft, and for a couple of seconds I wonder if she knows what's just happened between my new boss and me. Does she have ESP? Am I so horny that I'm sending out signals to the city at large that I just had a made-for-TV X-rated moment? Okay, so maybe not X-rated, but at least PG-13. Parents would not want their kids witnessing what just occurred between Max and I.

My face burns like I'm standing next to a fire. Way too close to the flames. Maybe I should see it as a warning that I'm out of my comfort zone, but I've never been one to stay in my lane. A part of the reason why I love acting is that I love the drama of it all; now that it's a part of my real life, I'm not sure how to feel.

Actually, that's a bit of a lie. I feel exhilarated.

I am finally living a life that is worthy of a daytime soap opera.

"How did you..." My voice trails off as it suddenly strikes me that she's talking about the audition and not my walk on the wild side.

"Oh, not well," I say quickly. For some reason, I feel embarrassed to tell Zara that I didn't go to the audition. I don't want her to know that I let my nerves and fear get the better of me. I really wanted to pursue my dream of acting full-time, but my low bank account balance means that I can't just give myself entirely to that endeavor.

I suppose that's a sign that I'm a real adult now. It's a cold slap in the face as I realize that my livelihood is completely on me now. I have no backup plan. I need to make money. And it's not like I'm the only person in the world with a boss that I'm unsure about.

"I'm so sorry, Lila. I'm sure you'll get the next one."

"Oh, I didn't even audition," I say quickly, not wanting to be duplicitous. She *is* my best friend, after all. "The line was tremendously long, like, over 100 girls, all of whom really seemed to know the part well and..."

"You didn't audition?" Zara is silent for a couple of seconds. "But you really wanted that role. You were so excited. What happened, Lila?"

Don't Quit The Day Job

"I just didn't think I was going to get it. And there was the job fair I wanted to go to and..." I pause. "I just figured it was smarter for me to try and get a job before trying to audition for a role I didn't think I was going to get."

"If this is about money, Lila, I told you I will—"

"No, Zara. No." I am emphatic. "I know you want to help me. I know that you want to be able to tell me that I can just focus on my acting. And as much as I would love that, a part of me would hate myself for it because I would feel like I didn't get there on my own. I would feel like I didn't—"

"But you were there for me," she says softly. "When I needed you, you were there."

"And you've paid me back tenfold," I say. "I'm in my own little apartment now." I pause. "And it's really great."

"Lila, I know you like I know the back of my hand," Zara says. "Do you want to come and live with me and—"

"No." I cut her off before she can finish. I know exactly what she's going to say, and while my life would be a lot easier, I know it isn't the path I want to take. Plus, I know Zara needs alone time with Jackson. They need to grow together without me all up in the business 24/7. No matter how much I miss her. "Yes, I'm lonely. I mean, I lived with you and Elise and the kids for ages, but I needed to take this step. I needed to be out in the real world by myself. I live in New York City and I've never really experienced everything there is to experience. I mean, we've had amazing times, but it was different, you know?"

"I know," she says softly, and I can hear slight disappointment in her tone. I know she misses me as much as I miss her. We were practically like twins for the last five years. It feels weird not waking up and chatting with her about life and goals and men. "I just worry about you."

"You don't need to worry about me. Trust me. If shit hits the fan and I can't pay my rent and I have nowhere to go, I will for sure be showing up on your doorstep."

"Okay," she says. "I love you."

"I love you too." I feel a bit emotional now. It's weird how much you can love a friend. And how much you can miss them when they no longer have a big role in your life. It's not like she's gone from my life, but now that she's engaged, she's moving forward. I'm no longer the first person she will come to about life events. It strikes me then that I feel a little bit heartbroken. I've never felt a bittersweet pain like this before. She's still in my life, but our relationship has shifted. "Guess what?" I lower my voice slightly because I don't want to be overheard by the other people walking down the street, just in case they know Max.

"What?" she asks excitedly, and I wonder if I'd been a bit too dramatic with my delivery.

"You are never going to believe this, but I am into something way over my head." I realize that my word choice is not optimal. I sound like a character in a movie that has just robbed a bank by mistake; if one can rob a bank by mistake, that is.

"What are you talking about?" She sounds confused.

"I got a job." My voice is still low.

"That's amazing! Congratulations, Lila. Wow. That was fast." She sounds more shocked than I feel. "Doing what, exactly?" she asks nervously, and I'm sure she's wondering if I'm somehow a paid escort or something and didn't realize it.

"It's at a law firm, but I kind of fucked up already."

"What do you mean you *kind of* fucked up? How can you fuck up in a couple of hours?" She pauses. "And what do you mean at a law firm? What are you doing at a law firm?"

"I'm an assistant to one of the partners." I say quickly. "But that's not how I fucked up."

"How did you fuck up, Lila?"

"I kind of asked my boss if he wanted to get into a dominant-submissive relationship with me." I know I'm being overdramatic. The conversation hadn't exactly gone that way, but in my brain it had been that bad.

"You did not." She screeches. "Oh my gosh, no way."

"I totally did. Well, I didn't say those words exactly, but I may or may not have made the point to ensure he knew I wasn't that kind of woman, I said that I wasn't interested in taking any offers for one night." I groan as the memories hit me. I can still picture the smug look on Max's handsome face as we'd spoken.

"Lila, what is going on? Did he offer you something to sleep with him for one night? Is that why he gave you the job?"

"He didn't offer me anything." I say quickly, "I just...he gets me so flustered." The fact of the matter is that the conversation hadn't been as bad as I was remembering, but...

"What do you mean he gets you flustered?" Zara sounds bemused. "Is this someone we know? Oh my gosh. You're not working for Hank, are you?" She says his name distastefully and I can't help but giggle. Hank is a guy I kind of went on a couple of dates with and made out with a couple of times. He's an actor that I met when we starred in a play together. He was extremely condescending to me and Zara had hated him. I hadn't really liked him that much either, but I thought if the play took off, well, it would be kind of cool if we were together. I had been wrong on all accounts. Being with him hadn't been cool and the play had been a dud. In fact, it had been canceled within a week.

"Lila." Zara sounds worried. "Please tell me you haven't let that weasel, Hank, worm his way back into your life."

"It's not Hank. His name is Max. Max Spector."

"Max?" she says slowly. "So you're working for an attorney named Max?" She pauses. "He's got you flustered and may or may not have offered you money to be his sub?"

"He didn't offer me anything." I groan. "Let's just say, I got caught up in a comment he made and maybe I overreacted and had verbal diarrhea, but trust me when I say, he's not into me like that. To be quite honest, I'm not even sure why he hired me."

"You're his assistant right? You didn't get hired as an attorney or anything."

"No! Of course not." I giggle. "Though, could you imagine how much money I'd be making? I'd be a baller, shot caller."

"Thank God for that. I didn't want to have to bail you out of jail for fraud. I know how you like to act sometimes, and I wasn't sure if you pretended you were an attorney to get a job. I could just picture you on the news and me standing by your side and—"

"My gosh, you have an overactive imagination, Zara," I say, though her concern isn't far from the truth. Max had heard me going on about being the best paralegal in The City. Though, he knew those had been only words from a script. "But no, I'm just his personal assistant. I'm not even his legal secretary or paralegal because I told him I don't really have experience and my number one concern in life is to be an actress."

There's silence on the other side of the phone. "And he hired you after hearing all that?"

"I know," I say. "I'm kind of in disbelief as well. That's why I said I'm not interested in being his submissive or signing any nondisclosure agreement for any sort of kinky goings-on. I don't really know why he hired me."

"You sure he's not trying to get into your pants?"

"No, but I doubt he'd need to hire me to try and get some. He's really good looking. Like, super tall, big blue amazing eyes that you could just take a deep dive and drown in. He has this dark blond silky hair that only models have. And he's tan and he's fit and...oh my gosh, I should quit, shouldn't I?" My stomach churns as I realize that I'm extremely attracted to Max Spector. He's an arrogant asshole, but there's also a spark to him that intrigues me.

"Well, you literally just got the job," she says. "So I don't even know if you have to quit. You can just not go back if you think there is more than a job offer going on here."

My heart thuds at the thought of never seeing Max again. "But I want to go back. I even met a really cool girl and she's most probably going to be working there as well."

"How did you meet a cool girl already?"

"Skye is her name and she was going to the audition, but she decided she didn't want to audition either because she also needed money. So she came with me to the law firm and she's also got me a weekend job so I don't even have to work at the law firm that long, even though I'll be dancing and popping out of cakes maybe, but—" I take a deep breath as the words tumble out of my mouth incoherently.

"Slow down, Lila. I have no idea what you're talking about. You're going to be popping out of cakes? For the law firm? Are you sure this is a real firm?"

"No," I say slowly. "My new friend Skye told me about another job she can help me to get. She works bachelor parties on the weekends and—"

"What? No way! You're not going to be a stripper. Lila,

I'm not going to let you be a stripper. I will make you take money from me and Jackson."

"No, she doesn't strip. We'd just dance around. It's nothing sordid, I promise." I cross my fingers behind my back because in all actuality I have no idea exactly what will occur, but I'm willing to try it at least once.

"How do you know it's not sordid? You've never even done it." Zara is too smart for her own good.

"Because I trust Skye and she said it's not dirty like that and you trust me and my intuition, right?"

"Yeah. What's trust got to do with anything though?"

"If I get to one of the parties and they're expecting me to give a naked lap dance, I will leave."

"But why do you even need to do this other job if you're working at a law firm now? I'm so confused."

"I'm working at the law firm because I need money and it pays well, but I don't really think I'm going to like the job because Max, my new boss, is really annoying. Even though he's good looking, he's really condescending and he already drives me up the wall."

"But you just met him."

"I know, but again, I don't know why he hired me. I think he thinks I'm crazy. But I really don't think he wants me for sex because I don't think he needs any woman for sex because he can get any woman wants."

"He's that good looking, huh?"

"He's gorgeous," I say, sighing. "Even better looking than Jackson or Ethan."

"Really?" She shakes her head in disbelief. "You think he's better looking than my very-good-looking fiancé?" She leans forward and raises her eyebrows while studying my face. I can tell that she's trying to figure out if I'm joking or not.

"I mean, yes, but that's why he's your fiancé and not mine."

"Touché," she says. "So you have no idea why he hired you?"

"I don't know why. Maybe he felt sorry for me, or maybe he's attracted to me a little, or maybe he really does want a dominant-submissive relationship with me and he's just not admitting it."

"Girl, you need to stop reading those romance books." Zara bursts out laughing. "Your mind is in the gutter."

"It's not my fault! It's TikTok. At least I'm not obsessing over a stalker or a serial killer that wants to make me his next victim/lover."

"Girl, I never understood why people would actually want a stalker. Like, what about this is romantic? Oh, is that you hiding behind my house and sneaking into my bathroom to watch me shower and killing every delivery man that comes to bring me food? No, I don't think that's weird. Thank you for loving me so much."

"Zara," I giggle. "You're awful."

"I just think standards for men have really gone downhill if that's what women want."

"It's not that we want that, we just don't want these fuckboys that seem to be occupying the dating pool these days."

"Not every sane man is a fuckboy, Lila."

"You're only saying that because you have the world's best boyfriend. Single women like me, we want an adventure. We want a fantasy. We want someone to grab us and pull us to the side of the room and run their fingers down our bodies and kiss our necks, and—" I pause as I realize that there's an old man walking next to me who is obviously listening to my conversation.

He winks and flicks something off of his top lip before saying, "I'll kiss you all over, Kiki."

I blush and shake my head before quickening my step. "Anyway, maybe I shouldn't be having this conversation as I'm walking down the street."

"Why are you walking down the street if you just got a new job?" Zara's back to sounding confused.

"Because my boss wants me to get him a bagel and a coffee."

"What?"

"He says it's part of the job." I wrinkle my nose. "He was kinda rude, if I'm honest, but then again I was going on a bit about my audition and then accusing him of wanting me to sign an NDA and have his wicked way with me." I pause. "I'm kind of a hot mess, right now, Zara. What am I doing with my life?" I wail. All of a sudden I feel like my life is spiraling out of control. "What am I doing? Is this all a big mistake?" I bite down on my lip and stop next to a light pole and lean against it. My breath is coming quickly and I realize that I'm having a mini anxiety attack. Everything in my life has been changing so quickly and I feel like I'm completely in over my head. I'm not used to so much change so quickly.

"I feel lost, Zara." My voice cracks. "What am I doing?"

"Where are you? Do you want me to come and get you?" She sounds concerned. "Lila, you are not alone. Please, let me be here for you."

"I'm okay." I take a couple of deep breaths and blink away the tears threatening to form. "I am overwhelmed, but also a little excited. I have no idea what I have to be excited about, but I am. Why am I such a hot mess?"

"What would life be like if we weren't hot messes?" she asks softly, and I can tell she's still worried. "So you think this Max guy is cute, huh? Because I have to believe that's the main reason you've decided to take this job."

I want to deny it, but I can't.

"He's really cute. But it would be totally unprofessional of me to date him, or even sleep with him."

"So you're already thinking of doing the dirty with him?"

"I mean I would be lying if I said it hadn't crossed my mind that he would be amazing in bed." I lick my lips as I whisper. "But he's my boss and he's totally inappropriate. And—"

"Girl, he may be your boss, but you don't think you're going to be working there for long, why not have some fun?"

"I totally cannot come on to this man. It would be so wrong."

"See if he comes on to you."

"I mean, he was looking at my legs a lot and I noticed him checking out my chest."

"Well, who wouldn't? You're gorgeous, Lila."

"Do you think it would be absolutely crazy of me to seduce him?"

"Um no. It would be crazy of you to seduce him if you actually wanted to keep this job forever. But you don't. Why not have some fun with it?" She pauses. "As long as you know what you're getting yourself into."

"What do you mean?"

"Only do this if you're just looking for a good time."

"You know I'm not the sort of girl that just looks for a good time, Zara." I sigh. "Though, I don't think Max looks for anything other than a good time."

"I think you just need to get out there and have some fun."

"So you're saying I should seduce my new boss?" I grin into the phone. The possibility sounds fun. I've never actually set out to seduce anyone, but then again, I've never had the instant attraction that I do with Max. I'm just not sure that I would be successful at it.

"I'm saying if the opportunity presents itself for you to have fun *and* make a little money, then you should do it."

"Even if he annoys the shit out of me?"

"If you want to get him to shut up, sleeping with him is certainly one way to make it happen," she says, laughing.

"I think he wants to get *me* to shut up. He will not know what's coming. I might be way too much for him. You should have seen the way he looked at me when I was like, 'I'm not going to sign the NDA to sleep with you.' He thinks I'm crazy."

"But he hired you. Maybe he wants a little bit of crazy in his life."

"Maybe," I say and think back to the events of the morning. "There's obviously something about me that he finds intriguing, right?"

"Girl, there has to be. Maybe he's looking for you to rock his world. I think every man needs his world rocked every now and again. You just have to make sure to protect your heart. You have to know exactly what it is you're looking for from him. Because you know how men can be."

"What do you mean?"

"I mean, he might want some sex, but it doesn't mean it's going to lead to a relationship."

"Oh, I don't want a relationship with him. He would get on every one of my last nerves. He seems like he's so serious and full of himself. And you know, as an actress, I need to be with a creative man that stimulates me, not some boring attorney."

"Hmm, but you want to sleep with a boring attorney and have boring vanilla sex?"

"He's hot and his eyes are smoldering. Maybe Mr. Vanilla can still rock my world. I mean, if I decide to go for it. I'll see how I feel after a few days of working for him."

"So is that his nickname then?" Zara asks. "Mr. Vanilla?"

"Why not?" I ask, thinking of Max's muscular body. It's a better nickname than "Sex On Legs," and one that won't make me want to picture him without clothes on half of the time. "Anyway, I better go. I'm sure he's waiting on his coffee and bagel and I don't need to get fired on my first day. Talk to you later, Zara."

Chapter Seven

Max

"Should I fire Lila Haversham?" I stare at the thick black ink at the top of the yellow legal pad. I've created a list of pros and cons for whether or not I should rid myself of this unnecessary distraction. The pro list consists of: 1. Win the bet 2. She's fun to flirt with and fluster 3. She's extremely sexy.

Though her being extremely sexy was also on the con list as well. I tap the pen against the pad as my mind wanders and my head jolts up when I realize someone has been rapping on the door.

"Hey, Max, can we talk?" There's another loud knock on the door and I see Kingston is standing there with a smirk on his face. Remy is behind him with an amused expression on his face as well. I fold over the pages on the legal pad and drop the pen onto the desk. The last thing I need is for these two to realize how conflicted I feel about hiring Lila.

"Sure. What is it?" I ask, ushering them in. I watch as Kingston looks around the room as if searching for something or someone and roll my eyes. "Is there something you're looking for?" I already know the answer.

"Yeah. Your new sexy smartass assistant." Kingston winks as he looks over at Remington. "Dude, Max has lost the bet. He hired the most kooky—"

"She's not kooky," I say, defending Lila even though she most certainly is the kookiest woman I've ever met in my life. "And you shouldn't be calling her sexy." I glare at him for being unprofessional. It requires some mental gymnastics to convince myself that I'm not being hypocritical, but I pull it off.

"Hey, I suppose you're right there. I don't know her like you do," Kingston says, shrugging, a glint in his eyes as he smirks, that knowing look annoying the shit out of me. "I mean, you certainly know her well enough to know she's not as kooky as a one-eyed flamingo, right?"

"What's your point, Kingston?"

"I'm just checking to see if you're sure she's the right assistant for you." He grins. "Wouldn't want her filing all your cases to the Court of Appeals or anything."

"What do you mean, am I sure she's the right assistant for me?" I ignore the latter part of his comment. He's trying to rile me up, but I won't let him.

Kingston doesn't take the bait. He and I were both on the debate team in college and he knows better than to let banal side chatter derail him from his path. "Just checking if you think she's going to last a month." He grins again in that cocky way that would have a lesser man ready to fight. "Remember, she can't quit and you can't fire her or you lose." He counts off the pertinent clauses of the bet on his fingers and I rue the day I ever let him convince me to go along with his immaturity. We were far too old to be caught up in workplace shenanigans.

"She will last a lot longer than a month." I say dryly, though the thud in the back of my head makes me nervous. I wonder how much extra work I'm giving myself just to win this bet. I wonder if I can hire a second assistant to take up the slack, but I know that would not be in the spirit of the bet.

"Guess that means you don't want to bang her then?"

"Really, Kingston?" I glare at him with narrowed eyes. Is he interested in Lila? Is he checking to see if I'm interested in order to figure out if he can try and date her? The thought irritates me. "I'm a professional."

"You are a professional player. I also know it's been a long time since you've dipped your quill into any ink."

"Since I've what?" I stand up, adjust my tie, then tap my fingers against my upper thigh. I ignore Remy's laughter. Of course he's loving the exchange. He's probably hoping we'll create a makeshift ring and start throwing punches. The man lives for drama. "What quill and ink? Did I go back in time and not know it? Am I the reincarnation of William Shakespeare? Double double, toil and trouble, fire burn and cauldron bubble."

"You know what I'm saying, Macbeth."

"If you're trying to imply that it's been a long time since I've had sex, you're very mistaken." I run my fingers through my hair nonchalantly and sneer. Marie would say that we were facing off like roosters, trying to show our dominance over each other. She's too young to understand that sometimes men rile each other up without there being animosity or competition. Kingston is my best friend and I know he loves to tease me.

"No, I'm not trying to imply that it's been a long time since you've had sex. I'm trying to imply that it's been a long time since you've had sex with someone that you've known for more than forty-eight hours."

I stare at him. "And your point is what, exactly?"

"My point being; you fuck for the night and then you leave. You don't have any sort of lasting relationships. So if you fuck your new assistant, I don't see her staying in the job very long." He snorts. "And then I win. So I'm just saying I see several paths to a win for me."

"She's my *assistant*. I'm a professional. I have no interest in her like that. And I will very much prove to you that I can take anyone and make them great assistants. Even so-called *kooky* women." I cross my arms. "Which she is not." I hope.

"This I have to see."

"You will see, and then you will eat your words."

"I suppose I was wrong in assuming that you had the hots for her. I hope that you don't want to hook up with her, because I'm pretty sure she won't be able to continue working with you if you subject her to your weekend special."

"Ah, the infamous Max Spector Special." Remy laughs as if he's at the greatest comedy show he's ever been to. Dickhead.

"I'm not going to hook up with my assistant," I say, my tone sharp with irritation, which only serves to make the two men grin even harder. I stare down at my watch, then back at them. "Is that all you guys came in here for? Because I have work to do." I snap my fingers. "I have money to make, billables to exceed. The associates want to see their partners working as hard as them."

"Because we don't work hard." Kingston rolls his steely gray-blue eyes and tousles his dark hair. The man could have been a model and he knows it.

"Look, I don't even know what's going on right now,"

Remy holds his hands up. "Kingston told me that we all needed to have a conversation about something."

"So what's the conversation about, Kingston? I have a call. Actually, I have several calls and I have to file a motion to—"

"There's a point for us all being here. Remember Jack Whittington?" Kingston says, his tone suddenly serious.

I stare at him for a couple of seconds, trying to place the name. "Not really."

"I'm sure you do. He owns Jack's Shacks."

"It sounds vaguely familiar," I say as Remington nods. "Oh, wait, he's the guy that owns all those hotels, right? Isn't he like a billionaire?"

"Yeah, that's him. Well, Jack of Jack's Shacks is going through a divorce right now."

"And what's that got to do with us?" I ask, sighing as I pick up my phone. "I told you I have a call."

"He has a prenup in place," Kingston continues.

"Okay, and?"

"He doesn't think he should have to pay her the ten million that she is entitled to for the five years they were married because she cheated."

"Okay, and?"

"And if we get him a good deal with the wife, we get his Jack's Shacks business. That's a ten million dollar retainer off the bat. Big money."

I stare at him for a couple of seconds and nod. "Okay, we'll take the case and—"

"Here's the thing: he wants *you*."

I stare at him for a couple of seconds. "What do you mean he wants me?"

"He's heard you're a shark in the courtroom."

Don't Quit The Day Job

"But we don't want this to go to court. I'm sure if he has a prenup in place, he can resolve this before then and—"

"Exactly," Kingston cuts me off.

"Exactly what?"

"He wants you to resolve it." Kingston shrugs. "There's a complication but he wouldn't tell me over the phone. He says he wants to tell you in person."

"So you're telling me that you want me to take this case?" Kingston nods. "He'd be a big client, Max."

"We've got plenty of big clients already. I don't know this guy. You know how I feel about handling clients that I do not know the backstory on."

"I'm telling you that he's a good guy to get into business with."

I stare at him for a couple of seconds. "Who's going to be in charge of the Jack's Shacks deals?" Because if there's one thing I know about Kingston, it's that he doesn't give away big clients.

"We can figure that out later," he says, and I grin.

"Fine. I'll do it, but you owe me. Has anyone heard from Gabriel?" I ask, talking about our fourth partner. He wasn't a named partner yet, but he didn't seem to care. In fact, Gabe seemed to prefer not having his name on the office door, so to speak. He hadn't been in the office for three weeks now.

"He's still in the Caribbean somewhere, sailing." Kingston shakes his head. "He should be back next week. He's going to need a new assistant as well."

I chuckle. "Good luck to him. Have you found *your* new assistant yet?" I ask Kingston, and he shakes his head.

"I was in HR a little bit ago and they said they're going to set up an interview for me in half an hour with some hopeful named Skye."

"Oh," I say, nodding, trying to withhold a grin.

"What? You know her?" His eyes narrow. "How do you know her?"

"I don't *know* her know her, but if it's the same Skye I'm thinking of, she came in with Lila."

"Lila, your new assistant?" He raises an eyebrow and shakes his head as he grimaces. "I might as well call HR right now because she is not about to get the job."

"You don't even know her."

"I know that if she's in any way affiliated or associated with Lila, she's not going to be a good assistant and I think with my brain and not my balls," he winks at me.

"I've never thought with my balls."

"Really?"

"Yeah, I do think with my dick sometimes, but never my balls." I chuckle then and we all laugh. There's a knock at the door and I look up and I see that Lila is standing there with wide eyes, a coffee in one hand and a brown bag in the other. I can tell by the expression on her face that she's heard the joke I just told about thinking with my dick. "Yes, Lila, come in," I say, not sounding regretful or sorrowful at what she's heard, even though I don't want her to think I hired her because she makes my cock hard.

"Um, I have your coffee and your bagel here," she says, blinking as she walks in. "Do you want me to bring them in or should I wait or...?" She looks at Kingston and juts her chin out. "By the way, you'd be lucky to work with Skye. She's really great and smart, but if I'm being honest, I hope that you don't hire her because she deserves to be with someone who is a good boss, not someone who would judge her just because she knows me. Also, I am going to be a really great assistant," she mumbles, and I feel her eyes on me again.

"He was just joking around, Lila, weren't you, Kingston?" I look over at him.

"No," he says bluntly and smirks. "I don't know exactly what's going on between you and Lila, but I'm not going to be hiring Skye, whoever she is. I'm not looking for a mouthy, disrespectful, and frankly, from what I can tell, not even qualified for the job."

"I *am* qualified. I have a bachelor's degree." Lila says stiffly. "You don't know me."

Kingston smirks and looks at me. "I'll send you the information on the Jack Whittington case."

"Yeah, send his files through," I say. "I'll have a look and see what I can do."

"Good," he says. "Because he wants to see you this afternoon before this all gets messy."

"What do you mean messy?"

"She's talking about going to the media."

"But why would she be going to the media if she's the one cheating?"

"Hell if I know, maybe because she knows that Jack's Shacks is a family vacation spot and any bad press is not going to look good." He shrugs.

I stare at him. "Fine, I'll have a look this afternoon."

"Good," he nods. "Let me head to HR now." He stares at Lila. "I really do hope that you are a great employee because Max here has a grand riding on your competency."

"Kingston," I chastise him.

"What?" He grins.

"Oh, you don't have to worry about that," she says, snarling at him. "I'll be the best assistant he's ever seen in his life."

"Will you now?" Kingston looks her over and I start to

feel annoyed. Is he flirting with her? Is he trying to make a move on my assistant?

"That's enough, Kingston," I say.

He looks up at me and smirks. "Yes, boss," he chuckles as he leaves the office and I can see that Lila is staring after him. "Anything else you want to discuss, Remington?" I ask.

"No, but I thought you would introduce me to your new assistant."

"Oh, yeah. I forgot you haven't met. Remington, this is Lila Haversham. Lila, this is my other partner, Remington."

"Nice to meet you," he says, shaking her hand.

"Nice to meet you as well," she says, smiling, and I can see her fluttering her eyelashes. "Are you looking for an assistant as well?" she asks, and I wonder if that's hope in her voice. Is she really trying to get a job with my partner right in front of me? For some reason, I feel infuriated.

"Oh, no. I have an assistant," he grins. "Juniper and I have a great working relationship."

"Oh." Lila presses her lips together. "Well, I guess that's good." She looks like she doesn't know what to say and he just chuckles.

"I am rather happy that I don't have the distraction of having a hot assistant in my office day in, day out." He looks at me and chuckles. "I know it's going to be pretty hard for you, Max."

"Very funny," I say. "Is there anything else Remy?"

"No, but HR did tell me to let you know that the meeting for the new hires is going to be this afternoon."

"Okay, I will make sure that Lila is there."

"Awesome," he says. Nice to meet you Miss Haversham."

"Nice to meet you too."

We stand there in silence as Remington leaves the office

before she hands me my coffee and bagel. "Here you go. And don't blame me if the coffee is cold. I had to walk like, five blocks and my feet are absolutely killing me."

"Excuse me," I stare at her.

"Excuse you for what?"

"You're really complaining to me about walking five blocks?"

"I'm just saying these shoes are not the most comfortable. Have you seen how high these heels are?"

"Then maybe you don't wear high heels if you can't walk in them for very long."

"I didn't expect to be walking in them for very long. I ended up getting off the train earlier than I should have this morning because there was this creepy guy that was staring at me and I didn't want to be a statistic." And then she pauses. "Well, I'm guessing you don't really want to know."

"No, please do tell me. I'm so interested in hearing the story as to why you got off the train early and had to walk many blocks in uncomfortable shoes. It's not like I have anything else going on today. I'm not a named partner at a top law firm. I don't have millions of dollars worth of lawsuits to figure out. And—"

"There's no need to be sarcastic," she says. "What do you want me to do?"

"What do you mean, what do I want you to—"

"Work-wise, what do you want me to do? I mean, you're paying me for a job and I assume it's not just to get you coffee and bagels."

"You know what, Lila?"

"Yes, Max."

"You can call me Mr. Spector by the way."

"I'm not calling you Mr. Spector. You're not my dad's friend."

"I'm your boss though."

"And because you're my boss, I should call you Mr. Spector?"

"It's respectful."

"Okay. Then call me Miss Haversham."

"I don't think so, Lila."

"But I am your employee, and as such, I deserve the same courtesy that you do."

"Are you always going to be like this?"

"What do you mean am I always going to be like this? This is my first day. This is my personality. Are you telling me you don't like my personality?" Her lower lip trembles.

"Don't even bother with the water works, Ms. Wannabe Actress."

"What?" She grins. "I was just going to see if I could cry. I told you I've been having a problem crying on cue these days, so it was unlikely to happen."

"You're not practicing your acting while you're at work."

"When else am I supposed to practice my acting?" She grins. "When I'm not being paid? What fun is that?" She tilts her head to the side, and for a moment I think she's flirting with me.

"Do you want me to fire you?"

"I literally just started this job. I don't think you want to fire me." She licks her lower lip and plays with her hair. I frown at the movement.

"And why do you think I don't want to fire you?"

"Let's be real here. Any regular, smart, intelligent attorney would never have hired me in the first place."

I stare at her for a couple of seconds, my lips twitching slightly. "Are you saying that I'm not intelligent?"

"I'm saying you're intelligent, but maybe not super intelligent."

"So you're calling me dumb?"

"You're either dumb or you are incredibly attracted to me." She steps forward. She's definitely flirting with me. And I don't hate it.

"You think I'm incredibly attracted to you?"

"I think so," she says. "Maybe it's my heels. Maybe it's my short skirt. Maybe it's even my tight top with the buttons undone." She undoes another button and my eyes widen. I'm not sure what is going on here, but I'm starting to feel turned on.

"I think..." she says as she takes another step towards me. "That I intrigue you. I think that you think I'm hot. Am I right?" She presses her palm against my chest and I know she can feel my heart beating. I stare at her for a couple of seconds, still not saying anything else. I can tell from the look in her eyes that she's not as brave as she's making it seem. She might be acting confident, but she's not. "I think," she says as she runs her finger down my chest. "That you—"

"I think it's time for you to get to work, Miss Haversham," I say, grabbing her hand and holding it tightly. "I don't really know what your game is, but you're here to do a job, be an assistant, remember? I really don't think you want a job on your back, am I correct?"

"What?" she says, her jaw dropping, and I grin at the wild look in her eyes.

"I'm saying that you came for an honest-day's-work job, not one where you spend all your time on your back. Am I correct?"

"Yes. What are you talking about on my back?"

"I mean, it seems to me that's where you want to be right now." I lick my lips slowly. "And don't get me wrong, I could slide that skirt up within five seconds and be in you so hard and fast that I'd have you calling out my name so the entire office could hear. But right now I have work to do, and that work doesn't include fucking you. No matter how badly you want it." I step away from her and sit down. Her face is beet red and I'm sure she's embarrassed, but as much as I want to push this and see how far she's willing to go, I really shouldn't. Not yet. Not like this. And for some reason, I don't think it's just because of the bet. For some reason, I actually want to see if I can figure out Lila and all of her intricacies.

I pull the top page off of the legal pad and rip it into pieces. I don't care about the pros and cons list anymore. I'm not about to fire Lila Haversham anytime soon. I want to see exactly where this is going to go.

Chapter Eight

Lila

Lila: **Mr. Vanilla is a jerk.**
Zara: **What happened?**
Lila: **I attempted to seduce him. Well, kinda.**
Zara: **Already? What?**
Lila: **I figured why not shoot my shot right away?**
Zara: **I take it it didn't go well?**
Lila: **Let's just say I'm no longer interested. I will never flirt with that jackass again. I will make my money and then leave as soon as I can.**

I slip my phone into my handbag as I walk into the large conference room feeling slightly embarrassed and a little bit nervous. I am utterly annoyed with myself and even more annoyed with Max Spector. I still can't believe what he said to me. I am mortified and feel like the biggest idiot on the planet. I shouldn't have come on to him.

I did not feel empowered.

I did not feel sexy.

In fact, I felt like a fool. I am going to absolutely kill Zara for making me think trying to seduce Max was a good idea. It was evident to me that he was not interested in me whatsoever.

"Over here, Lila." I hear my name and I look around the crowded room. I spot Skye sitting at the back next to a girl with long, dark hair. I make my way over to them and Skye beams at me, a twinkle in her green eyes. "How's it going?"

"Just brilliantly," I say, rolling my eyes as I take a seat. "Hi." I look at the brunette. "I'm Lila."

"Nice to meet you, I'm Juniper."

"Is today your first day as well?" I ask, though suddenly I realize I've heard her name before.

"No," she says, shaking her head. "I've worked here for a couple of weeks. I work for one of the partners."

"Oh, which one?" I ask. "Actually, I think I know. I met them this afternoon, I believe. Not Kingston because he's looking for someone, but the other guy, what was his name? Remy? Remington?"

"Remington Parker," she confirms, nodding. "He's the bane of my existence."

"Oh?" I ask her as she fumbles with her thick black glasses. They are way too big for her face and kind of make her look like an owl.

"He is the sort of boss that makes you not want to work."

"Oh, so he's just as great as my boss." I start laughing, the sound filling the room a bit too loudly so I quickly stop.

"Who's your boss?" she asks, curious.

"Max. Max Spector."

"Oh." She grins with a nod. "Yeah. He's just as bad as Remington."

"So did you get a job yet, Skye?" I lick my lips nervously.

I don't want to tell her about the conversation I'd overheard between Max, Remy, and Kingston.

"I have an interview with Kingston Chase in a couple of hours," she says. "He's another one of the partners. It was supposed to be before lunch, but for some reason it got pushed back, but they told me I should attend this meeting just in case I was hired."

"Oh, okay, so you think you'll get the job?"

"I don't know," she says. "But they said with my qualifications, it looked like I was a shoo-in."

"Oh?" I ask her in surprise. "I didn't realize you had great qualifications. Have you worked at a law firm before?"

She giggles slightly. "Does it look like I've worked at a law firm before?"

"I don't really know what to say. Is there a look for a law firm?"

"I think she means like me," Juniper says, with a self-deprecating smile. "Dowdy."

"No, no, no, I didn't," Skye says quickly.

"It's fine. I know I'm nerdy." Juniper lets out a deep sigh and adjusts the bun on the top of her hair. She's wearing an oversized white shirt and a long, ugly gray skirt that does nothing for her body. Her glasses are too thick for her face and her hairstyle is not doing her any favors. Add to that the fact that she's not wearing any makeup and you could almost believe she didn't even try to get ready this morning. "I know that I'm a bit of a plain Jane," she says. "I just...I am not one of those women that ever learned how to do makeup and stuff, you know?"

"Hey, I can teach you any time of day," I say with a small smile. "I'm not an expert, but one summer I went into six different Sephoras and had them do makeovers, pretending that I was going to buy the makeup. I mean, I bought a lip gloss. Anyway, I know tricks and tips if you want me to give you a makeover someday."

"Oh, that would be really nice," she says, pushing her falling glasses up her nose again. "I've always said that I wanted to have some incredible makeover, but it's just never happened, you know? I guess I'm just too busy working here and trying to write."

"Oh, what do you write?" I ask her. "Newspaper articles?" I don't know why I imagined her as a Dear Abby columnist.

"I want to be an author," she says shyly.

"Romance books?" I ask her eagerly.

"No, no," she says, shaking her head and looking down. "Well, kind of."

"What do you mean kind of?"

"I write fantasy with a little romance. I guess they call it romantasy now." She looks up and blushes slightly as she turns her face to the side. I can tell from her profile that she's actually quite pretty. She'd be beautiful if she wanted to be.

"Oh, I don't know that I've read much fantasy," I say honestly. "But I love romance books. In fact..." I lower my voice and look around the room to make sure no one's listening. "I kind of told Max about it and I kind of embarrassed myself." I don't know why I'm bringing it up to these two women who I don't really know, but even though I've already told Zara, I feel like I need to talk about it again.

"You told your boss that you like to read romance?" Juniper looks surprised. "Why?"

Skye is laughing loudly and I haven't even answered.

"What's so funny?" I ask her.

"You and that Max, there's just something about the chemistry that you have that I find hilarious."

Don't Quit The Day Job

"We don't have chemistry. He thinks I'm an idiot. Trust me. I have so much to tell you two, but I don't want to say it here in the conference room, just in case they have listening devices or something. But let's just say I may or may not have come on to him and had it blow up in my face." The rejection still stings in my heart. I felt like I was slapped when he dismissed me so casually.

"No way..." Skye looks shocked. "I was just joking. So are you guys going to hook up?" She gasps suddenly. "Wait, don't tell me it's already happened." I stare at her for a few seconds and shake my head slowly. Does she really think I'm that easy?

"He's not interested," I say, blushing and looking down at the table.

"Are you kidding? Skye looks surprised. "I could see the way he was looking at you. He's totally interested."

"Well, he may have been interested when he offered me the job, but then he got to know me." I grimace. "But that's the story of my life. I'm a bit too much for most men."

"Aren't we all?" Skye says, giggling.

"I have not dated in several years," Juniper adds with a small frown. "My best friend says it's because I'm always writing and reading, but I feel like the characters in books are just so much better than real people."

"I know what you mean," I say. "But there's nothing better than real life experiences." I suddenly have an idea. "Shall we all go out for a drink after work. Are you girls down?"

"I'm down!" Skye nods eagerly. "But you knew that already."

"What about you, Juniper?" I ask the brunette.

"Um." She bites down on her lower lip. "I was going to

go home and make lasagna and try to write a chapter of my book."

"Nope," I say, shaking my head. "We're going for a drink."

"Well, I mean, maybe one drink. I don't really drink that much because alcohol goes to my head and I kind of act a little bit weird and—"

"Juniper," I say. "Do you not want to have fun?"

"I mean, yeah." She nods. "Okay, fine. I'll go with you girls. It sounds like it will be a good time."

"It will be great," I say and let out a deep sigh. "I haven't worked here for very long and I don't even know if I'm going to have the job for very long either, but this whole experience has been worth it just to meet you two. I've been wanting more girlfriends for such a long time."

"Me too. It's so hard to make friends in The City." Skye nods.

"I know," Juniper says. "I have one really good friend, but that's about it. I've had a hard time making friends since I graduated from college."

"Yeah, I get that," I say. "My best friend, Zara, is in The City, but she just got engaged to this gorgeous guy and now they're living together and you know what that's like." I wave my hands in a goodbye and wrinkle my nose. "They spend most of their time together now and it'd be nice to hang out with some single girls." I pause. "We are all single, right?"

"I am as single as the day is long," Skye says, laughing.

"And I'm as single as Cinderella was when she went to the ball on that dark, gloomy night." Juniper's voice is sweet, and I laugh.

"You really are a writer, aren't you?"

"I hope to be. I'm just not published yet, but maybe one day," she says hopefully. "But it will never happen if Remington has anything to say about it. I will never be able to finish my book with the constant amount of work he gives me morning, noon, and night." She leans forward and lowers her voice. "Sometimes I just want to tell him to do it himself."

"So why don't you?" I ask. "If he's such a jackass, you should let him know how you feel. If Max tries to work me like a horse, I will let him know that he's the only ass I see in the office."

Both Skye and Juniper burst out laughing and I grin at them as my heart warms. I already know we're going to be great friends. The three musketeers of Chase, Parker & Spector.

"I wish, but I'm not brave like you are and I would be scared witless to let Remington know what I think. Plus, he barely knows that I exist."

"What do you mean he doesn't know that you exist?"

"I think he sees me as some kind of robot. I don't even think he sees me as a woman," she admits. "He even got me to send flowers to three different women last week," she says, shaking her head. "He's such a dog."

"He's cute though," I say, my brain racing at the slight change in her voice. Was Juniper interested in Remington? He's definitely extremely handsome. In fact, all of the partners are. "Don't you think?"

"He's okay." She looks away and blushes. My eyes meet Skye's and we smile at each other. I have a feeling that Skye can also see that Juniper thinks Remington is way more than okay, but I'm not going to push her to admit that. While the three men might be gorgeous, they all seem like jerks based on the conversation I'd overheard earlier. I'm pretty confident that Juniper was correct, Remington hasn't noticed her as a woman. I have a feeling that the reason he hired her in the first place was because she didn't look like much of anything, which is crazy because even I can see that she's beautiful. She just needs a better hairstyle, a little bit of makeup, and a better wardrobe. I know that men don't always see what's right in front of their eyes, but come on. Juniper is a diamond in the rough and I'm determined to give her the best makeover possible. Juniper will blossom from an ugly duckling to a swan and that will make Remington take notice.

"Good Afternoon, new staffers. Welcome to Chase, Parker, and Spector, the number one law firm in New York City." The door slams shut and I look up to see a middle-aged woman with short, curly black hair standing at the front. She is dressed in a smart navy-blue suit and she reminds me of the dean at my last school. "My name is Vivian Johnson and I am in charge of HR training. As many of you may know, we've been going through a lot of turnover recently and that's not good. As a law firm, the attorneys have to focus on the cases and we are meant to make their life easier." She crosses her arms and looks around the room, her dark eyes seeming to issue a warning to everyone. "You're not here to flirt. You're not here to find a husband. You're not here to get free meals. You're here to make the attorneys' lives easier, and I'm here to ensure that you do your job well. Please raise your hand if you feel like you are not a good candidate for a personal or legal assistant position." She pauses and walks around the room, a pursed look on her face. I can tell that Vivian Johnson takes her job very seriously.

The room is silent as we all look around and wait to see

if anyone will raise their hand. There are about fifteen of us in the room and I wonder how much more experience the others have over me. I'm not surprised when nobody puts their hand up. I'm sure we all want to, but we're all too scared.

"Good," She nods and heads back to the front of the room. "Today we're going to go through the HR handbook and discuss the upcoming trainings." There's a loud knock on the door and she frowns. "Hold on, please." She heads over to the door, opens it, and steps outside. A few moments later, she comes back into the room and looks around. "Is there a Skye in the room?"

"Yeah, that's me," Skye says from beside me, looking nervous. "Is everything okay?" She stands up.

"I understand that you have not been hired as of yet. Kingston Chase has just alerted me to the fact that you have an interview right now and he would like you to make your way to his office."

"Oh wow, now? I thought it was going to be afterwards."

"He wants to see you now. Please, gather your stuff. If you get the job I will have to catch you up tomorrow morning with what we discuss this afternoon. There will be another training tomorrow afternoon if you do get the job."

"Okay, well, thank you." Skye looks at me and wrinkles her nose. "You have my number, right?" she whispers. I nod. "Text me, let me know the plan for drinks."

"Will do," I say. I look over at Juniper. "I'll get your number afterwards as well."

"Sounds good," she smiles.

Skye takes a deep breath. "Wish me luck. I hope I get the job. I hope this Kingston is nicer than Max and the Remington guy that you two were talking about."

"Me too," I say, though I really want to tell her that he seems like he's the biggest jerk of them all.

"Good luck," Juniper says, and we watch as Skye walks out of the room. I look over at Juniper and she makes a face.

"Kingston sucks, huh?"

"He kind of does," Juniper says with a little giggle and nod.

"I didn't want to say that to Skye, but he did seem like a jerk. I still hope she gets the job. It'll be cool if we all work together. We can go to lunch and stuff."

"That would be really nice." Juniper nods.

The door closes behind Skye and Vivian starts up again. "Hopefully we won't have any more interruptions. Ladies and gentlemen, I'd like you to take out a pen. We're going to start filling out some forms. I hope you all have your social security cards and a form of ID. We will also complete some tax paperwork as well and—"

There's another knock on the door and she lets out an irritated grunt. "Do people not know I'm trying to run a meeting here?" she says in a self-important voice before opening the door. "Can I help you?" Immediately, her voice lowers. "Oh, sorry. Mr. Spector. I didn't realize it was you." I freeze. What does Max Spector want? "Yes, she must be in here. I was about to start the training, but..." She nods. "Yes, sir. Of course." She steps back into the room. "Is there a Lila Haversham?"

"That's me," I say, holding my hand up.

"Mr. Spector needs you to do some urgent work, so I'm going to have to speak to you tomorrow morning along with Skye to go over this paperwork."

"Oh, okay," I say. I look down at Juniper and watch as she scribbles her number on a piece of paper and hands it to me. "Thank you, I will text you later." I stand up and head toward the door. "Thank you, Vivian. I—"

"I'll see you in the morning." She sounds pissed as she shakes her head, as if I'm the one that said I had to go and not Max.

I step outside and find Max standing there looking at something on his phone. "Okay, let's go," he says, without looking up at me.

"Really?" I say, feeling pissed at myself. "That's how you're going to speak to me?"

He looks up at me slowly, his eyes boring into mine as he frowns. "Sorry, what?"

"I was just in a meeting, filling out paperwork and trying to ensure that I am set up for this job. You just pulled me out of the training that you sent me to and—"

He just stares at me. I hate that he doesn't say anything. It unnerves me. "Are you going to keep going?" he asks. "Or are you done?"

"I just think you're so rude."

"Is this because I didn't offer you a million dollars to sleep with me, even though I know you would've slept with me for free?"

I bite down on my lip to stop from cussing him. "I wouldn't sleep with you if you were the last man on Earth. In fact, I wouldn't sleep with you if you were the last man in the universe."

"Tell me how that's different," he says, his blue eyes twinkling, and I ignore the flutter in my heart. Why does he affect me so?

"What?"

"Tell me how it's different."

"Tell you how what's different?"

"You said you wouldn't sleep with me if I was the last man on Earth."

"I wouldn't," I say, glaring at him disdainfully.

"And then you said you wouldn't sleep with me if I was the last man in the universe."

"I wouldn't." I raise my chin.

"But how is it different? How is me being the last man on Earth different from being the last man in the universe? Or do you think there are other life-sustaining planets out there or something?"

I stare at him for a couple of seconds and I can feel that my blood is about to boil over. I want to go off on him so badly. I can tell by the smirk on his face that he thinks he's so intelligent and superior. This man is getting on my last nerves, and what's worse is I'm so madly attracted to him that I want to rip the buttons off his shirt and just kiss him. Why is he doing this to me? Why am I so attracted to him?

"I was just making a point, Mr. Spector. I wanted you to clearly understand that I don't want you and I couldn't care less if you offered me a million dollars or not."

"Really? Hmm. It didn't seem that way an hour ago. In fact, I was thinking about..."

"Thinking about what?" I ask.

"I was thinking about us having a specific deal with each other."

"What do you mean?" I ask, my lips trembling slightly. Is he about to say what I think he is? Is he about to come on to me? Is he about to offer me some sort of kinky deal to be his lover? And will I take it? I'm not sure. "What is the offer?" I ask.

"Wouldn't you like to know?" He grins as he brings his mouth to my ear.

"Well, yeah, you brought it up, so..." I step back, feeling flustered.

"Come with me and you'll find out."

"Where are we going? You're not taking me to a hotel, are you? Look, I am not that type of girl."

"Lila, I was joking. There is no deal."

I cross my arms and glare at him. I don't find his joke funny whatsoever.

"Moving on. I removed you from the training because we're going to meet a client." He taps his watch.

"A client?" I raise an eyebrow. "What client?"

"His name is Jack Whittington and he needs help with a divorce."

"Okay." I press my lips together. "Let's go then."

"To the Plaza?" He winks and I gasp.

"I should quit right now."

"We both know you're not quitting, Lila. Just like we both know if I took you to the Plaza Hotel right now, your skirt and panties would be on the ground before I could say the word ground."

"Dude, you wish."

"Maybe I do," he says, his eyes looking me up and down. "And maybe I don't, but you'll never know."

"You think this is a joke, don't you?"

"Not at all," he says softly. "I just think that when I have you, it's going to be because neither of us can keep our hands off of each other, and who knows? Maybe I am the crazy one. Maybe this banter is going to drive me absolutely bonkers and maybe it's going to drive you bonkers too. I guess we'll just have to wait and see. But you can't say that you don't enjoy it."

I bite down on my lower lip. "I do not get you."

"That's understandable," he says. "You didn't know me until today. I don't get you either, but I have a feeling I will."

"What do you mean you have a feeling you will? Are you saying you have a feeling that you'll sleep with me? Because I already told you I'm not interested."

"I know what you said, Miss Haversham, but I think we both know how you feel right now. Like the ocean, right baby?"

Chapter Nine

Max

I can tell by the look on Lila's face that she's nonplussed. She doesn't know how to take our interactions, and if I'm quite honest with myself, I don't know how to take our interactions either. We've gone back and forth so often in such a short time that I already feel like she's changed a part of my life. It feels like I've known her forever as opposed to less than a day.

A part of me now understands the sentiment that life can be changed in a moment. I already feel like the air I'm breathing is slightly sweeter. I wonder if I was hit over the head in my sleep last night and didn't realize it.

"So where are we going, exactly?" she asks, her blue eyes studying me curiously as we wait outside the building for the driver to pick us up. I wonder if she's considering quitting. I haven't exactly made her first day the most seamless. The thought of her quitting is unpleasant to the brain and I know it has nothing to do with the bet. I will have to be nicer. But not too nice. I make a vow to stop the teasing and flirting. It's been so long since I've even wanted to flirt.

"Jack Whittington has an office in Midtown West, the car will take us there." I step forward as I see the black Cadillac Escalade Sport pull up to the front of the building. "If you have your phone on you, I'd like you to Google him so that we can get some more information."

"You want me to Google him?" She raises an eyebrow as I open the door for her. I watch her step up and take a seat and I can't help but stare at her long legs as her skirt rides up her thighs.

"That's what I said." I realize my voice sounds a bit obnoxious and soften my tone. "I don't know much about him and I'd like to be well informed before I meet him for the first time."

"You've never met him before?" She sounds surprised as I get in behind her and close the door.

"No, I have not." I buckle my seatbelt. "Good Afternoon, Henry. This is my new assistant, Lila. Lila, this is Henry, one of the drivers for the firm."

"Nice to meet you, Henry." She raises her head and smiles at the older man as he gives her a quick look back.

"Very nice to make your acquaintance Lila." He nods and starts the engine again. I look over at Lila and watch as she types something on her phone. Her fingernails are painted a light pink and I notice she's not wearing much jewelry. I wonder if she really does have a boyfriend. I wonder how serious the relationship is.

"So...tell me more about your boyfriend." I say before I can stop myself. I'm irritated that I'm digging for more personal information, even after I told myself I was going to keep it professional.

"I thought you wanted to know about Jack..." she says, looking up at me and showing me her phone screen. There's a photo of a middle-aged man on the screen and I can tell from the smug look on his face that he definitely has more money than he knows what to do with. "Oh, wow! He owns Jack's Shacks," she says in an awed voice. "My best friend, Zara, and I wanted to rent one of his beach shacks in Bali, but they were so expensive we said we'd wait until we retired." She leans back into the leather seat. "Though, I suppose Zara can go now if she wants."

"But you can't?"

"I mean, she'll go with her boyfriend." Her voice trails off and she blushes, that pinkish hue that makes my heart shift every time I see it.

"Your boyfriend can't take you? Or is he broke?" The question comes across as rude, but I'm curious. My instincts tell me that he doesn't have two brass pennies to rub together, but I know from my legal work that you can never assume anything in life. For all I know, she's dating Bill Gates and is just trying to prove to him that she isn't a gold digger. It's highly unlikely, but you never know.

"He's not broke." She shifts in the seat, clearly uncomfortable, and turns away from me. I wonder if she's uncomfortable talking about her boyfriend with me, or if she feels guilty about the way she reacts to me. The thought delights me that her attraction to me is something she can't hide. Not that I would pursue her or continue our weird little flirtation if I thought she was actually in a relationship; even though I'm not actually looking for a relationship, I have no interest in being a homewrecker.

"How long have you been dating, exactly?" I push it a little further. "Is he on the path to becoming your fiancé?"

"I don't really think that's important, or any of your business, do you?" she snaps, her eyes shifting back and forth like a criminal's does in an interrogation room. I'm getting under her skin. I'd prefer to be getting under her clothes. If the circumstances were different, of course.

"Does this guy that you're *dating* know that you're calling him your boyfriend?" I pause dramatically and run my fingers through my hair. The car hums along slowly, darting in and out of traffic to get us to our destination in a timely fashion. Lila's jaw drops open like I've offended her and she shifts back into the seat again, causing her already short skirt to ride up again. Her thighs look toned and tan and I look away before my thoughts start becoming inappropriate.

"You what?" She sputters and coughs slightly.

I can't quite stop myself from laughing as I see her face going scarlet red. "I'm not trying to judge or make you uncomfortable. But this boyfriend? Is he a friend with benefits? Does he know you're telling people he's your boyfriend." I pause as she licks her lips nervously. She's definitely uncomfortable. "Does he even exist?"

She stills and I chuckle. There is definitely no boyfriend, but I won't let her know how confident I am of that just yet.

"I'm just curious how your boyfriend, the man you love, the man you make sweet love to, would feel knowing you were flirting with and offering yourself to me today?"

"Say what?" She sits forward, her hair falling over her shoulders as her body shakes in agitation. "I didn't offer myself to you. You wish I offered myself to you. Do you know what I want to know? I want to know why you offered me this job! Is it because you thought and hoped that you were going to get a piece of me?" She looks me up and down and shakes her head. "I've been trying to figure out why you gave me this job, because let's be real, we both know I'm not exactly qualified. I mean, I am a fast learner, but you don't know that. I think you just want to torment and torture me until I agree to sleep with you." She takes a deep breath. "But I'm not lucky enough to be offered a million dollars. You probably want me to do it for a hundred, but I am not a whore, Mr. Spector. I'm not about to sleep with you for a hundred bucks." She crosses her arms and gives me a smug look. "Sorry about your luck."

I consider telling her about the supermodels and A-list actresses I've bedded in the last couple of years. I could pull out my phone and show her that a princess in a small country had been texting me for three months straight, begging me to fly over and take her to dinner. The fact that Lila really seems to think I would offer her anything to sleep with her is laughable. I could, quite frankly, get any woman I wanted, if I wanted them.

I decide not to come off as a smug prick though. I don't want her to think I'm a player. I don't want her to think that I'm the sort of man that only dates glamorous women.

"So you consider a woman who sleeps with a man for a hundred dollars a whore, but you think it's OK if she does it for a million?" I raise an eyebrow and tilt my head to the side as if I'm pondering the meaning of life. "Double standards much?" I shake my head slowly before continuing. "Also, dear Lila, you really need to stop accusing me of wanting to sleep with you; especially with the caveat of me paying. I am not the sort of man that would offer money to a woman for anything physical. I don't really find movies like *Pretty Woman* to be romantic, but rather a poor spotlight on how rich men can get away with almost anything and still be celebrated."

"Are you saying that you're not a rich man?" she asks in disbelief, and I can see her shaking her head. Lila wears her heart and her emotions on her sleeve. I quite like how transparent she is and I wonder how well she can hide her emotions as an actress. I don't want to judge her, but I have a feeling that Hollywood won't be calling her anytime soon. She doesn't seem to be able to fake any of her emotions.

"Oh, honey," I chuckle as I think about just how many zeroes I have in my accounts. "That's the sort of question that doesn't even warrant a response." For some reason, I don't want her to know just how much money I'm worth. She's not from South Carolina, she's never heard of the Spectors. I have a feeling she's not interested in horse racing either, so she wouldn't know or care about the family dynasty.

"Tell me what else you found out about Jack Whittington." I fold my arms and lean back.

A slight quiver of disappointment crosses her face and I wonder if she expected me to tell her exactly what my net worth was.

I'm not the sort of man to show off by talking about my bank account. The very thought of it is uncouth. Not that that sentiment is normal for many bachelors in The City; most men I know love to show off their wealth. They love to impress women and money has a way of appealing to demographics that you thought would never be interested in you, but I've always disliked people gravitating toward me because of my family's net worth. I'm more than a figure in the bank. I think that was why Kingston, Remington, and Gabe had all been drawn to each other. We'd all grown up in families with money. We all knew what it was to want to prove ourselves outside of that wealth. And we're doing it. We're succeeding, though I know Marie would ask if we feel we were living full lives. She feels that a life without love is a life not worth living. But she's a teen and a true romantic and hasn't yet experienced the realities of love and relationships. It isn't all sugar, candy, and flowers. Love is an intricate puzzle made of pieces that could disintegrate in a minute. You can try and fit a piece into another, and for a while, even think it was in the correct spot, but then as it worms its way out and you realize it was in the wrong spot all along. Emotions are not to be trusted. They aren't black and white and there's no science that can explain how love works.

I like to work with concrete facts. I like to work with reason. If A happens, then B will also happen. And if C is added, then we have X. I need to be able to understand how things fit together and you just can't fully understand emotions. I think that's part of the reason why I've never really fallen in love. I don't want to lose control of any part of my life.

"I will tell you everything that I can find." She taps away on her phone, her nose wrinkled as she sets about her task. "So this is what Google has to say about our man, Jack: he's worth an estimated eight hundred sixty-three million. Wow, that's a lot of money." Her eyes widen. "He's been married twice. He has two sons from his first marriage. It looks like he's only been married to his current wife for four years. And she is significantly younger than him." She pauses and looks up at me. "You will never guess how old she is." She shakes her head. "Wow, she looks younger than me."

"So she's fifty-two?" I ask with a straight face. "Because you look like you're about fifty-five." I lean back and I chuckle as she rolls her eyes and starts laughing.

"I know I do not look like I'm fifty-five." She grins. "Stop comparing everyone to yourself. You're about sixty right?"

"I wouldn't say that." I lean toward her and watch as she swallows hard and wonders what I'm going to do next. "If you're worried that I need the little blue pill, you don't need to be. Sir Spector does his—"

"Not interested." She cuts me off. "Looks like Jack has investments all over the world and supposedly has aspirations to run for president one day." She rubs the side of her face. "So perhaps we're about to meet a future president."

"Perhaps." I nod. Interesting that Jack Whittington would specifically request me to work on his divorce. There has to be some sort of catch.

"So, you said his wife cheated on him?"

"Yes, that's what Kingston said." I nod. "It should be straight-forward if there was a prenup with a cheating clause; which I assume there would be."

"Why isn't he using the attorney that drafted the prenup for the divorce?" Lila asks and I shake my head. The question has crossed my mind several times.

"We shall see." I say. "When we get to his home, please do not ask any questions."

"Why would I do that?" She rolls her eyes.

"I know you think you're Maria Conchita Estella whoever, the best paralegal in all the land, but..."

"That was for a role, Max." She glares at me, but I can see her blue eyes sparkling. "You're really trying hard to get on my nerves, aren't you?"

"Why would I want to do that?" I ask softly, and we just stare at each other for a few moments. There's static in the air, a spark that threatens to burst into flames. My throat feels dry for a moment, my legs stiff. We can't seem to look away from each other. Then she leans forward and brushes something off of my chin and the touch of her fingers against my skin scorches me.

"You had a crumb." She licks her lips nervously. "I didn't

think you'd want Jack Whittington to see part of your breakfast bagel on your chin and think you're a messy eater."

"No, I don't think I would have wanted that." I nod and smile slightly, taken aback by the moment we just shared. It makes me uncomfortable. This blonde, flirty, vivacious, beautiful woman is like a tornado in my life and I have a feeling that she could do a lot of damage if I let her.

I'm not going to though.

I'm not Dorothy from *The Wizard of Oz*.

I don't want to get swept off anywhere.

I refuse to allow Lila Haversham disrupt my life.

Chapter Ten

Lila

I am playing with fire and I am definitely going to be burned. I cannot believe that Max and I haven't kissed or killed each other yet.

I cannot believe that we only met each other this morning. I feel like I've known the man a lifetime.

And I might just be a little crazy because I have an overwhelming desire to feel his lips on mine.

I now understand what it is to be both drawn to someone and want to run away at the same time. Max confuses and enrages me in the most delicious of ways, and if he wasn't my boss, I'd go all in to see what sort of crazy he could bring to my life. I've always thought a great love affair could take my acting and emotional vulnerability to the next level.

However, he is my boss. I need the paycheck more than I need oxygen, and I don't really need the emotional entanglement of being with a man like Max. Though, the more I think about it, the more I think that Max could be the perfect man to break my heart. My acting could really go to the next level if I got involved with a man like him.

I peek at him on the other side of the elevator. He's staring at something on his phone and there's a slight frown on his face, that for once is not directed at me.

The elevator doors open and we step out into the lobby of what appears to be a penthouse apartment. It's luxurious to the point that I wouldn't be surprised if the King of England himself stepped out. The expansive floors are all shining white marble and there's a huge crystal chandelier glittering from the embossed ceiling. A tall man with prominent features, who I recognize from my research as Jack Whittington, stands there waiting for us. I'm taken aback by how tight his gray suit fits his body. The trousers look like they could have been let out a little bit because his bulge is there for all to see.

"Do my eyes deceive me or do you look like you could become my third wife," Jack asks in dulcet tones as he takes my hand and kisses my palm. My heart races as I stare at him. It's weird because I really don't find him attractive, but still I'm drawn to him. I guess that's the magic of men with money. My palm tingles as he reluctantly lets go of my hand and takes a step back. He hums something under his breath and I feel my uncomfortability monitor rising quickly.

I hear Max clear his throat and turn to look at him. He's frowning slightly as he steps forward with his hand held out. "I'm Max Spector. It's good to meet you, Jack. Or would you rather I call you, Mr. Whittington?" He stands in front of me so that he is now next to Jack and I feel like he's just become my shield. I wonder if he's done that on purpose or not. Is he being my knight in shining armor or just trying to cockblock me?

He's either sweet or a douchebag.

I need to stop thinking about him as anything other than my boss.

Note to self: This is real life, Lila. This is not a play. Or a role. Max Spector is not your leading man. This is not going to end up with me receiving a Golden Globe or an Oscar.

Those golden statues would be like my babies, if I ever won one.

The only golden baby I could possibly end up with would be puking all over me with chubby cheeks and irresistible blue eyes. And I'm not quite ready to be a mother. Not that Max is ready to be a father. Or that I'd even want him to be the father of my children.

I need to stop letting my imagination run away with me.

"Call me Jack." Jack gives me a smoldering smile, then turns to size up Max. He holds out his hand and gives it a solid shake. I watch as the two men take stock of each other. Jack nods as if he's impressed by what he sees. "I've heard good things about you."

"Really?" Max says, though there's no surprise in his tone. Suddenly, I want to Google Max and find out everything I can about him. Our interaction in the car had been taut with tension, and I'd almost felt like he was going to pull me onto his lap and devour me. Or maybe that had been wishful thinking. He's gorgeous, and I'm drawn to him in ways that I've never been drawn to any other man before in my life.

I need a lobotomy.

"So, are you another one of the attorneys at the firm?" Jack turns back to me and looks me up and down. I feel his eyes on my legs and shiver slightly, but not from warmth and butterflies, but rather coldness. Jack's lookover is creepy. He's making me feel like a pig in a butcher shop, hung upside down and skinned. I suddenly don't find it a compliment that he thinks I could be wife number three.

I immediately feel sorry for his ex-wife. I don't care what she's done to him. I can tell that he deserves it. Not that I will tell Max my thoughts on his newest client. He's most probably taken some sort of oath that makes him look out for his client, no matter how smarmy he is.

I'm definitely not going to tell him that Jack Whittington reminds me of a used snake oil salesman, dripping in his own product from head to toe.

"Or would you like to be my personal...attorney..." He chuckles and all I feel is distaste. His words don't even make sense.

I press my lips together so I don't show him my emotions and have him demand Max fire me. "No, I'm not an attorney. Not even close. I'm Max's assistant, Lila," I say with a small embarrassed smile. "I'm just accompanying him so that I can take notes and ensure we give you the best representation possible." *Very professional! Good one, Lila!* "He is the best attorney in all of the—"

"Great!" Jack cuts me off and moves closer, going around Max to get to me. His eyes shift downward again and I have the distinct feeling that he is trying to look down my shirt. What a pervert. If I wasn't here for a job, I'd slap him.

"If you were *my* assistant, I'd take you everywhere as well. All hours of the day and night." He licks his lips. "Only, if you were my assistant, I'd make sure that skirt was just a little bit shorter." He winks and blows me a kiss. "If you know what I mean."

I blush and look over at Max, whose lips are thinner than I've ever seen them. I wonder what he's thinking. He's angry for sure, but I'm not sure if it's at me for wearing the short skirt or Jack for pointing it out. I wonder if he regrets hiring me. I guess I really don't look appropriate for a professional job like this.

"Jack, I think you're making Lila uncomfortable." His voice is grim, and I wouldn't be surprised if fire soared out of his mouth. "Let's you and I talk about your marriage and the dissolution process. Is there somewhere we can sit? I take it you have the signed prenuptial paperwork for me to review?"

"I do." Jack turns to him, his expression now serious. "There's a slight complication."

"I've heard." Max stares at him. "Are you going to tell me what that complication is?"

"My wife cheated on me." He stares at me and smiles that creepy smile again. "I have a feeling you wouldn't cheat on me. Would you, Lila?"

"I don't cheat," I say, swallowing hard. Why is this man asking me all these questions? I don't understand why he's focusing so much of his attention on me.

"Exactly. I feel like you're a good girl. I like good girls." He almost whispers, like some creep in a movie on Lifetime. I shiver slightly and look over at Max. His eyes look furious. I can tell that he's not happy with the conversation, but I don't want him to say something that would cause him to lose this potential client. I know that a client like Jack Whittington that's worth millions of dollars would be very valuable to any law firm.

"Why don't we focus on the matter at hand?" Max says, stepping forward and expertly guiding the conversation back to business. "My assistant, Lila, and I don't have very long to chat with you. We have some other appointments later today." This is the first I've heard about that, but I don't say anything.

"Appointments, eh?" Jack looks at Max with a knowing

glance. "I'd have an appointment every afternoon with Lila if..."

"That's enough," Max says, shaking his head and clenching his fists. "You have a prenuptial agreement that states if your wife cheats, what happens?"

"She gets nothing," Jack says, shrugging, his smirk back on his face. "If she cheats, she gets nothing."

"So what's the complication then?" Max asks, frowning. "And why did you need me to help with this case?"

"Because I don't want to be embarrassed," Jack is annoyed as Max grabs my arm and moves me to the other side of him. "I don't want this to get out into the media. You understand? I have a company that has a very wholesome image."

"So what does your wife cheating have to do with your company's wholesome image? It's her that looks bad," I say, unable to stop myself from asking the question.

He stares at me for a couple of seconds then smirks. "The fact of the matter is, my wife and I attended a very exclusive club." He pauses. "And while I was only there to watch, it may not go down well that I was there in the first place," he says softly.

"An exclusive club?" I ask. "Like a nightclub?" I know I shouldn't be talking, and I can see Max frowning, but I can't stop myself.

"Something like that," he says, then looks over at Max. "I think you know what I mean."

Max stares at him for a couple of seconds and nods. "I think I do."

"So discretion is very important," Jack continues. "In fact, I need to ensure that this doesn't get out."

"Are you willing to pay your wife anything to ensure that that happens?" Max asks.

"I'm willing to give her a hundred thousand dollars." Jack licks his lips. "No more."

"A hundred thousand dollars," Max says, frowning slightly. "That's it?"

"She screwed two men." Jack shakes his head. "She can't get away with that." My eyes widen at his comment. What is going on here? I'm pretty sure that the exclusive club he mentioned is a sex club, but why had Jack gone if he wasn't going to partake? For some reason, I don't believe that he'd only gone to watch, especially not after the way he'd just been talking about me.

"Well, I can definitely try to make a deal with your wife," Max says, nodding. "Is there anything else that I should know?"

Jack shakes his head. "No. I just need this done within the next two weeks."

"The next two weeks?" Max raises an eyebrow. "Is there a particular reason why it needs to be completed so quickly?"

"We have an IPO coming up." Jack says. "It's going to be launched in two weeks, and I don't need any bad publicity coming out. This is a deal that is worth billions of dollars."

"And the firm that's handling the IPO cannot handle the divorce?" Max asks, frowning slightly.

"I'm looking to change firms. If you can take care of this for me, then I know that you can be trusted to take care of the bigger matters as well."

Max nods and types something into his phone. He looks over at me for a couple of seconds. "Do you have all of that information, Lila?"

I just stare at him. I'm not sure what he's talking about or what I was meant to have written down. I assumed that he would tell me if he wanted me to take notes. I nod quickly. "I have all of it, sir." I say. And because I'm an idiot, I salute him. Jack raises an eyebrow and Max just shakes his head.

"She's new," he says, as if that explains it.

"Oh." Jack grins. "Well, if you're ever looking for a job, Lila..." He leans toward me. "I think I know someone who's hiring." He licks his lips. "As long as you don't mind being on your back for..."

"I think that I have enough information," Max says, cutting him off with a frown. "Lila, we do have some more meetings this afternoon. Are you ready to go?"

"Sure, but..."

"Okay," he says, pulling his phone out without another thought. "I will tell Henry that we're ready." Max holds out his hand. "It was nice to meet you, Mr. Whittington."

"You're done already?" Jack asks, frowning. He looks as confused as I feel. We've literally just arrived. I'd hoped to get to explore the penthouse. It's not often I get to hobnob with the rich and famous. I was hoping to excuse myself and check out one of the restrooms and see if he had real gold faucets. I mean, I don't think he would, but I know really rich people buy really ostentatious home decor. "But—"

"But nothing." Max's tone is polite, but firm. I feel a certain thrill at how he's taking charge of the situation. "I have the paperwork now and I will read it over. I understand the urgency of the deal you wish to make with your wife. I'll see if I can do it. You're a busy man and so am I," Max says as he nods. "Nice to meet you. Come on, Lila." He gestures toward me and heads back to the front door. He holds it open for me and we walk out toward the elevator, which we ride down in silence. My heart is racing as I glance at him. Max looks furious and I'm not even sure why.

"Did you have to flirt with the man?" Max asks, shaking his head, and my jaw drops.

"What?" I stare at him in disbelief. "What are you talking about? I didn't flirt with him. I couldn't stand the jerk."

Max looks up at me. "You need to wear more appropriate attire tomorrow."

"Oh, so it's my fault that that pig basically asked me to sleep with him? I mean, that's my fault, right? Because I'm a woman and ooze sex and men can't be held accountable for being dickheads, right?"

"It's not your fault," Max says, shaking his head and holding up his hands. There's a chagrined look on his face as if he's embarrassed by what he's just said. I'm glad to see he's not doubling down on blaming me because I'd never be able to look past that disrespect, no matter how handsome he is. "He was totally inappropriate and I did not appreciate the way that he spoke to you. I apologize if any of my own words or actions came off that way earlier today. Now that I see it from the perspective of a bystander, I realize how inappropriate such comments are." I stare at him in surprise. That was not what I'd expected him to say. At all. Is the guy nice after all?

"It's fine," I say, offering him a sincere smile. "You and I had banter...this guy was just a dick."

Max's lips twitch. "He was a dick, wasn't he?"

"And if I'm being honest, I just don't trust him," I say quickly.

"What do you mean?" he asks as we get out of the elevator and walk toward the lobby to wait for Henry to pick us up.

"I just don't think someone like Jack Whittington is going to a sex club with his wife so that they can both watch. It just doesn't ring true to me. The type of man that's flirting with me the first time he meets me is not going to a sex club just to watch people experiment."

Max tilts his head to the side. "You may have a point there."

"So what are you going to do about it?" I ask, crossing my arms.

He stares at me blankly. "What do you mean what am I going to do about it?"

"I mean, if there's more to the story than what he's saying, then we should find out because it's not fair to Mrs. Whittington."

"Life is not about what's fair. The law is not about what's fair," he signals to Henry and we step forward. "The firm represents Jack Whittington and we will try to get him what he wants."

"But that just doesn't seem right." I say, frowning.

"But nothing," he says, opening the back door for me. I slide into the back of the car and offer Henry a small wave. "I'll go through the paperwork and I'll present an offer to Mrs. Whittington in the next few days. She either takes it or she doesn't." He opens the file that Jack gave him and I watch him going through papers and photos. His eyes widen slightly before he closes it.

"What? What is it that was in there?" I ask him. "Can I see?"

"There are photos," he says as he glances at me and shakes his head. "Compromising photos."

"Of Mrs. Whittington?" I raise my eyebrows.

"I assume so," he says, nodding. "She's definitely naked on a bed with two men, neither of whom are Jack." He shrugs. "I think this will be a fairly open and shut case."

"But, that's awful." I stare at him and shift closer to him. "It just seems so wrong."

He shrugs. "She obviously knew the man she was marrying. Maybe she shouldn't have cheated?"

I stare at him for a couple of seconds. "I think there's more to the story, Max."

"What more could there be?" he says, holding up the folder. The proof is in the pudding."

"I guess. But who took the photos?" I shrug. "I'm not an attorney, and this is my first day as a paralegal—"

"Assistant," he interrupts, but I ignore him.

"So obviously I'm not an expert, but it just doesn't ring true. Where did the photos come from? He just happened to decide to take photos of her banging two other men? I just don't think it's fair that Mrs. Whittington is only going to get a hundred grand when her husband is worth hundreds of millions. And maybe there is more to the story."

"Like what?" he asks.

"I don't know. He's a pig and a slime ball. I just don't feel like a slime ball like that should get away with paying next to nothing."

"You don't know that she's not one as well."

"True," I say. "But..." I pause.

"What is it?" he asks.

"Can I at least meet her, have a conversation with her, see what her side is?"

He stares at me for a couple of seconds and sighs deeply. "Why do you want to do that?"

"I'm not going to say that I'm with the law firm. I'm not going to say that I'm your assistant. I just want to see if there's more to the story."

"But it doesn't matter if..."

"Please, Max."

He sighs. "We're not therapists. We're not here to make things equal. We are here to get our client what he wants."

"It doesn't matter if we're therapists or not. I'm just curious if my instinct is correct. I could've just tried to find her and had a conversation with her without telling you. But you're my boss so I wanted to at least pass it by you first."

"Are you interested in being some sort of detective or something? Is that what you'd rather be doing instead of being my assistant?"

"No, I want to be an actress," I say. "But I also care about people. And I feel like I can sense good people and bad people, and Jack Whittington is not a good man. I just want to see what I think about Mrs. Whittington."

"You can do whatever you want to do. Just do not tell her anything about this case." He stares at me. "Do you understand?"

"Yes." I nod slowly.

"Good," he says. "So Lila, I'm curious about something now."

"Yes, Max?" I ask him, wondering if he thinks I may have been a detective in another life.

"What do your instincts say about me?" He looks at me as if he doesn't care about the answer, but for some reason I can sense that he's waiting on tenterhooks for whatever words pass my lips next.

"I think that you're outwardly arrogant," I say with a small smile as he smirks. "I think that your work comes first in your life."

"What gave that away?" he says with a chuckle, though his eyes are keen as they watch me.

"I think that you have a better sense of humor than you initially let on to most people." I grin as he grunts. "And I think that maybe you're not as horrible as I thought a few hours ago."

"So you're saying you don't think I'm a slime ball?" He's grinning now and his face is transformed. It's like a light has come on inside of him and the warmth and humor radiating from him has my heart racing. And not just because he's handsome, but because there's a real connection between us. He's looking at me like I'm the only woman in the world and it makes me feel like dancing. It's probably all in my head, but I like how this feels.

The earthy side of me now thinks that he and I met for a reason.

The earthy side of me feels like maybe this man has something to teach me.

But that could just be my hormones and the lack of good sex speaking.

It's funny how sometimes we try to find meaning in any and every exchange we have to give ourselves a purpose or reason to believe in something.

"Oh, I didn't say that," I say with a grin as I try to ignore the feel of his hard warm thigh against me. He's leaning toward me now and I can feel the heat emanating from his body.

"So you *do* think I'm a slime ball?"

"No," I say honestly. "I don't."

"Even though I flirted with you and you thought I was trying to offer you a million dollars for sex?"

"Oh my God. Let's agree to never bring that up again. I don't really think you were offering me money for sex." I lick my lips nervously. "Let's be real. You don't have to offer anyone money for sex. You're a very good-looking man."

"Thank you. I'm glad that you realize that."

"Uh-huh," I say, rolling my eyes.

"But don't sell yourself short, Lila. You're a very beautiful woman," he says softly. "And if I was the sort of man to offer money for sex, I'd give you way more than a million dollars."

I stare at him in shock, my heart racing. "What?"

"If I were to offer you money for one night," he says softly, grabbing my hand and running a finger down my palm. "I'd offer you a billion dollars because I'd want to change your life as much as you were about to change mine."

I stare at him in shock, wondering if I just heard what I think I heard. Does Max like me? Is he as attracted to me as I am to him? Is this his way of saying that?

He bursts out laughing then, and I frown as he pulls back and runs his fingers through his hair. "You really do need to stop watching so many movies." He smirks. "That was way too easy."

"What?" I blink at him. "That was an act?"

"Yes, darling," he says. "I guess you're not the only actor in this car after all."

"You're such a jackass," I mumble under my breath and look out of the window. I'm mortified that I thought for a second that he was being genuine and sincere. I'm absolutely cringing inside that I thought he was interested in me.

I need to get a life.

I've only known this man a day and I already know that it's not going to take long for him to drive me crazy. I already know that I cannot stay in his employ for too long because the simple fact of the matter is, Max Spector is the most handsome man I've ever met in my life, while also being the most annoying.

I don't know if I will be able to survive working with him day in and day out for a significant amount of time.

However, as I think about my empty studio apartment—the lack of furniture and my empty fridge—I know I need to get as many paychecks as possible because I don't want to starve or live on a blowup mattress forever.

I have to change my mindset. I'll stay at this job for the money and the work experience. Everything I learn will help me to become a better actress. I just need to think of it as real-life research for a role. As long as I compartmentalize the emotions Max brings out in me, I'll be okay.

At least that was what I hope.

Chapter Eleven

Max

My apartment feels empty when I finally arrive home. I'm hungry but I don't feel like cooking. I head to the fridge to see if I have any leftovers worth heating up. It's been a long day and I'm glad to finally be able to relax.

The sight of moldy cheese greets me as I open the fridge and I release a small sigh. I'm about to order a pizza when my phone starts ringing. For a moment, I'm hopeful that Lila is calling me for some reason, but I don't even think she has my number. I see Marie's number on the screen and smile as I answer.

"Hey, little sis. How are you trying to bother me this evening?"

"Is that any way to talk to your favorite sister?"

"How much?" I chuckle as I open an empty cupboard door.

"How much what?" she asks innocently.

"How much money do you want that Dad won't give you?"

"I don't want any money, my darling brother." She sounds like she's shocked I would even ask. "Plus, Dad would give me money if I needed it."

"So if you don't need money from me, what is it you need, darling sister?" I ask her, running my fingers through my hair.

Marie is only my half-sister, but I love her more than life itself. I never thought that I would ever enjoy having a little sister, but she keeps me in check and I love that she seems to have no fear when communicating with me. She's quite possibly the only person in my life that tells me exactly what she's thinking when she's thinking it and doesn't hold back.

"So I was wondering just how much you love me," she says softly and I frown.

"Marie, what is it you want?"

"I told you I don't want anything. Well, not anything with a monetary value."

"Do you want me to charter a plane for you to Europe?"

"No. Why would I want that?"

"I don't know. Maybe you and your friends want to go party or something."

"If I asked you to charter me a plane to Europe, would you do it?"

"No," I say, chuckling. "But you're acting like you're asking for something major."

"It's not really major. In fact, it's not even that big a deal."

"So if it's not that big a deal, why are you taking so much time to ask me?"

"Fine. Can I come and stay with you for a little bit?"

I pause.

"Max," she squeals into the phone.

Don't Quit The Day Job

"I'm here."

"So is that a yes?"

"I didn't say yes."

"You didn't say anything."

"Exactly. Read between the lines, darling."

"Max, you're horrible. Please let me come. It's not going to be for long. I just really need to get away."

I let out a deep sigh. "Marie, you cannot just come to New York City. I can't be your chaperone. I can't take care of you. You know that your mother and Dad will not be happy with you staying in my apartment all alone. You know I work long hours and you know—"

"Fine," she says. "I should have known you'd say no."

I pause. "I thought we agreed you'd come for a weekend to look at schools later on this year and then—"

"It's fine. I'll figure something out."

I can tell by her tone that she's upset, but I can also tell that she's hurt, and if there's one thing I can't stand, it's hearing her hurt. She's a good little actress, but I have a feeling she's not faking it this time.

"What's wrong, Marie?"

"Nothing," she says, gulping.

"Marie, tell me."

"Dad's cheating on Mom," she says softly.

"And does your mom know?" I ask, my heart breaking for her because I know exactly what she's going through.

My dad had cheated on my mom when I was young and that's how he'd ended up with Marie's mom. My mom had never really gotten over her heartbreak, though she had moved on in her life. She's now married to a very quiet man named David, and even though they get along and I can tell that he loves her, I know she hasn't given him her entire heart.

119

"Yeah, my mom knows," she says. "They shout and scream about it every night. In fact, I think Mom has someone herself..." She lets her voice trail off and my heart breaks.

"Fine," I say. "What are you going to do about school though?"

"Actually, I'm in the program right now where I don't even have to attend classes in person, so it's perfect. I can work from New York City. I just have to make sure that you have good Internet so I can do some Zoom classes and meet with my—" She giggles. "What am I talking about? You're an attorney and you're rich. You have good Internet."

"But I still cannot be here to chaperone you," I say.

"I'm eighteen, Max. I don't need a chaperone."

"You're also my little sister and you're a high school student, and if I'm going to take custody of you..."

"It's not custody if I'm just hanging out with my big brother."

"To your parents, to my dad and your mom, it will be me taking full responsibility and custody of you. So we need to ensure..."

"I'll be good. It's not like I'm going to sneak out or anything. It's not even like I have a boyfriend." She lets out a deep sigh. "Because guys aren't interested in me."

I press my lips together to stop from laughing. Marie is absolutely gorgeous and she's still young enough to have no idea that she is. But I'm not going to be the one to tell her that she could have almost any man that she wanted to because she's my little sister and the longer she stays away from men, the better it will be for me.

"I think that when you graduate from college, you can start dating and I'm sure that—"

"I don't want to wait until I graduate from college. Are you crazy? You're just as bad as Dad."

I start laughing then. "I'm just saying, you're not missing out on anything by not dating."

"I just don't fit in with these people here in South Carolina. I am meant to be a big city girl. I want to live in New York. I want to be with you, my big brother, and I mean, you're single, right?"

"As the day is long," I say, and she starts laughing.

"I mean, you could totally be in a relationship, but I guess you don't want to commit because there are so many women that want you."

"You sound like my ex-girlfriends, Marie. Have you been talking to them?"

"No," she sighs dramatically. "But I know men like you."

"Excuse me?" I say, frowning. "What do you mean you know men like me? I sure hope that is just an off-the-cuff comment and not an actual factual statement because—"

"Oh my gosh, I am joking, Max. Obviously, I don't really know any men like you. I'm in high school. I don't know any men aside from you and Dad. I just mean I've watched a lot of movies."

I groan loudly. How many women in my life are learning about life from fictional characters?

"What?"

"You're the second woman I have had this conversation with today. You cannot get your information about men from movies and romance books."

"I mean I've had real experience as well, Max." She mumbles. "That's why I'm in this shitty position."

"What are you talking about?"

"Uhm...nothing. So who's the other woman?"

I frown at her question. I'm not ready to talk about Lila

with anyone, not even Marie. I'm still trying to process our relationship with each other because it's happened so quickly.

"What are you talking about?" I say quickly, trying to distract her. "Also, are you saying you haven't been dating?"

"You said I'm not the only woman today you've had to tell they rely too heavily upon movies and romance books to get their information about men. Well, who's the other woman that you had to speak to about this? Not a woman you're dating," she says, giggling. "Oh my gosh, that would be hilarious."

"No. You know I'm not dating anyone, Marie. I was actually referring to my new assistant."

"Oh my gosh. You have another new assistant? You have a new assistant every other week."

"It's not quite every other week, but this one will last at least a month, I'm sure."

"What do you mean she'll last at least a month?"

"Let's just say there's a little bet that she'll last a month."

I groan as I think about Lila.

"Huh? What are you talking about, Max?"

"My new assistant might not really be the best person for the job, but due to a bet with Kingston, I decided to hire her. And she lives with her head in the clouds and she's totally unrealistic. I just want to make sure that when you get to her age that you are not the same way."

"Oh my gosh. Is your new assistant like, fifty or something?'.

"No, she's not."

"How old is she then?"

"I don't know. In her twenties."

"Ooh." Marie sounds excited. "Is she pretty?"

"What do you mean is she pretty? I don't know. I haven't noticed."

"You haven't noticed if your new assistant is pretty?"

"No, I have not. She works for me and as such, I—"

"Oh my gosh. Okay, so she's either absolutely stunningly gorgeous or she's a dog," she deduces. "Because there's no way you don't know if she's attractive. You just don't want to tell me."

"Do you or do you not want to come to New York?" I challenge, changing the subject.

"Why are you changing the subject Max? Oh my gosh. She's gotten under your skin, hasn't she?"

"She has not gotten under my skin. I mean, has she gotten under my skin in the fact that she is annoying and doesn't really do a good job?" I pause. "Okay. I'm being unfair. I don't know if she's going to do a good job or not yet. She doesn't really have the experience that tells me she's going to do a great job, but I shouldn't judge her before she's actually done anything for me."

"Okay. When did you hire this lady again?"

"Today," I say, and Marie bursts out laughing. "What is so funny?" I ask her.

"We are talking about your new assistant like you've known her forever. This is just some lady you met today. She's really gotten under your skin, huh?"

"Marie."

"Ooh, now *I'm* getting under your skin. I want to meet her. What's her name?"

"I don't think you need to meet her. You've never asked to meet any of my other assistants and—"

"Yeah, but it was quite obvious to me that you weren't interested in them."

"And I'm not interested in Lila either." I groan as I realize I said her name.

"Lila, that's a pretty name," Marie says. "Ooh, I can't wait to meet her."

"Marie, I have to go now. I have work to do."

"Okay, fine. So can I come up this weekend?"

"No," I say. "That's a bit soon."

"But—"

"But nothing. Let's schedule it for the beginning of next month. Okay? I still have to speak to Dad."

"You're not going to tell him what I said, right?" she says softly.

"No, I won't tell him that you know about him cheating or that your mom is cheating as well."

"Why are they like that?" she asks, her voice low and vulnerable. "Why can't they just be in love and just be with each other?"

"Because they weren't made that way," I explain as gently as I can. "I don't know."

"Is that why you can't settle with one woman?" she asks.

"Why, I'm not sure what you mean."

"Is it because you know you can't be faithful and you just want a different woman every night?"

"Marie, I know you think I'm a player and I know you think that I have all these women, but trust me when I say I do not have a different woman every night. If I did, do you think I would be on the phone with you right now?"

"That's true," she admits. "But you never settle down and you never talk about wanting to get married or have kids or…"

"Because I don't know that I see that in my life plan," I say. "Not that I have anything against it, but it's just not my dream right now. It's not a goal of mine."

"You don't want to be in love and have that special person in your life that you can just chat with and hang out with and..." She sighs. "I mean, don't you ever feel lonely, Max?"

I pause for a second and think about her words. "Sometimes," I say, realizing that it's true. "Sometimes when I'm sitting on the couch and watching a movie and I laugh or get sad, I think about turning to the person next to me and seeing how they feel. But there's no one there."

"I know the feeling," Marie says. "I hate watching movies by myself."

"I know, but what about your best friend? What's her name again?" I feel bad that I can't remember her best friend's name.

"You can't remember my best friend's name?" she says, feeling hurt.

"It's Poppy," I say, laughing.

"You're crazy," she says. "Poppy and I are no longer best friends. My new best friend is Bella."

"Oh yeah," I say, vaguely remembering a long story involving Poppy, Bella, and a handbag that they'd all wanted. "You're not going to miss her when you come to New York?"

"No, because I never see her. She got a boyfriend and all they do is make out and I don't want to be a third wheel."

"You don't mind being a third wheel with me?" I ask her.

"Well, you don't have a girlfriend, so why would I be a third wheel?"

"Touché," I say, laughing. "You do realize that I work a lot and I'm going to have to get a nanny or something, or a live-in governess, right?"

"A live-in governess. Are you kidding me, Max? I'm eighteen, not eight."

"Well, I'm just saying there's going to have to be someone here to help with chores and cooking and looking after you and making sure you don't sneak out or have men over or boys or whatever you call the guys that you date."

"I don't date."

"Yeah. Well, maybe when you come to The City, you'll feel differently about that."

"Fine," she says. "Do whatever you've got to do just as long as I can get out of here."

"Okay. I'll give Dad a call tomorrow and we'll figure it out. Okay?"

"Thank you, Max. That's why you're my favorite big brother ever."

"That's because I'm your only big brother."

"I know, but I love you."

"I love you too, little sis. You have a good night. Okay?"

"You too. And don't spend too much time not thinking about Lila."

"I don't—" I start protesting, but she hangs up.

I shake my head as I place the phone down on the counter and stare off into the night.

"Lila." I say her name out loud. "Lila, Lila, Lila." I repeat her name and an image of her beautiful face pops into my head. Her beguiling blue eyes, her blonde, silky hair. Marie had been correct in her statement. Lila is drop-dead gorgeous, and even though I don't want to admit it to anyone, especially myself, I can't stop thinking about how perfectly proportioned her body is and how sparkling her blue eyes are or how luscious and pink her lips are.

She's going to be trouble. The fact that she has a sense of humor and makes me laugh is even more damning. I don't need this complication in my life. And now she wanted to complicate the case with Jack Whittington, who I couldn't stand. He is obviously a jackass and when he started flirting with Lila, I'd been about to smack him. But he's a potential client. A potential client worth hundreds of millions of dollars, millions of which would be poured into my law firm. I can't lose him as a client.

I let out a deep sigh and before I know what's happening, I've picked up my phone and went to log into the HR database so I can find Lila's phone number. It's easy enough. Her name isn't exactly common. I stare at the number on the screen and debate calling it. I have no reason to be calling her at this time, but for some reason I just need to have some contact with her. I wonder if she's thinking about me. I wonder if she's even going to come back into work tomorrow. I feel a dip in my stomach as I think about the possibility that she won't come back to work. I need to ensure that wasn't so. I need to see her again.

Before I can talk myself out of it, I've typed her phone number into my phone and sent a message.

"You up?" I text, then put the phone back down.

I don't know what I'm doing. Maybe this was the biggest mistake of my life. Maybe she won't even respond, but as the phone pings a few seconds later, a smile crosses my face. She's up and ready to flirt back. At least that's what I'm hoping.

"Who is this?" The message reads.

"It's your boss."

"Mrs. Cartwright?"

"This is Max Spector."

"Do you have the right number? I have no idea who you are."

"Lila?"

"My name is Bob."

"Sorry." I frown as I stare at the phone. Had Lila

deliberately given us an incorrect phone number? I go back into the database and find her email address and try emailing instead.

From: MaxSpector@Chaseparkerspector.com
To: Lilathethespian@gmail.com
Re: My bagel
Please let me know if you need my bagel order for the morning.

I send the email and wait. Five minutes later, a response comes through.

From: Lilathethespian@gmail.com
To: MaxSpector@Chaseparkerspector.com
Re: My bagel
Get your own. Also, I'm not your assistant after hours.

A warm feeling settles in my stomach when I see her response. Email isn't as good as texting, but it will have to do for now. I just need a distraction for the evening that doesn't involve the law or my very messed up family.

Chapter Twelve

Lila

I can feel the air dissipating from my blow-up mattress and I sigh as my back approaches the floor. I look around my small apartment and stare out of the window into the night sky. I can't see stars, but there are a lot of street lights that resemble stars. I almost wish I lived in the countryside somewhere so I could stare into an unpolluted night sky, but if I was in the country, I wouldn't be working for Max Spector and exchanging emails with him before I went to bed. I pull out my phone to see if he responded to my last email.

From: MaxSpector@Chaseparkerspector.com
To: Lilathethespian@gmail.com
Re: My bagel
I think you're still my assistant at all hours of the day.
From: Lilathethespian@gmail.com
To: MaxSpector@Chaseparkerspector.com
Re: My bagel
So you're saying you think I need to work for you all hours of the day.

From: MaxSpector@Chaseparkerspector.com
To: Lilathethespian@gmail.com
Re: My bagel

No, I'm saying that technically your role as my assistant isn't based on time. It's not like you leave work and no longer have a job, is it?

From: Lilathethespian@gmail.com
To: MaxSpector@Chaseparkerspector.com
Re: My bagel

I am trying to sleep.

From: MaxSpector@Chaseparkerspector.com
To: Lilathethespian@gmail.com
Re: My bagel

Why do I not believe that?

From: Lilathethespian@gmail.com
To: MaxSpector@Chaseparkerspector.com
Re: My bagel

I have no idea why you don't believe that, but you're keeping me up past my bedtime.

From: MaxSpector@Chaseparkerspector.com
To: Lilathethespian@gmail.com
Re: My bagel

Is that an invitation?

From: Lilathethespian@gmail.com
To: MaxSpector@Chaseparkerspector.com
Re: My bagel

To do what?

From: MaxSpector@Chaseparkerspector.com
To: Lilathethespian@gmail.com
Re: My bagel

Sing you a lullaby?

From: Lilathethespian@gmail.com
To: MaxSpector@Chaseparkerspector.com

Re: My bagel
Can you sing?
From: MaxSpector@Chaseparkerspector.com
To: Lilathethespian@gmail.com
Re: My bagel
Not very well.
From: Lilathethespian@gmail.com
To: MaxSpector@Chaseparkerspector.com
Re: My bagel
Then no thanks.
From: MaxSpector@Chaseparkerspector.com
To: Lilathethespian@gmail.com
Re: My bagel
Did you find out any information on Mrs. Whittington.
From: Lilathethespian@gmail.com
To: MaxSpector@Chaseparkerspector.com
Re: My bagel
I'm not on the clock right now, but not yet.
From: MaxSpector@Chaseparkerspector.com
To: Lilathethespian@gmail.com
Re: My bagel
Your detective hat came off?
From: Lilathethespian@gmail.com
To: MaxSpector@Chaseparkerspector.com
Re: My bagel
I suppose so.
From: MaxSpector@Chaseparkerspector.com
To: Lilathethespian@gmail.com
Re: My bagel
You do realize it doesn't matter what you find out, right? I still have to do my job.
From: Lilathethespian@gmail.com
To: MaxSpector@Chaseparkerspector.com

Re: My bagel
And I still have to live with myself.
From: MaxSpector@Chaseparkerspector.com
To: Lilathethespian@gmail.com
Re: My bagel
You're an interesting one, Lila Haversham.
From: Lilathethespian@gmail.com
To: MaxSpector@Chaseparkerspector.com
Re: My bagel
Is that a good thing?
From: MaxSpector@Chaseparkerspector.com
To: Lilathethespian@gmail.com
Re: My bagel
I guess we shall see. Sweet dreams.
From: Lilathethespian@gmail.com
To: MaxSpector@Chaseparkerspector.com
Re: My bagel
Thanks! To you as well.

I roll over and get up off of the mattress, then walk over to the window to look outside, then I look back into my empty apartment. I don't have any furniture. I don't even really have plates or pots, but the place is mine. A feeling of happiness surges through me as I realize that I'm doing it. I'm living my life as a single, independent woman. A momentary glimpse of nostalgia enters my brain as I think about Zara and how I miss her. How I've not really been an adult without her in my life.

"You're finally a grown woman, Lila," I say to myself.

I feel suddenly overwhelmed and excited at the same time. I'm entering new territory. It feels weird and wonderful, and I'm hopeful for the future. I move back to the bed and pick up my phone to read the email thread from Max asking me to bring his bagel for breakfast tomorrow.

Don't Quit The Day Job

I roll my eyes as I wait for a response to my last email. It's late and I'm kinda shocked that he emailed me in the first place, but also kind of excited. I lick my lower lip and realize that it's dry so I head to the fridge and pull out a bottle of water. I twist the cap and drink it down halfway before regretting that I'm drinking water so late. I don't have the biggest bladder, so I know that at about five o'clock in the morning I'm going to have a decision to make: get up and go pee or lay in bed and hope that I can hold it in.

My phone beeps again and I grin, wondering if it's Max, but it's Zara's name that pops up on my screen.

"Hey, you up?"

I immediately call her.

"Hey," she answers, whispering. "How are you?"

"What do you mean how am I? You're not my grandma."

"What's up, bitch?" Zara says, and we both burst out laughing. We rarely speak to each other like that, but when we do it always makes us laugh. "I was just thinking about you," she says.

"Oh? Before or after your crazy love making with your absolutely gorgeous rich fiancé?"

"Goofy, he's working. Plus, if I was in bed with him, I would definitely not be thinking about you. No offense."

"No offense taken. Thank you very much," I say, giggling. "I was just looking at my apartment and thinking how bare it is and—wait. Do not offer to buy me furniture."

She giggles. "You know me too well."

"Of course I do. I'm your best friend. Duh."

"You are," she says. "But come on. I can get you a couch and a table and—"

"No, I want to do it on my own. I want to have the exhilaration of scrimping and saving, and—"

"It's really not all it's made out to be," she says, laughing. "You and I both know that."

"I know, but I feel like I want something to be proud of, you know?"

"Lila, what are you talking about? You have so many things to be proud of. You are absolutely amazing. You—"

"And I'm mad at myself, Zara."

"Oh, no. Why are you mad?"

"I'm upset that I didn't go to the audition. I mean, even if I didn't get the role, I still should have tried. I can't just not go."

"I know," she says. "But obviously you didn't go for a reason."

"I think because when I saw that long line of women, I really didn't think I was going to get the role and I really knew I needed to get a job. But if I want to be an actress, that has to come first. Even if I can't eat, that has to come first."

"Lila, I love you, but I'm not going to let you be a starving artist, okay? If you can't eat, I will be buying you groceries. I don't care what you say."

"Fine," I giggle. "If I can't afford groceries, I will let you buy them for me, but then I will pay you back when I make it as an A-list star...or B-list, or even C-list."

"Girl, aim for the stars," Zara says. "No one aims to be a C-list star."

"Hey, when you're a zero star, you'd be very happy to be a C-list," I say, laughing. I twirl around the room, my hands in the air as I hold the phone out on speaker. "Can you hear me?" I ask.

"Yeah, what are you doing?"

"I'm just dancing around my very own apartment like I'm Audrey Hepburn."

"I love you, Lila. You're so goofy."

"I love you too. Guess what?" I say.

"What?" she asks.

"My jackass of a boss literally just emailed me telling me not to forget his bagel tomorrow morning."

"No way," she says. "Are you for real?"

"Yeah. I was like, these aren't work hours and you can't tell me what to do."

"You did not say that."

"No, I didn't actually say that in those particular words, but I think he got the hint based on what I did say."

"Lila, you can't speak to your new boss that way."

"I'm not planning on staying there long. I think I just need to get a couple of paychecks because I'm making so much money. Then I can buy a couple of pieces of furniture and then really focus on my acting."

"A couple of paychecks?" she says. "What does that mean?"

"Girl, I don't think I'm going to last working for him, and I don't even know that I actually like the work. We met with one of the clients today that we're supposed to be taking care of through his divorce from his wife, and he was such a jackass and he was hitting on me and he was the biggest slime ball, and I was just thinking to myself, you're going to represent that douche bag? I don't want to be a part of that."

There's silence on the phone.

"Hello? Are you there, Zara?"

"Yeah, I'm here, but you do realize most people who need attorneys are slime balls, right?"

"No," I say. "Most people that need attorneys are not slime balls. Maybe most people that need criminal attorneys are slime balls."

Zara giggles. "Oh, yeah, you're right. For some reason, I

was thinking of *Law and Order: SVU* and everyone that needs an attorney on that show is an asshole."

"Well, you mean a defense attorney. If they're with the prosecution—"

"Yeah. Yeah. You know what I mean, Lila."

"I do. I don't know Max. Obviously, I just got this job and obviously, I don't know the law that well, but I would think that if I was an attorney I would want to work with and for people that I respect. And just because Jack Whittington has a lot of money doesn't mean that he should..." I pause. "Oh my gosh. I hope I didn't just break the Hippocratic Oath."

"What?" Zara says.

"Isn't that that the oath that they take as attorneys to keep your mouth shut?"

"One, doctors take the Hippocratic Oath, girl."

"Oh, yeah," I say, giggling.

"And two, Lila, you're not an attorney. So you wouldn't have taken any oath."

"I know, but I work for an attorney and I feel like maybe the client information should be confidential. I mean, it's not like Max told me I can't tell anyone, but I assume I can't tell anyone."

"It's not like I'm the *New York Post* or the *National Enquirer*, but yeah, I wouldn't go blabbing your mouth," Zara says, laughing. "You do want to get a couple of paychecks, right?"

"Yep. I looked at the paycheck schedule and I don't even think I have to be there a month to get my first two paychecks, and then I will be like, 'sayonara bitches'." I giggle.

"There's no way you're going to say that to your boss."

"I don't know, but he's a jerk."

"He's a jerk, huh?"

"He's a jerk with the biggest sparkling blue eyes I've ever seen, and—"

"So he's got blue eyes, does he?"

"Yes, he's hot and yes, if I'd met him in other circumstances, I would bang him all night long. I'm not going to lie. He has got a body that could give Magic Mike a run for his money."

"Not Magic Mike!"

"Girl, he's got the body of Magic Mike, but the face of fricking Brad Pitt, but cuter."

"He sounds very delicious."

"He is, and that's why I can only work there for a month or so, because he's either going to drive me crazy or I'm going to have my wicked way with him, and neither one of us is going to want that."

"If you're feeling him that much, why don't you just have your wicked way with him? I mean, when we spoke earlier..." She pauses. "Nothing happened, did it, since we spoke earlier?"

"No, Zara. I'm not the wicked whore of the east."

"Did you just say the wicked whore of the east?"

"Well, yeah. Wouldn't that be kind of a cool name?"

"I could just see it on Broadway," she says. "Lila Haversham starring in *The Wicked Whore of the East*."

"With my co-star Max Spector as the timid scarecrow."

Zara starts laughing. "Oh my gosh. If I ever meet him, all I'm going to think about is a timid scarecrow."

I giggle. "He doesn't really look like a timid scarecrow, but once the wicked whore of the east has had her wicked way with him, he'll be one."

"It sounds like you've really thought about this a lot, Lila."

"I totally haven't, I promise. I literally just made it up in my head."

"So you're not going to have your wicked way with him?"

"No, because knowing me, I'd be the one that got burned and I do not have time for heartache right now, especially after Hank."

"Girl, he did not leave you in heartache," Zara says, and I can tell she's rolling her eyes. She couldn't stand Hank.

"No, he didn't leave me in heartache, but I did feel a little bit used and I did feel—"

"Girl, you only made out with him. It's not like you guys had sex."

"I know, and he wasn't even a good kisser. He's lucky he got my lips on his." I burst out laughing. "Anyway, I want to do way more with Max than kiss. Not that I would ever tell him that."

"You should see..."

"No, Zara. I'm not going to see anything. Anyway, I have to get up early tomorrow because I guess I have to go and get my boss a bagel and coffee before I get to work."

"You're going to do it?"

"Oh, girl. Of course I'm going to do it. I'm going to be the best little employee he's ever had so that when I leave in a month, he's going to regret the day he was ever rude to me and made fun of me and acted like I sucked."

"He did not act like you suck."

"I mean, he didn't say I suck, but he and I both know that I am not the best assistant on the market." I giggle. "Like I said before, I don't really know why he hired me. I don't really *care* why he hired me, but it's just weird."

"It is weird," she says. "Did you ask him?"

"I did ask him and he didn't really say. Maybe I'll ask again tomorrow?"

"No, girl," Zara says. "You don't want to give him an excuse to say, 'oh, you know what? I regret the decision' and fire you before you ever get those first two paychecks."

"That's true," I say. "That would be the last thing I need. Anyway, I'm going to go and wash my face and maybe I'll look to see if there are any other auditions coming up. I love you, Zara."

"I love you Lila. Talk to you soon?"

"Okay, bye."

Chapter Thirteen

Max

It's seven AM and I'm excited to head to the office, which is absolutely crazy. I love my job and I love my office—my work is my life—but it isn't that I particularly enjoy going there. But today feels different. Today, there's a pep in my step that I haven't felt for a really long time and I don't want to analyze why that is.

"Morning, Max," Kingston says as I get out of the elevator and head toward my office.

"Morning," I say, looking at him in surprise. "You're here early."

"I had some paperwork I needed to take care of before I go to court this morning." He looks at me. "But that doesn't explain why *you* are here this early."

"I wanted to get ahead on a couple of cases because Marie is actually going to join me in a couple of weeks."

"She's joining you?" Kingston says in surprise. "What do you mean joining you?"

"She called me last night and asked if she could come and stay. Turns out my dad is still a douche bag and is cheating on her mom and I don't want her to have any sort of emotional issues."

"Marie?" He looks at me and shakes his head. "Your sister is the last person I would ever expect to have emotional issues."

"Yeah, because she has a big brother like me taking care of her," I say with a chuckle. "But anyway, even though she knows I have to work, I want to ensure that I've got some time for her when she first gets to town."

"You're a good big brother," Kingston says, laughing. "She's lucky to have you."

"Don't be getting all sentimental on me, Kingston."

"I'm not, trust me. Just make sure you're getting your shit done."

"You're talking to me like you think you're my boss instead of my partner."

"Hey," he says. "What can I say? Am I not really the big boss around here?"

I laugh. "You wish."

"So how's it going with your new assistant?" he asks, grinning at me.

"Fabulously," I say, my heart racing slightly as I think of Lila. "She's going to be a real asset to the firm."

"Yeah, right," Kingston says. "Does she even know what a brief is?"

I stare at him and just shake my head. "No comment."

"Well, let's just hope she lasts a month," he says, grinning.

"She will be here a lot longer than a month. I can assure you of that."

"I just hope that doesn't mean your work is going to suffer."

I laugh suddenly. "You know what, Kingston? Not funny."

"Well, what can I say?" He pauses. "Oh yeah, and you will never believe what happened to me last night."

"What happened?"

"Do you remember that girl, Ashley?"

"No, Kingston. I do not remember Ashley."

"You know. Big boobs, long blonde hair, brown eyes."

I stare at him. "That could be any number of women you've slept with in the last decade."

"Whatever. You know who I'm talking about. Remember she said she wanted to be my maid?" He holds out his fingers and does quotes.

"No, I don't really remember this."

"Remember she had a thing for role play? She used to like to be a maid and she wanted me to act like I was her boss."

"Okay. Well, what about her?"

"Dude, she came over last night in a trench coat."

"Okay, and?"

"And she opened it and she had nothing on underneath."

"Oh, you dirty dog!" I laugh. "You did *not* fulfill one of every man's fantasies."

He chuckles. "I will neither confirm nor deny what happened at my apartment around 11:22 PM last night, but I will say that the Trojan manufacturing plant thanks me for my service."

"Dude."

"What? It was Ashley's idea, not mine."

"I'm going to my office now."

I turn to do just that but turn back to him before I've taken two steps.

"Oh, yeah. Did you hire your new assistant yet?"

"Actually I hired that girl, Skye. She had a good résumè." He shrugs. "And she doesn't really know Lila very well. They just met that morning on the way to the office."

I stare at him. "You know they met on the way to an audition to be actresses, right?"

He cocks his head to the side and frowns. "No, she didn't tell me that part."

"I'm just saying." I shrug. "But good luck to you."

"Hmm, I will have to speak to her when she gets in." He shrugs. "Anyway, I'll talk to you later?"

"Sounds good. Is Remy in the office yet?"

He shakes his head. "I don't think so, but I did hear from Gabe. He will be back on Monday."

"Great. We'll have a partners meeting Monday morning?"

"Sounds good. I'll let everyone know," Kingston says.

"Great. Thanks."

I head to my office and I'm surprised to see that there's a light on. Had someone been into my office? I frown slightly as I hurry toward my desk and my jaw drops when I see a brown bag and a white styrofoam cup on the desk. I open the bag and sniff. It's a freshly made bagel. I open the top of the cup and there's coffee. Is Lila here already? I look around for a couple of seconds, frowning, and she walks in with a big smile on her face.

"Good morning, Mr. Spector. How are you today?" she says in an almost-robotic fashion, and I freeze for a couple of moments.

I am slightly disappointed to realize that she's wearing a much more appropriate suit today. A long skirt and an almost-Victorian-looking white shirt with buttons all the way up her neck. Maybe she's trying to let me know that she is no longer interested in flirting.

"Did you poison this?" I hold up the coffee cup and sniff.

"No, I would never do that to you, Mr. Spector," she says demurely, and my eyes narrow as she steps forward, a serene smile on her face. "I just want to let you know that I want to be the best, most professional assistant you've ever seen." She holds her hands together. "Is there anything that I can do for you, Mr. Spector? Or do you need any sugar for your coffee?"

I take a sip of the coffee. Surprisingly, it's not that bad, so I shake my head.

"Why are you here so early?"

"Well, when I got your email last night, I decided I can let this go one of two ways. I can appreciate that my boss wants a bagel for breakfast and get it, or I can email him and tell him to stuff the bagel up his ass. I decided to go with the former."

I can't stop myself from chuckling. "I'd like to see you try and stuff a bagel up my ass."

"Would you?" She breaks the demure smile off her face, her eyes sparkling as she smirks. "Because I can pull that bagel out of the bag and have you bend over if you want."

"Really, Lila?"

She blushes lightly. "But I would never do such a thing," she says in her Stepford wife voice again.

"What is up with your outfit and the way you're talking to me?"

"I have no idea what you mean, Mr. Spector. I am the epitome of a perfect legal assistant, and while I may not have the experience, I am going to do my very best to be the sort of assistant that you deserve and need."

"Are you like an AI robot? Did the world change

overnight and create AI robots that look like real people and I didn't know it?"

"No, Mr. Spector," she giggles. "It's me, Lila Haversham and I—"

"Lila." I hold my hand up. "You were annoying as fuck yesterday, but this shit is even more annoying."

She bites down on her lower lip. "But I thought you wanted me to be the perfect assistant."

"The perfect assistant doesn't talk like a robot and act like a Stepford wife. I hired you because I think you can eventually learn to do a good job and..."

"Because you want to..." She grins as I glare at her.

"Go ahead. I want to what?"

"You want to do a good job at your firm," she says quickly.

"Okay, because if you were going to say I want to sleep with you one more time..."

"No, sir. You are a professional. You would never sleep with your assistant, would you?"

"No, I would not," I confirm.

"And I'm a professional too. I would never sleep with my boss. Especially not one that looks like you."

"Excuse me?"

"I mean you're handsome in an obvious way, but I like men that are distinguished looking and have a little bit of uniqueness to them. You're like a carbon copy frat guy."

"I'll have you know I was never in a frat."

"Well, you're just like a carbon copy of a generic, good-looking guy. Yeah, you could go to Hollywood and make it as an A-list star, and yeah, a lot of women probably want you, but that's not what I'm attracted to. Like sure, you may have a six-pack, but ew. Who really wants to be with a guy with a six pack? All six packs do is make you feel self-conscious about your own body."

"Is that your way of telling me you don't have a six pack, or is that your way of telling me you want to see *my* six pack?"

"No," she says, shaking her head. "I don't want to see your six pack."

"Good," I say as I step around my desk and come to her. I take another sip of the coffee and swallow slowly. "Because there's one thing you should know, Lila."

"Yes?" she says, blinking rapidly as I take another step toward her.

"I don't have a six pack."

"You don't?" Her eyes widen and she looks down toward my stomach in disbelief.

"I have an eight pack," I say as I bring my lips close to her ear and blow lightly before pulling back.

Her face is red and I watch as she swallows hard. "An eight pack?" She rolls her eyes. "Of course you would have an eight pack."

"I'm a perfectionist." I shrug. "What can I say?"

"Nothing," she says.

"Well, good for you, but of course you wouldn't want to see my eight pack, would you?"

"No, of course not," she says. "Why would I?"

"I don't know. Maybe because you were thinking about it all night."

"No, I was not," she says, blinking. "Why would you say that?"

"Why are you acting like I read your mind? Were you thinking about me last night?" I ask, looking her up and down.

I realize that even though the white shirt she's wearing

is Victorian in style, the material is also quite thin and I can see the outline of her bra. Dirty thoughts run through my mind as I picture undoing one button at a time and ripping that shirt off of her. I bet she has a beautiful chest. I bet her breasts are perky and...

"Sorry, what did you say, Mr. Spector?" she says, and I realized that I have completely spaced out.

"I said that I think you should do some research on Mrs. Whittington this morning and give me a bullet list of everything you find out around one o'clock."

"Okay," she says, nodding. "Is there anything else you'd like me to do?"

"No. I think that is good for now," I say. "And you do see your office desk right outside there?"

"Yes," she says. "Should I go there now or..."

"I think that would be best," I say. "Thank you for the bagel and the coffee."

"You're welcome," she says, turning to me with a small smile. "Let me know if there's anything else you want me to do or you know, paperwork to file. Or..."

"Don't forget you're meeting with HR again later today. I do not want to get in trouble for having you miss a second day."

"I know," she says. "I won't forget."

There's a warm smile on her face as she runs her fingers through her hair.

"And Lila?" I ask her as she heads toward the door.

"Yes, Mr. Spector?" She turns and looks back at me.

"I'm glad to see you this morning."

"Thank you," she says, looking surprised. "Just don't think you can text me or email me every evening and demand a bagel."

"Well, I don't need to do that now, do I? You already know."

"I guess I do," she says, shaking her head. "Okay. I'll do the research now."

"Sounds good."

I watch as she goes to her desk, then I head back to mine and sit down. My phone rings and I groan when I see it's my father.

"Hi, Dad," I say, answering quickly. "Can't talk long. I'm busy doing work."

"It's not even eight o'clock in the morning yet."

"I know, but as an attorney, that's when I'm at the top of my game—"

"Marie says that she is going to be living with you?" My father cuts me off and I sigh.

I had wanted to speak to him before Marie. "Dad, she seems like she's having a hard time there and—"

"I mean, if you think you can deal with her and her attitude, go right ahead."

"What?" I say in surprise. "You and—"

"If you want to deal with Marie, let her go to New York. She'll realize very quickly that the life she has here is amazing and cannot be beat."

"Dad..."

"What? You're her big brother and you know best, right? Just like you knew that I—"

"Dad, we're not getting into this right now," I say, cutting him off.

"Whatever. Just know that I'm going to be putting her on a plane next week."

"Fine. You know I love her and she can stay with me as long as she needs to."

"Good. I suppose she told you that her mother and I are having some issues."

"Yes, Dad," I say snidely. "That's part of the reason why she wants to leave the house."

He sighs. "Well, that's none of her business, is it? She shouldn't involve herself in grown people's issues."

"Dad, I'm going to go now. Okay?"

I hang up before he can answer and put my face in my hands and squeeze my temples. "Oh, Marie," I think out loud. "Oh, Marie."

Chapter Fourteen

Lila

"Who the hell is Marie?" I mumble to myself as I sit at my desk and try not to look back into Max's office. I'm supposed to be trying to figure out if Mrs. Whittington is an innocent or guilty party, but all I can think about is the name I had just heard Max mumbling to himself. Is Marie his girlfriend? His ex-girlfriend? A woman he wants to be with? I have no clue, but just the thought of her makes me annoyed.

Why was he sitting at his desk mumbling her name like he was concerned about her?

It really shouldn't matter to me, but I feel annoyed for her and for me, because if she's someone special in his life, why the hell was he flirting with me so much, and why was he giving me those looks that told me he wanted to rip my clothes off? Why is he making me feel like we're in a chemistry lab and about to explode together? It doesn't make sense. I take a deep breath and open my company-issued laptop. I cannot fixate on the Marie issue.

"Hey, Lila, I'm just going to—"

"Yes," I look up and snap at Max, who raises a single eyebrow.

"So I guess the Stepford wife thing is done already?"

"It wasn't a thing. I was just trying to be the perfect employee for the not-so-perfect boss. But I don't think that you actually deserve me to be perfect."

"Erm, okay..." He looks confused. "Number one, I never said you needed to be perfect. Number two, even when you were doing the Stepford wife thing, you weren't perfect. And number three, what's with the attitude? Two seconds ago you were smiling and laughing, and now?"

"And now nothing, Mr. Spector," I say, glaring at him. "I have work to do, and I think you do as well."

"Yes. I was just going to say that my calls are being forwarded to your desk, so if you could take messages..." He pauses then adds, "*Detailed* messages, including a name, number, and reason for the call, that would be great."

"Why, of course, Mr. Spector. There's nothing I would like to do more."

"I am sure there are a couple of things you'd like to do more," he says, putting his hands on the desk and leaning toward me. "I mean, I can think of a couple of things I'd like you to do." My eyes widen as he licks his lips. There's no way he's flirting with me again, is there? Just after he was mumbling about Marie?

"I know there are a couple of things I'd like to do to you as well," I say, leaning forward, a small smile on my face. I look over his handsome face, then down. "Actually, I think that..."

"Yes?" he says. "Continue..."

"I'd love to..." I lick my lips. "If you stand up straight for me for a second." He shrugs and stands up straight and I looked him directly in the crotch, then I look back in his eyes, which are sparkling, and I'm not sure if he thinks I'm about to tell him I'd love to give him a blowjob, but if he is, he's absolutely crazy.

"Continue, Ms. Haversham," he says.

"I'd love to be able to knee you right there," I say succinctly. "It's always been my dream to kick a guy in the balls." He bursts out laughing then.

"That's not exactly what I expected to hear. And I do hope that you do not try it on me. I would not like to be your first victim."

"Erm, then don't act like a jackass," I say.

"Wow, you really went from zero to 180 in, like, ten seconds. Did I do something and not know about it?"

"No," I say. "And please, let me get back to my research on Mrs. Whittington."

"Okie dokie," he says. "I most likely won't be back for a couple of hours, so feel free to have your lunch break, and I'll see you this afternoon."

"Oh, okay," I say in surprise. "Are you going somewhere that you wish for me to accompany you, or..."

"No," he says. "What I have to do you'll be no help with."

"Thanks a lot," I say.

"I'm not trying to be rude, but this is your second day on the job and you're going to an HR meeting, which you should check with them and see exactly what time that's scheduled for. When you go, just forward the calls to the receptionist."

"Okay, I will." I stare at him for a couple of seconds and he just looks at me.

"So if that's all," he says, clearing his throat. "I'll be off."

"Okay then," I say, watching his back as he heads toward the elevator. He's tall, and his shoulders are broad and wide, and my mind thinks back to his comment from earlier.

"Does he really have an eight pack?" I mumble to myself. There's no way. I don't even think eight packs are humanly possible unless you're a bodybuilder.

And he doesn't have the body of a bodybuilder. Though, it's not like I've seen him naked. But I mean, I wouldn't *mind* seeing him naked, if I'm completely honest with myself. If I'm being completely honest with myself, I can only imagine just how dynamite he is in bed.

I think the reason my mind cannot move away from him is because I haven't been in a real relationship with a guy I find really attractive in a long time. And it's not like Mr. Spector is going to be...that. He would suck as a boyfriend. I have no doubt in my mind that he'd be so self-absorbed and buried in his work that I'd barely see him if we were actually dating.

But I have a feeling that, in bed, he would be the Fourth of July and Halloween all rolled into one. He'd be the bag of sweets and the fireworks.

I sigh as I realized that my mind is in the gutter and it really has no reason to be, because even if I did want to be with him, that doesn't mean he wants to be with me. I have a feeling he just likes playing with me.

That's what good-looking guys do, they just want to see if they can get you. It doesn't even mean they actually want you.

My phone beeps then, and I look down and smile. It's a text message from Skye.

"Hey, you girls want to grab lunch?" I realize that she's texted me and Juniper.

Juniper responds immediately.

"I am so in."

"Me too." I send back, smiling. I really like them. And I really hope that we grow to be good friends. I was really happy that Skye had received a job offer from Kingston, even though it had shocked me. I hadn't wanted to tell her what I'd overheard him saying to Max about the possibility of hiring her.

It just doesn't even make sense to me that she got hired. She has about as much experience as I do, which is none. I want to ask her how she'd gotten the job, but a part of me is nervous that maybe she'd lied, and I don't want to be burdened with her truth just in case HR or Max come to me with questions.

I don't mind a little white lie every now and then, but I really hate having to lie frequently. And as much as I like Skye, I don't want to have to lie for her. And I have a teenzie-weenzie suspicion that she hadn't been utterly honest about her qualifications. I'm not sure why I have that feeling, but I can't shake it.

Maybe it's just my female instinct, but I'm suspicious that a man like Kingston, who had seemed like he wanted someone with a lot of experience, would hire Skye. Almost as suspicious as I am about the reason behind why Max had hired me. It just doesn't make sense, unless they were trying to hire the worst assistants for the jobs. But why would they do that?

I realize that I've been sitting at the desk for thirty minutes already and have done absolutely no work, so I quickly type into Google, "Lucinda Whittington" and wait for the results to show so I can do a deep dive into her life and personality. I'm kinda hoping that I'll find enough information to somehow take down Jack Whittington, that I find something to make Max question taking him on as a client. I'm hoping to impress him.

Because even though I have no interest in being a personal assistant to an attorney for a long amount of time, I want Max to eat his words. I want Max to really believe that I'm a great assistant. I want to leave and make him feel disappointed. I want him to regret every negative word he's said to me, because even though I want to make it as an A-list actress, I also want to be the sort of assistant that people don't want to let go.

Maybe that's just my nature. Maybe I've just always wanted to be the best. I don't care that I have no knowledge of the law. I don't really like being subservient to people. I just know that when I take on a role, I do it to the best of my ability.

"Aha," I say as I bring up Lucinda Whittington's Facebook account. I frown slightly as I see her profile picture. She's dressed in a bikini at the beach. Not the very best sign for someone that I'm trying to prove is innocent and demure, especially because the bikini's a thong bikini and there's a guy slapping her ass who is definitely *not* her husband.

I bite down on my lower lip. Maybe Mrs. Whittington did cheat on her husband. Maybe Jack does deserve to keep every penny that he's made. Maybe I'd gotten it wrong. Maybe she isn't someone who needs my help. But still, I know I'm going to continue looking to see if there is anything else I can do.

Chapter Fifteen

Max

I make my way back to the office, curious about what information Lila may have dug up on Mrs. Whittington. Not that it will affect my decision, but Jack had been an asshole and I'd been literally seconds from punching the shit out of him. The comments he kept making towards Lila were completely inappropriate, and I felt like he was disrespecting both her and myself with the way he'd been flirting with her.

I hold the brown bag in my hand and look down at it as I make my way back to my office. I wonder if Lila's going to be surprised at the little present I've gotten for her. I know I surprised myself when I purchased it. I'm not normally the sort of man that buys gifts for my assistant.

"How is lunch Lila?" I ask her. She's sitting at her desk staring at her laptop as if she's seen a ghost. She looks up at me, blinking slowly, and offers me a wide smile. When she smiles at me it's like the Earth stands still. There's something so calming and pleasant in her spirit.

"It was great. I went with some of the girls. We're actually going to be going to HR in an hour for some paperwork."

"Great," I say, standing by the desk and looking down at her. So did you find any information on Mrs. Whittington?"

"A little," she says, frowning slightly, and I can tell by the distress in her expression that whatever she's found isn't as great as she would've hoped.

"And are you going to impart that knowledge on me?"

"No, because I haven't finished my research and it wouldn't be smart of me to give you any sort of opinion without fully knowing what I'm talking about." A slow smile spreads across my face and I chuckle.

"Well, you are a thorough detective, aren't you?"

"I try to do my best." She grins at me.

"Well, then I'm glad I got you this." I hand her the small brown bag quickly and she takes it from me with a surprised expression.

"What's this?" she asks, raising an eyebrow, not opening the bag.

"A little gift."

"A gift? For me?" Her eyes widen. "What sort of gift?" She looks at the bag. "You didn't get me..." She blushes and my heart races.

"What do you think is in that bag, Lila?"

"I don't know. You didn't get me a thong or something, did you?"

"A thong?" I ask her, grinning. "Do you wear thongs?"

"Not that it's any of your business, but no, I don't wear thongs. I mean, unless, you know..."

"I think I get what you're saying, Lila. But no, I didn't get you a thong."

"It's not any sort of underwear like a bra or panties or...?"

"Lila, get your mind out of the gutter. Would I do such a thing?"

"I don't know." She shrugs. "Maybe this was your way of telling me that..." She looks down at her desk. Her face is deep red now.

"This is my way of telling you what, Lila?"

"I don't know. Forget it. You're right. I do watch too many romance movies and I'm definitely reading too many steamy romance books."

"You like the smut, huh?"

"I mean, the men in those books are always way better than the men I meet in real life."

"Well, that's a shame," I say, though a part of me is happy at her comment, because if she had met a man that she considered to be as good as a fictional character, then it would make me slightly disappointed. "So are you going to open it or are we just going to stand here awkwardly with you accusing me of buying you sexy underwear or sex toys?"

"I never accused you of buying me a sex toy."

"I have a feeling that was going to be your next question."

She giggles slightly. "Maybe." She puts her hand into the bag and pulls out the present I got her. There's a confused expression on her face as she stares down at the magnifying glass. "What's this?"

"You've never seen a magnifying glass before? You must get out more, Lila."

"No, I mean, I know it's a magnifying glass, but why did you get me one?"

"Because you're a regular Sherlock Holmes now," I say, laughing. "Or should I say Sherlocka Holmes?"

"You can call me Enola Holmes." She grins. "Thank you." She holds it up gingerly and studies the circular glass before lowering it to her desk and looking at a paperclip through it. "This is really cool. Thank you so much. You really didn't have to get me this."

"I thought it was a nice welcome gift to welcome you to the team. I mean, I know it's not a million dollars or a contract asking you to be my naughty little secretary, but I thought—"

"No, this is great," she cuts me off. "This is really, really cool. You're really nice." She jumps up and gives me a quick hug, her arms wrapped around my neck. I hug her back, and for a couple of seconds we just stand there holding each other close. I can smell her shampoo as she pulls away from me. "Sorry, maybe that wasn't appropriate."

"It's fine," I say. "I'm your boss, sure, but you can hug me anytime you want."

"Well, thank you, I think?" She bites down on her lip. "You're really not as bad as I thought."

"I'm glad to hear that. Though maybe I should be. I don't want to lose my touch."

"Your touch?" she asks curiously.

"You know, as the big bad wolf of the law firm?"

"Oh," she giggles again, the girlish sound delighting my ears. "So is there any other work you need me to do this afternoon or...?"

"I think that you continue your research on Mrs. Whittington and I'd like a full update tomorrow morning as I will be contacting her then."

"Oh. Really?"

"Yes. I've put in an appointment with her personal assistant and we're talking sometime next week, but I'd like the full intel before then."

"Oh, wow. Without her attorney?"

"I assume her attorney will likely be on the call as well."

I shrug. "I have some other work to finish up right now, but you feel free to go to your meeting and also feel free to leave at whatever time you need to today. It's going to be a long day tomorrow, I think."

"Oh, really? Why is that?"

"Because we'll be going to New Jersey."

"New Jersey?" she asks in surprise. "Why are we going to New Jersey?"

"Before you ask me if I'm taking you to a hotel, the answer is no. We're going to meet the CEO of a bank."

"Oh, what, is he going to just give us money or something? That would be cool."

"No, but he needs help *getting* money."

"What?" she asks.

"I'll explain to you tomorrow. I don't want to fill your head with too much information."

"I'm not a little kid. I can handle information in my brain."

"I know," I say. "But I wouldn't want you to think I'm overworking you in your first week."

"You don't care if you're overworking me. That's why you message me at night to get you bagels."

"Oh, about that," I say. "I need your phone number."

"What?" She looks at me in confusion. "Why?"

"Because I would like to be able to text you instead of email."

"I don't think that's needed," she says, laughing. "I don't need to give you any more access. Plus, I only get a limited amount of data."

"Really?" I say, staring at her.

She nods slowly, a wicked expression in her eyes, "Yep, so I don't really want to waste it on messaging back and forth with you about what I should or shouldn't be having ready for the next day."

"Then I guess I'll get you a work phone." I grin. "That way, you'll be available twenty-four seven and you don't have to worry about the data."

"But..." Her jaw drops. "I don't need a work phone. I'm only..."

"You're only what?" I ask.

"I'm only an assistant. It's not like I'm running the company."

"No, but you do work for one of the managing partners, and as such," I pause, she rolls her eyes.

"And as such, I need to be available at any moment, et cetera, et cetera. La-di-da-di-da Pooh-Bye-Ah, Kum ba yah, my Lord," she says dramatically, and I can't stop myself from laughing. I can see why Lila is in the acting field. She is super dramatic, super over the top, and super funny. I feel slightly sad for a moment because I know that's where her heart lies, and as such, it's unrealistic to think that she'll work for me forever. In reality, I'll be lucky if she stays for the month, and maybe not just because I'd want to fire her, but maybe because she wouldn't feel like she was being engaged enough.

I realize then that I like the banter back and forth with her and she's not a bad assistant. Sure, she has no idea what she's doing and she doesn't really understand what it means to be a lawyer, but I kind of like having the yin to my yang, the devil's advocate on my shoulder, reminding me that sometimes representing a client is not just about helping them win. It's about the fairness of the situation as well. I swallow hard as that thought hits me. Have I lost my mind? Is Lila working a spell on me and I'm already losing focus on what my task should be as an attorney.

"Anyway," I say abruptly. "I have a phone call and I'll be busy for the rest of the afternoon, so please just take any messages. Unless, of course, Marie calls me." She looks up at me, a question in her eyes, but she doesn't ask it. "By the way, may I have your phone number, just in case I need to get in contact with you before your work phone arrives?"

"You can send me emails."

"I'd like to be able to call or text, just in case it's an emergency."

"What sort of emergency?"

"Really Lila? Who can predict which emergencies are going to pop up?"

"Fine." She reaches down for a piece of paper and scribbles her number on it. "You better not text me to fetch you dinner or anything."

"Would I do that?" She nods enthusiastically and I can't stop myself from snort laughing. She knows me too well. "Thanks." I say as I take the paper from her. "I'll see you later, okay?"

"Okay," she says. "Thank you again for the magnifying glass. It means a lot and I will strive to do my best detective work."

"I'm pretty sure that you will. Thank you." I nod and head right into my office and close the door behind me. Even though the walls are made of glass and I can see her sitting there, it feels nice to be back behind a barrier. It feels nice to be in my own space again. Lila Haversham is already under my skin and I don't know why. Maybe hiring her hadn't been the best decision. My assessment has nothing to do with the fact that she had no legal experience and everything to do with the way she's making my heart feel.

"It's only lust," I mutter to myself as I start to wonder if love at first sight is actually real. "It's lust, Max," I repeat. "Trust me, there is no such thing as love at first sight."

Chapter Sixteen

Lila

"Hey, Skye. What are you up to this evening?" I ask my new friend as we make our way to the elevator at the end of the day. I'm glad to be leaving the office.

"Not much," she says, shaking her head. "I think I'm going to go and have a drink. Do you want to join me?"

"I would, but I'm going to do some reconnaissance work tonight."

"Reconnaissance work?" She looks at me in surprise. "What are you talking about?"

"So..." I lower my voice and look around to ensure no one's listening to me. "Max has this new case where he is helping a client, a very rich client, file for divorce. Problem is, there's a prenuptial agreement in place that states if she cheats, he doesn't have to pay her anything, and she cheated and there's photographic proof of her cheating."

"What's the problem then?" Skye looks confused as we step inside the elevator.

"Well, he's nervous that the wife is going to go to the

press, which I don't even know why she would, but anyway, he wants her to accept a hundred thousand dollars as a settlement."

"I'd accept a hundred thousand dollars," she says. "That's a lot of money."

"He's worth millions of dollars. Hundreds of millions, actually."

"Oh, okay. But I still don't get it. If there's a prenup..."

"Exactly." I stare her in the eyes.

"Why is he so worried? Why is this such a big deal? It seems to me there's more to the story." She looks at me. "So what are you going to do?"

"I need to try and find her and figure out what the real story is."

"You are going to do what?" she says as we get out of the elevator and walk toward the lobby.

"I want to try and meet her and figure out the real story and then try and persuade Max to do the right thing."

She giggles. "Are you crazy, Lila?"

"What?" I am slightly taken aback by her question. "I just don't like the client. I haven't said his name because privacy or something, but I think it's okay with you. We both work at the same law firm, right?"

"True."

"Well, his name is Jack Whittington."

"No way. Not *the* Jack Whittington of Jack's Shacks."

"Yeah, him. I met him and he's such a jerk off and I just feel like he's trying to screw his wife."

"Okay, and she looks like a sweet, innocent woman?"

"No," I say, shaking my head. "I saw some pictures of her and her social media is all her in bikinis. But I want to give her the benefit of the doubt because he was just so creepy."

"And you think you're going to find out something that's

going to make Max not do what his client wants?" she asks with an eyebrow raised.

"I don't know, but I'm hopeful," I admit. "I mean, I just want to see if my hunch is correct."

"Okay, so then what's the plan?"

"So, I was looking on her social media and it looked like she goes to a spin class tonight, and after that, they all head out to a smoothie shop next door. I figure if I go to the spin class, I might get an invite to the smoothie shop and then I can speak to her. You want to come?"

Skye shakes her head. "I would, but I absolutely hate exercise and I am just exhausted. But if you really want me to..."

"No, it's okay." I smile at her. "I don't want you to burn out. Plus, it's an hour-long class."

"Oh, yeah. Then definitely no. There's no way I could handle that."

My phone rings and I look down at it and groan. It's Max. "I have to take this," I say. "I'll see you tomorrow?"

"Okay, see you tomorrow. Good luck tonight."

"Thanks, Skye," I say as I answer the phone. "Hello, can I help you?"

"Hey there, Lila. It's me. Max."

"I know it's you. What do you want? I'm just leaving the office."

"Oh, so you're still here?"

"I'm not here. I literally just walked out the building and I'm about to—"

"Are you planning on doing any work this evening?" he asks.

"Um, not technically. Why?"

"What do you mean not technically?"

"I mean I'm trying to do some reconnaissance on Mrs.

Whittington, but I don't think you really consider that work."

"I would like to come with you," he says.

"What do you mean you'd like to come with me? You don't even know where I'm going."

"I know that your plan is to try and have a conversation with her, right?"

"Yeah, but..."

"But nothing. I'd like to see you in action."

"What do you mean see me in action? It's not like I really am Sherlock Holmes."

"I know." He chuckles. "But this is my case and I would like—"

"Fine," I say, cutting him off. "If you can be outside within five minutes, you can come with me. But if you're not, then you can't."

"I'll be there in three," he says and hangs up. I take a deep breath and quickly brush my fingers through my hair. I don't know why my heart is racing like this.

A few minutes later, Max walks out of the front of the building, a wry smile on his handsome face. "So, where are we off to?" he asks.

"We're going to a spin class." I look him up and down. "So you really are not going to be able to wear that suit."

"I don't think you're going to be able to wear what you're wearing either."

"And that's why I'm headed home first."

"Well, I guess I will have to head home as well."

"Okay. I'll text you the location of the—"

"No," he says, cutting me off. I see him signal to Henry and I frown.

"What do you mean no?"

"Henry will drive you home, and then he'll drive me,

and then he'll drive *us* to the class and take us home afterwards."

"Oh, he doesn't have to do that. I am perfectly capable of getting there by myself."

"You're doing work so you can use work resources."

"But—"

"But nothing, Lila," he says, smiling. "Plus, I'd quite like to see where you live."

"Oh, you don't have to come in or anything. I'm literally just going to run upstairs, change my clothes, and come back out."

"You don't want me to see where you live?"

"Not particularly. It's not like I'm going to see where *you* live."

"You can see where I live if you want." He grins. "I have no bodies buried in my apartment."

"I have no bodies buried in mine either," I say.

"Will your boyfriend be there?" he asks, and I just roll my eyes.

"You and I both know I don't really have a boyfriend."

"I know." He grins. "But I was just waiting for you to admit it."

"What do you mean you were waiting for me to admit it? I just..." I pause. "Anyway, so there you have it. That doesn't mean you're coming inside."

"We'll see." Henry pulls up to the front and Max opens the back of the car and I slide in.

"Hi, Henry."

"Hello, Miss Haversham," he says, nodding his head. Max slides in beside me.

"Give him your address, Lila," he says.

"Henry, we're going to drop Lila off for a second. We'll

wait. She'll change. Then we'll go to my place, I'll change, and then we're going to a spin class."

"Yes, Mr. Spector," he says.

I look over at Max. "Poor Henry should get the afternoon off."

"Henry doesn't mind driving in the afternoon, do you?"

"No sir. You pay me very well, sir."

I roll my eyes. "Just because you pay him well doesn't mean he doesn't want to have a life."

I can see Henry grinning from the front as I look over at Max.

"Yes, well, I guess we all make sacrifices," Max says as he leans back and pulls out his phone. "So spin, huh?"

"If you're nervous about it, you don't have to come."

"Why would I be nervous?" He looks confused as he glances up at me.

"Because, it's..." I pause as I look over his body. "I guess maybe you're in better shape than me, so maybe you wouldn't be nervous. Maybe you know you're going to ace it."

"You don't think you're going to ace it?" He stares at my lips for some reason.

"Let's just say it's an hour-long class and I will be grateful if I can last twenty minutes without falling to the ground."

"Sounds like you're not getting enough cardio." He grins.

"I mean, I could definitely work out a little bit more."

"I could help you with that if you want."

I stare at him without saying anything.

"I mean, would you like that, Lila?"

"What exactly are you saying?" I lean forward. "Are you saying what I think you're saying?"

"What do you think I'm saying?" He grins.

"Are you trying to say you can help me with cardio in the bedroom?"

"I don't know. Do you have an elliptical or a treadmill in your bedroom?" He chuckles and I roll my eyes.

"I know you weren't talking about an elliptical or a treadmill."

"What do you think I was talking about?"

"You were talking about me being some sort of cowgirl."

"Is that what you like?" He chuckles.

I stare at him as I blush. "I plead the Fifth."

"You're not on the stand, Lila. You don't have to plead the Fifth."

"Well, then it's none of your business," I say, and he laughs.

"I guess that's true, but I am curious."

"What are you curious about if that's your favorite position?"

"Max!" I say. "You can't ask me that."

"I'll tell you mine if you tell me yours."

"I'm not telling you my favorite position right now," I say, staring at him.

"Later, then?"

I shake my head and I pull out my phone.

"I'm not having this conversation with you, Mr. Spector."

"Pity," he says.

We drive in companionable silence for the next fifteen minutes until Henry pulls up outside my apartment building. I open the door and jump out.

"I'll be back."

"Okay," Max says. "You sure I can't come up with you and—"

"You have no reason to come up into my building," I say, flustered. "It's not like you really want to come up anyway."

"I mean, I wouldn't say no if you invited me up." He makes to get out of the car and I'm not sure why my heart races. It's not like he wants to come up so we can share a kiss or anything. This is a post-date mating ritual.

"But I'm not inviting you up," I say, stepping back as he attempts to slide out of the car. "Max...you're not coming up."

"This time." He grins. "But next time, maybe?"

"Who says there will be a next time?"

"I think we both know there will be a next time." The smug look on his face infuriates me and I slam the door shut before hurrying into my building.

Chapter Seventeen

Max

I watch as Lila slides into the back seat of the car. She's wearing a white T-shirt, which is pretty transparent, and I can see she's got on a pink sports bra underneath. She's wearing tight black leggings that accentuate every curve of her body. I try not to stare at her juicy ass as she plops it down next to me. Her hair is up in a high ponytail and it looks like she's put on a little mascara. She eyes me and puts her finger to her lips. I frown slightly as I stare at her. "What is it?"

"Don't you dare say anything, Max Spector."

"What would I say?" I glance at her lips curiously. Has she put on a different color lip gloss?

"Don't say that I look like a peppy cheerleader or—"

"I wasn't even thinking it," I say, which is true. I hadn't been thinking it until she brought it up, but now that she has, she really does look like a cheerleader. Only, I wish she had on a short skirt. I grin to myself. We'd be in trouble if she had on a short skirt.

"Henry, will you drive us to my place?" I ask the driver.

Don't Quit The Day Job

"And then I'll change." I look over at Lila. "I can't believe that I'm doing this, you know?"

"Why? Because you're a stick in the mud?" she asks.

I shake my head, not answering her. Maybe to her I'm a stick in the mud, but I do feel like I'm quite close to crossing the professional lines of the code of conduct period. But I suppose if I'm not going to be engaging Mrs. Whittington in any ex parte communication, then it should be okay. Plus, I quite like the idea of going on an adventure with Lila. She swept into my life like a hurricane and I'm definitely along for the ride.

We pull up outside my place all too soon.

"Would you like to come in with me?" I ask her.

She blinks at me for a couple of seconds. "I guess it's not really fair," she says. "Seeing as I didn't let you come into my place."

"It's okay," I say. "You can come up. We won't be long."

"Are you sure? I *would* really like to see how someone super rich lives."

"You keep saying that, but I'm not Bill Gates."

"You might not be Bill Gates, but you're certainly not Lila Haversham either."

"Now you make me even more curious about your place."

"Trust me. You wouldn't believe it even if you saw it," she says, laughing.

I watch as she jumps out of the car before me and chuckle. "I'll be right back, Henry."

"Take your time, sir," he says, grinning with a slight nod. "I'll pull around, so just text me when you're coming back down."

"Sounds good." I nod then get out of the car and see Lila standing there. "Eager, are we?"

"I want to see your place, Mr. Spector."

"Ooh, because you want to...?"

She holds a hand up. "You know I just want to see how rich you are."

"You think that sounds better than saying you want to bang me?" I ask, And she throws her head back and laughs. I watch as her ponytail bobs up and down. I picture her on my lap bouncing up and down and me pulling that ponytail hard. Shit, I'm going to make myself horny if I don't stop it. "Come on, let's go inside."

I take her up to my apartment and watch as she looks around and ooh's and ah's at everything I take for granted. "I'm just going to go and change," I say, pointing toward the kitchen. "Feel free to help yourself to a drink."

"Maybe I'll grab some bottles of water if you have some," she says. "If you don't mind, I forgot to bring some with me."

"No worries. Go ahead." I head toward my bedroom and leave the door open as I change my clothes. A part of me hopes that she'll walk in, catch sight of me naked, and change her mind about wanting to go to the gym. I wouldn't mind having a workout right here and right now. Unfortunately for me, she doesn't even venture toward my bedroom. I pull on a T-shirt and some shorts and my tennis shoes and head back out.

"Make your way around my entire house?"

"No, but close enough," she says. "It's really beautiful. You have an amazing view."

"Thank you," I say.

"How many bedrooms do you have?"

"Three bedrooms, two baths. You know, if I have company and whatnot."

"Of course. I mean, if I could afford it, I'd have three bedrooms and two baths as well," she says.

"How big is your place?" I ask her.

"It's a studio, but it's really cute and I love it and I'm not complaining."

"I didn't say that you were."

"I just didn't want to come across as one of those people that was envious because I was in a studio and you were in a three bedroom, two bath and we're both single and living by ourselves." She pauses. "Well, I assume you live by yourself."

"I live by myself, Lila. I do. Let's head back down." I grab my phone and text Henry to let him know that we're coming back.

"So what's the plan of action?"

"I'm not sure yet," she says. "I just want to have a conversation with her. I want to see what she's like. I need to feel good about what we're doing, and I'll know better once we get to the class and I sense her aura."

"Once you sense her aura, huh?"

"Why am I already regretting this? I'm not trying to say I'm a psychic or anything. I don't have any sort of powers, but I feel like I can read people."

"True. You did read me and you were pretty accurate."

"See?" she says, grinning, her blue eyes sparkling. "And I even know what you're thinking right now."

"What's that?" I ask her.

"You're thinking that you would love for me to grab your hand, take you to your bedroom and say forget the workout at the gym."

I stare at her with wide eyes and a huge smirk on my face. "Are you a mind reader?"

She giggles and shakes her head. "No, I'm not, but maybe the thought did cross my mind for a second."

I gasp at her words and she gives me a little wave as we head out of the apartment. Holy shit. Lila is unlike any

175

woman I've ever met before in my life. Most women are not open enough to tell me that they want me sexually. It's usually much more of a game, and while I enjoy the game, sometimes I really like straightforwardness as well. I really like Lila a lot more than I thought I would when I first saw her. I mean, she's gorgeous, of course. I've known that since I first met her. But her personality, she's honest and straightforward and matter-of-fact, in a way that I appreciate more than she could ever know. We ride along to the gym in companionable silence and walk inside.

Lila pays while I stand there and pull out my driver's license.

"You're going to be in room G, right over there." The bored-looking attendant says, pointing to the door.

Lila nods at me and we head over and wait outside. There's a gaggle of women all staring at me and I wonder if I've made a mistake in accompanying Lila, but then I noticed that they're all kind of checking me out and flirting and I offer them all a wide smile. I'm about to say something when my phone beeps. I look down and see it's Marie. "Hey," I say, answering quickly.

"Can you talk to me for a second?" she asks, sounding upset.

"I'm just about to take a class. Can it wait?"

"Please, Max. I need to talk to you for just one second. Please."

"Fine," I say, letting out a deep sigh. I point to the phone, look over at Lila, then head back outside.

"Hey, what's going on? Is everything okay?"

"I have to come in a couple of days. I can't wait until next week."

"What's going on, Marie?"

"I don't want to tell you, but it's really serious and I don't want you to be mad at me and I don't want you to judge me, but—"

"Marie, what's going on? Tell me now."

"I'm not going to tell you till I get there, okay? Please let me come in two days. Please let me stay with you. I can't stand it here anymore."

"Of course, you know you always have a home with me, no questions asked." I take a deep breath. "Send me your flight information and I'll pick you up at the airport."

"Oh my gosh. Thank you so much. I love you, Max."

"I love you too. Okay. I don't want to miss the beginning of this class, so I'll talk to you later?"

"Okay," she hiccups. "I'll email you the information for the flight. Oh, and can I use your credit card?"

"I assumed that's what you were going to do," I say, laughing.

"And Max?"

"Yes, you can book a first class ticket," I say. She bursts out laughing.

"How can you read my mind?"

"I don't know. Maybe my new assistant passed her powers on to me," I say, chuckling slightly.

"What?" Marie sounds confused.

"Nothing. I'll talk to you later." I hang up the phone and head back inside to the class. As soon as I walk in, I see all the women looking over at me. I search for Lila and find her grinning at me.

"Hey, darling," she says. "I'm so glad you made it before the class started."

"Hey," I say, feeling very confused at her words. Did she just call me darling? She blows me a kiss and I realize that something is really off.

"Come sit next to me. I saved you a bike, my love."

"Um, okay," I say, heading over to the other side of the room. As I get closer to her, I lower my voice. "What's going on?"

"What do you mean what's going on, Goofy? You're my adoring boyfriend and I'm so grateful that you took this class with me."

"Um, okay," I say, getting onto the bike. I look around and see all the women looking at Lila enviously, including one that looks suspiciously like Lucinda Whittington from the Google photographs that Lila had showed me previously. I don't know what happened while I was outside, but if she wants to pretend that I'm her boyfriend, I'm not going to say no.

The class goes by much faster than I thought it would, and I also enjoy it a lot more than I thought it would. Lila, however, looks absolutely exhausted by the time the teacher starts clapping and telling us to congratulate ourselves.

"You guys killed it. Who wants to go again?" the teacher says. A bunch of the women start clapping and screaming, but Lila just moans. I get off the bike and walk over to her and rub her back. "You okay?"

"I am literally exhausted," she says. Her face is bright red and blotchy and I can't help but chuckle slightly. "It's not funny. I'm so out of shape."

"I think you're okay, darling."

"Hey, you two." A blonde heads over to us. The same blonde that I'm pretty sure is Lucinda Whittington. "How did you guys like the class? You're new, right?"

"Yeah, we're new," Lila says. "I did okay, but I think my boyfriend here absolutely loved it. He's so sporty and muscular. I'm so jealous." She puts her hand on my arm and I grab it and hold it, squeezing affectionately. She looks at me with a quick shot of surprise, but if she wants to be touchy-feely, I'm going to go for it.

"Well, he definitely looks muscular to me," Lucinda says as she looks me up and down, an appreciative look in her eyes. I look over at Lila and find her wearing a frown. If this is how Lucinda acts with every man she comes into contact with, I can certainly understand why Jack is divorcing her and doesn't want to give her a penny, because Lucinda is a flirt and I can tell by the bedroom eyes that she's giving me that if I agree to go into the bathroom with her and fuck her right here and now, she would definitely be going for it.

I'm about to tell Lila that we should just leave when Lucinda puts her hand on Lila's shoulder. "Do you guys want to grab some smoothies with us? A bunch of us usually go after class to the place next door, get to know each other."

"Oh, that would be great," Lila says. "Do you mind if my boyfriend comes? He's the love of my life and we just love spending so much time together."

"Yeah, we really do," I say. "I just can't be apart from this woman." I pull Lila into my side and she looks over at me, her eyes widening. "Darling, I know I tell you this all the time, but you are just so fricking sexy," I say as I grab her head and lean down and give her a long, soft kiss. She melts against me and I feel her arms wrap around my neck, her fingers in my hair, and all of a sudden my tongue is in her mouth and I'm just loving the feel of her wet body against mine. She's so feminine against my hardness and I just want to take her.

Then I hear coughing. I look up and I see Lucinda is grinning at us. "Well, I know spinning turns some people on, but maybe you guys can wait until after the smoothie?"

"Oh, of course," Lila says, blushing as she pulls away

from me. "Sorry, my boyfriend just really gets out of control sometimes."

"It's because I just love to be with you so much," I say. "Right, darling?"

"Yeah," she says, wrinkling her nose in the cutest way, and I realize that I am enjoying playing the part of her doting boyfriend.

Chapter Eighteen

Lila

"What was that?" I say to Max as we head toward the changing rooms. My lips feel like they're on fire and I'm walking with wobbly legs, and I don't know if my legs are wobbly because the class just took everything I had or because Max's kiss was the most fantastic kiss I've ever had in my life.

"What?" he says. "You're not the only actor around here."

I glare at him, and I'm about to tell him off when I see Lucinda Whittington approaching us.

"Oh, hey, you two. I just want to make sure that you know the name of the place. It's Smoothie King."

"Oh, thank you. That sounds great. We'll probably just shower quickly then meet you there."

"Of course. That sounds really good. I'm Lucinda, by the way." I nod slowly because I had nearly said her name before she'd introduced herself. I had nearly blown it.

"I'm Lila, and this is Max, my—"

"I know, your boyfriend."

"Yeah. We are kind of new to the relationship. I guess that's why we're so touchy-feely."

"No worries. I love that," she says.

"Hey, honey." Max grabs my hand and pulls me into him again. I feel his hard, muscular body pressed up against mine and reach over to run my fingers down the front of his T-shirt. If he wants to go for gold, I'm willing to do it as well. I'm quite enjoying this little charade we have going.

"Yes, darling? You want to shower together?" he says, licking his lips.

"Max." I shake my head slowly and Lucinda laughs.

"Well, I'll see you guys later," she says.

I watch as she walks into the locker room, then put my hands on my hips. "Max, you are really, really, really trying too hard. It's not going to look realistic."

"What part of it is not going to look realistic?" he asks, shaking his head. I watch droplets of sweat run down his forehead. How is it that he's even sexier sweaty than he is when he's dry?

"Lila, you may think you look a hot mess right now, but I think you look slamming."

"I never said I thought I looked a hot mess," I bite back, glaring at him, and he chuckles.

"I mean, I'm surprised you survived the ride. Let's be real."

"Max, that's so rude."

"But true, right?"

"Yes," I admit, laughing.

"Could you hear me huffing and puffing?"

"I could hear you doing something."

"But, to be honest, do you know what it made me think about?"

"No. What?"

"It just made me think about you on top of me and the sounds you might make if we were making love."

I stare at him with my jaw open. He winks.

"And that may have been true, or maybe it was a line for me, as part of my role as your boyfriend."

"What?" I say, dumbfounded and slightly confused.

"Nothing." He grins, and I watch as he walks into the male locker room.

I run my fingers through my hair and slowly walk into the female locker room. I touch my lips softly. All I can think about is the kiss, the way my body had felt pressed against his, the way he teased me, and the look in his eyes when he'd said he wanted to shower with me. A part of me had wanted to be like, "Well, come on then. Let's do it." Because what did I have to lose?

"Get it together, Lila," I mumble to myself as I head to my locker. I'm totally losing it. Maybe it's because of all the endorphins that were released from the exercise, but I'm feeling higher than a kite and way too happy for someone who is realistically still working. I grab my towel and head to a narrow corridor where there's a row of showers. I walk into one of the stalls and pull off my clothes, hanging them on the small little hook before turning the shower on.

The water is cool and feels amazing against my hot body. As I stand there and close my eyes, all of a sudden, all I can think about is Max and the kiss again and how he'd made me feel. I'm suddenly feeling hornier than I've ever felt in my life, and I feel my fingers sliding down my stomach toward my thighs. I slip my fingers between my legs and lean back against the shower wall, letting the water cascade down my body as I start to play with myself. As I think of Max, his blue eyes, his silky hair, his strong arms, his muscular legs, I think about him kissing me and touching me, and I pause suddenly as I realize there's someone in the shower next to me and they're humming. My fingers stop moving and my eyes fly open as I realize it's a male voice. I think it's Max. I gasp suddenly and the singing stops.

"Is that you, Lila?" he asks, and I lick my lips nervously, not wanting to say anything. What in the hell is going on here? "Lila, is that you?"

"What are you doing in the women's shower?" I demand.

"Weren't you paying attention?" He chuckles. "When we checked in, the locker rooms are private, but the shower's are co-ed."

"What? How can they have co-ed showers?" I press my lips together. "But no, I didn't know that was you."

"Are you scared?"

"Scared of what?" I say, standing there with my eyes wide open.

"Scared that I'm only feet away from you. Naked."

"No. Why would I be scared about that? I'm naked as well."

"I know, and that's all I can think about." He growls and butterflies fly in my stomach. I think I must be crazy or losing my mind because I suddenly feel my feet moving.

"Are *you* scared, Max?"

"No. Why should I be scared?"

"Because..." I say. I quickly head out of my shower, move to the side, and step into his shower. My eyes widen as I see him naked. His body is gold and tan except for his butt and his cock, which is long and thick, and I swallow hard as I take him in. He is the most magnificent-looking man I've ever seen in my life. He's staring at me, and I'm sure he's not sure what I'm going to do, but I want to tease him. I want him to see that I'm not the sort of woman that's intimidated by a hot guy. I close the curtain behind me, brush past him, and grab the soap from his hand.

He looks down at me and I stare up at him and smile. A little seductive smile because I want him to want me more than he's ever wanted anyone before in the world. I rub the soap slowly across my body, focusing it on my breasts. His jaw drops slightly as I lift my arms up and continue rubbing the soap along my skin. He licks his lips and I can see his breath against the glass mirror. He's hot and his cock is getting harder, and then, because I'm a naughty girl, I slip the soap between my legs, my eyes never losing contact with his. He steps forward slightly and I feel my breast pushed up against his arm.

"What are you doing, Lila?" he asks, softly gazing at me. There's a question in his eyes and I don't know how to answer it. I don't know what to say. I don't know what to do. I just keep moving the soap back and forth, and before I know what's happening, his right hand has slipped between my legs and is now covering mine, and he's guiding the soap back and forth. I gasp as I look up at him.

There's a question in his eyes, and I nod. He grins as he steps forward and pushes me to the side so that my back is now against the wall. I bite down on my lip. I don't know what's about to happen, but I know it's going to be good. I know this is a moment I have been thinking of and dreaming of for years. I just never actually thought something like this would happen to me. "So, Lila," he says softly. "Is this part of the game? Is this part of the act, or do you want to see where this goes?"

Chapter Nineteen

Max

"What do you mean?" Lila asks softly. Her hands are trembling beneath mine and I'm still in shock that she actually walked into the shower with me, naked. We've been teasing each other back and forth for the last couple of days, and I definitely wanted it to lead somewhere. I just didn't anticipate it leading somewhere like this so quickly. I'm more turned on than I've ever been in my life.

"Is this part of the act? Do you want me to stop?" I say.

"No," she whispers, and I grin. I pull her hand away from her pussy, because as much as I want to rub her clit and make her orgasm, I want to make it last. I want this moment to last longer than the five seconds that it will take me to make her come.

I pull the soap from between her legs and she just stares at me as I guide the soap back to her breasts. They're voluptuous and big and I just want to lean down and suck on her nipples, but I don't want to take things too quickly, too fast.

I gently rub the soap across her breasts, my fingers

flicking her nipples softly. She gasps and leans back against the wall, her body trembling slightly. I drop the soap to the ground and she stares at me. I lean forward and kiss the side of her neck and run my thumbs around each nipple, cupping her breasts gently as I push myself up against her.

My cock is pushed up against her stomach and it feels glorious next to the slippery soap coating her skin. She reaches up and touches my shoulders, her fingernails running down my back, and I grunt as she moves her face toward mine, a question in her eyes.

"You're so wet," I say, laughing as the water cascades down on us.

"Showers will do that to you," she says, laughing, her lips parted slightly.

I lean down and kiss her again. Her lips are like the sweetest sugar and I groan as her fingers run through my hair again. I pull out her hair band and let her hair down, before running my fingers through the wet tresses. I slide my hands down the side of her body to her ass and squeeze before slipping them between her thighs again. She gasps as my bare fingers rub along her slit and gently flick against her clit. Her legs tremble.

As I increase the pressure, she reacts to me just as I wanted, just how I need it, and I groan as my cock becomes harder against her. I slip a finger inside of her and she leans forward and bites down on my shoulder to stop herself from screaming. I'm about to slide another in when we hear someone walk in. She gasps, her eyes widening as I grin down at her, not stopping the movement of my fingers. They enter one of the stalls and turn it on. I have no idea who it is or if they know we're in here, and I don't care.

"Oh, shit," she says as I feel her body trembling.

My thumb flicks against her clit as my fingers plunge

into her more and more quickly. She reaches down and holds on to my cock, her fingers sliding up and down, and I know that if she continues to do that, everything is going to become even crazier. I lift her up slightly.

"Wrap your legs around my waist," I say as I push her up against the wall. Her breasts are now pressed against my chest as I slip my fingers out and rub my cock against her entrance. She moans, grabbing my head and kissing me hard. I'm about to thrust inside of her when she gasps. I stare at her in confusion and pause.

"We have to get to this smoothie place before they leave," she says, biting down on her lower lip.

"Are you fucking kidding me?" I say.

She shakes her head and I let her down slowly as I groan. I slap her on the bottom and she giggles slightly. "Are you just saying that because you don't want me to fuck you, or are you saying that because—"

"Oh, trust me," she says. "I want you to fuck me. Desperately. But we came here for a mission, and if we leave without the mission being completed, I won't feel right."

"You owe me an orgasm," I say, grinning at her. She flicks her tongue out at me and I lean down and suck on it. She gasps as my fingers once again caress her breast, and I feel her thumb rubbing the tip of my cock. I groan slightly. Going to be left with blue balls and there's nothing I can do about it. "We have to stop," I say, pushing her back reluctantly. "If we keep this up, we're never going to make it."

"I know," she says as she grabs the towel. "It's a pity, isn't it?" She winks at me, and for a couple of moments, I wonder if this whole thing has been one big tease. Has she deliberately come into the shower to seduce me so she can walk out?

I stare at her for a couple of seconds, but then I realize

from the way that she's breathing and the reluctant tone of her voice that she doesn't want this to end either. I lean down and blow into her ear, caressing the side of her face as I brush her hair back. "We're not finished here, Lila Havesham. We're not finished by a long shot."

"I know," she says. "Trust me." She looks down at my cock and licks her lips. "I'm hungry, and it's not just for food." I growl as she pulls away and leaves the shower. She is going to be the death of me.

I wait a couple of minutes before I grab my own towel and head out. I don't want anyone to think we were doing anything untoward, even though we most definitely were. I take a deep breath as I put my clothes on and lean back against the wall as I run my fingers through my wet hair and just think about the moment with Lila in the shower, how close I'd been to fucking her, how willing she'd been to have that happen, how cheeky and beautiful her breasts had been.

I needed her and I wanted her, and I will have her before the night is over, because there's no way that I'll be able to go another twenty-four hours without being inside of her. It just isn't possible. And I have a feeling that she wants it just as badly as I do.

Chapter Twenty

Lila

My heart is racing as I stand in the lobby waiting for Max to come out. I have no idea what just happened or why it felt so good, but my body is on fire and I desperately need to talk to Zara about it. That was not about playing games. It wasn't about me playing a role. That was all about my attraction to Max and how sexy I think he is, even his personality, which annoys the life out of me, I'm beginning to somehow find charming. I'm not sure if it's because of the endorphins released by the exercise or because I haven't gotten any in a while, but there's no arguing that Max is changing my body chemistry. I'm literally walking around like I'm on fire.

I'm jerked from my thoughts as Max hurries out with his bag.

"Hey," he says, his eyes searching mine as if he's nervous that I might regret what happened. He has nothing to worry about. I could never regret the greatest sexual experience of my life.

"Hey," I say, tilting my head to the side and grinning. "That was something, huh?"

"We should talk about this later," he says, and I stare up at him. His eyes are sparkling as he reaches down and rubs my shoulder. His fingers feel like Heaven and I want to push him back and kiss him. "I think we need to."

"Hey, guys! We're over here," Lucinda calls out as we step outside. She's waiting outside the smoothie place with another one of the women whose name I don't know.

"Oh, hey," I say, smiling and waving. "Sorry, we're a little slow."

"It's okay." Lucinda grins. "If I was with someone that hot, I would be taking my time getting ready as well, especially with the co-ed showers."

I blush and Max grins. "Well, you know what they say about co-ed showers?"

"No," Lucinda says, flirting. "What do they say?" I can feel the slight niggling of jealousy in the pit of my stomach, but I try not to let it show.

"You guys are engaged or what?" Lucinda asks as she stares at Max, affording me barely more than a cursory glance.

I shake my head slowly. "No. Are you married?" I ask casually, as if that's not the entire reason we're here this evening.

"I am," Lucinda says, nodding. "To a very rich man." She grins. "Kind of handsome as well."

"Oh, cool," I say, wondering what she feels about the relationship. If she knows that Jack's about to file for divorce, she's certainly hiding it.

"Yeah, he is really great and we're in a very open relationship."

"Open?" I ask as we walk into this smoothie shop.

"Yeah," she grins. "Why? Are you curious to know what that means?"

"Yes," I say enthusiastically, looking over at Max.

"Hey, darling, I'm going to get us some smoothies." He places his palm at the small of my back and leans in to kiss my cheek, sending an unexpected tightening need through my body. "Do you know what you want?"

"Choose for me, honey. You always pick the best stuff," I say, fighting to keep my voice steady.

"Well, okay then." He gives me a little wink and I just shake my head.

"Come, let's have a seat," Lucinda says as she sips from her smoothie.

"Okay." I nod and follow her to a booth at the back that's set apart from the other women. "Is your friend going to join us?" I ask, nodding back outside to the woman still standing there. It looks like she's on the phone.

"Oh, yeah. She's just arguing with her husband, Billy."

"Oh?" I ask.

"They argue frequently."

"Oh, okay." That's sad.

"It's fine," she says. "I think she likes it. She always gets amazing gifts when they make up."

"Oh, cool."

"So, how long have you and Max been together?"

"A good couple of months," I say, not really wanting to lie, but knowing that I can't tell the truth.

"He's really cute."

"He is. Thank you."

"How did you meet?" she asks.

I gnaw on my lip. This is not how I'd intended the conversation to go. She was grilling me and I was supposed to be the one grilling her. "We actually met at a work event,"

I say, smiling. "I guess we just saw each other and we were both single and ready to mingle."

"Cute. So do you guys like to play around?"

"Play around?" I stumble over the words and lean back. "Sorry, I'm not really sure what you're talking about."

"Oh, well..." Lucinda grins. "How open are you?"

"Um, what do you mean?" She'd use that word again. Open. What does open mean?

"Are you guys experimental in the bedroom?"

"Oh, yeah, sure. We're both curious about trying stuff."

"Great," she smiles, leaning toward me. "My husband... well, he's a little bit older and sometimes he has a hard time getting it up, which is unfortunate, but he's rich, so..." She shrugs, "And I love him, of course."

"Oh, of course," I say, nodding. Though, I'm not sure how true that is.

"Anyway, we're in this kind of cool, open relationship. He likes to take me to sex clubs and watch me have sex with other men."

"He what?" I asked, my jaw dropping. And she giggles.

"I know, right?"

"You asked him for this?"

"No," she says, looking shocked. "I mean, I was actually hell-bent against it at first. I was not interested in sleeping with another man, being a married woman and all, but when the sex kind of got a little bit boring and he started struggling to get it up, he asked if I wanted a threesome to spice up our life."

"Oh," I say. "Wow."

"Yeah, I was a little bit taken aback and I assumed that it was going to be with another woman, which I was okay with. You know, I'm curious."

"Oh, of course," I say quickly, not wanting her to know

that I'm not really curious at all, but not wanting her to feel judged by it. To each their own.

"So anyway, there we are at home. I'm in a bubble bath that he's drawn for me with these beautiful, fragrant rose petals, and there's a knock on the door."

"Yeah?" I prompt. I don't know much about Lucinda, but she's an amazing storyteller.

"Anyway, there's this gorgeous man standing there."

"Your husband?"

"No, a much younger, much more...well-built man. Very young. Very, very good-looking, very well-endowed, if you know what I mean?"

"Um, sure. I do."

"Anyway, they both walk in and they pull me out of the bath, each of them holding a different hand."

"Wow..." I'm not sure if it's overflow from my shower with Max or what, but it's getting really hot in here.

"And then they take me to the bedroom..." My eyes widen as she continues talking. I'd wanted to get some dirt from her, I just hadn't expected to get this much dirt.

"Anyway, both of them start pleasuring me at the same time."

"What?" I'm struggling to believe that she's divulging all this information to me. I mean, we just met.

"It was the best sex I've ever had in my life, and surprisingly, my husband was harder than he's ever been in his life."

"Oh, wow. That sounds cool."

"It was amazing. So anyway, we had that experience and he asked if I felt like I was open to trying other stuff."

"Oh," I frown slightly. "So you didn't feel like you were cheating?"

"I mean, no. He's the one that brought the other man

and he was right there. We all had a lot of fun." She licks her lips.

"True. Yeah. He wouldn't really be able to say you were cheating if he was the one that brought the other man." My brain is racing and I can't wait to tell Max everything that I've heard.

"Exactly," she says. "I feel like if both people are open to new experiences and trying stuff, then what's the big deal?"

"And you said your husband suggested it, right?" I press my lips together because I nearly let his name slip, and she doesn't know that I know exactly who her husband is.

"Yeah, he suggested it," she says, leaning forward and touching the side of my face. My eyes widen slightly as she plays with my hair. "So...are you and your boyfriend, Max, open?"

"Um..." I lick my lips nervously. I'm not really sure what to say. I want to get some more information, but I do not want to find myself in a threesome with this woman and Max when I've never even had sex with Max in the first place.

"He just looks like he would be such an amazing lover, and you are pretty hot yourself," she says, looking me up and down. I swallow hard and smile.

"Thank you." I look over to the counter to see where Max is. He needs to hurry up before my stupid mouth lands us both in a pretty awkward position.

"So what do you think?" she asks, her voice low, and I'm happy when she leans back and takes another sip of her smoothie.

"You want us to have a threesome, or...?"

"No," she says. "I mean, I'd love that, but my husband likes to be involved."

"You want a foursome?" I ask, my eyes widening even further. "Like a swap?"

"I mean more like an orgy," she says, grinning.

"Have you ever had an orgy?"

"No, I actually haven't. I mean, my husband and I, we can definitely teach the two of you, and I know he'd love you. He loves blondes with big boobs." She looks me up and down. "He would love to fuck you. I just know it."

"Oh, I'm sure..." I say, my voice trailing off. Do I tell her that he's already planning for me to replace her? Part of me wishes I could, but then I'd have to tell her that it would take a billion gazillion dollars for me to sleep with the two of them.

"Thank you for the offer, but Max and I are very monogamous. He is the love of my life and I just could not imagine sharing him."

"I get it," Lucinda says, looking disappointed. "I wouldn't want to share that hunk either, but you know what they say, you might as well shoot your shot. You just never know."

"Yeah," I agree, looking at Max as he heads back toward us with the smoothies. There's a wide smile on his face and my heart flips as I stare at him. He really is good looking, and for a few moments, I wish that this wasn't an act. I wish that he was my boyfriend. I wish that we were having wild, crazy sex and monogamous and madly in love.

"You know," Lucinda says as she stares at me. "When I look at you and Max..."

"Yeah?" I say, my heart racing with the possibility of her calling us out for our charade.

"I just see that look that the two of you share," she says, her voice tinged slightly with envy. A wash of sadness crosses over her face and she blinks rapidly before she looks to the side.

"Hey, is everything okay?" I touch her shoulder lightly.

She nods quickly. "Yeah. I mean, when I see happy couples like you and Max, it just reminds me that a part of me would much rather be monogamous. I love my husband. I want to make him happy, but I just feel like I'm not good enough, you know? I just feel like..." She sighs and shakes her head. "I guess this is the life I have to lead for love."

"If you don't want to do it, you should tell him," I say. I feel horrible for her because she looks like she's about to cry.

"He wants me to be with other men," she says. "It's weird. I know he loves me. I know he wants me to be happy, but all I want is him. I don't want those other men. I mean, sure, I'd love to be with a man like Max for one night, but that's not the rest of my life, you know? I just want me and Jack to enjoy forever together. That's why I married him." My heart sinks for her and I nod slowly.

"Hey there, talking about me?" Max says as he plops into the seat next to mine and hands me a smoothie. "I got you strawberry kiwi. I hope that's okay."

"It's great. Thank you." I say, taking the cup from him gratefully. "You're so sweet, Max." I lean over and give him a kiss on the cheek.

"What's that for?" he asks, his eyes crinkled at the side.

"Just wanted to say that I'm appreciative of you."

"I'm appreciative of you as well." He takes a sip of his smoothie, then reaches over and grabs my hand and squeezes. "I'm ready for bed," he says, winking. He looks way too sexy for his own good and I know that I'm in trouble.

Lucinda laughs as she stares at us. "Oh, to be young and in love." She leans back and pulls her phone out of her bag. I want to tell her that I know she's about the same age as me, but I can't. I can't tell her that I know exactly who she is. I can't tell her that her husband is looking to divorce her, that he doesn't love her, that he wants to get rid of her and not even give her a penny. But I can't. I look over at Max and give him a warm, sweet smile. He might not be my man, but I know he's a good guy in the depths of my soul.

"You two go and have some fun," she says. "I think I'm going to go and see about getting something to eat before I head home. Maybe I'll surprise Jack, my husband, and see if he wants to have some fun tonight."

"Cool," I say. "Well, it was nice meeting you, Lucinda."

"It was great meeting you as well. And if you ever change your mind, know that the door is always open." She winks at me. "Even if it's just you and me. If you're ever curious, of course."

"Thanks," I say, nodding.

I squeeze Max's arm and he shrugs. "What is it?"

"I'll tell you later," I whisper. I watch as Lucinda heads to the door. "I have so much to tell you."

"Good news, I hope?"

"I mean yes and no, but you are not going to believe what she asked."

"What?" he says, a twinkle in his eyes that tells me he's enjoying this far more than he should be.

"She wanted to have an orgy with us." His eyes light up and he nods eagerly. The motion makes me roll my eyes as I laugh. "It's not happening, stupid." I poke him in the shoulder. "Sorry, bud, but that particular dream is not coming true tonight."

"I never say never."

Chapter Twenty-One

Max

"So what are you thinking now about the case?" Lila asks me, her eyes narrowed. I can feel the heat in her gaze and I know what she's really asking. She wants to know if I'm going to drop the case.

I stare at her for a couple of seconds. "Sorry. What?" I don't want to disappoint her or make her feel badly about me, but I've already told her several times that my job isn't to ensure that Mrs. Whittington is provided for. The nuances of this particular case are none of my business.

She either accepts the settlement offer or she doesn't.

A momentary ripple of guilt spreads through my stomach, which I try to ignore. Why have I let Lila infiltrate my brain and heart like this?

I blink as she leans forward. I want to kiss her again, but I'm not sure if she really wants that or not.

"Are you going to drop the case?"

"Am I going to drop a potentially multi-million dollar case because you had one conversation in a smoothie bar with someone?" I shake my head. "That's not how life works, Lila. I think I told you that."

"You said you were willing to see what her side of the story was and—"

"And you found out that her and her husband have fun at clubs, and she openly admitted that she has slept with other men."

"But it was her husband that set it up and she didn't even want to."

"She was coming onto me, Lila. She said she wanted an orgy with the two of us and God knows who else."

Lila lets out a deep sigh. "Yeah, but you should have heard her when she was looking at us and she thought we were so in love. And I could tell from the look in her eyes, that's what she really wants. She doesn't want to be sleeping with these random men. She just wants the love from her husband. He's manipulated her. Can't you see that?"

"Lila, I cannot not take this case because you are now an actress, personal assistant to an attorney, and psychotherapist all rolled into one infuriating female."

"I'm not a psychotherapist just because I care about people."

Henry pulls up outside her apartment. She leans back and I wonder if this is how the night is going to end. What had been an amazingly sexy, fun, and flirtatious night full of banter had turned into something quite awkward. I have a professional responsibility toward my client. Unfortunately, that client is Jack Whittington. It doesn't matter if he persuaded his wife to have threesomes, that isn't my business.

"So this is me," Lila says, running her fingers through her hair. She gives me a small little smile and my heart races slightly.

"This is you," I say, nodding.

"So..."

"Yes?" I ask her, leaning forward.

"You interested in coming up for a nightcap?" she asks, and I stare at her in shock.

Did she just say what I imagined she did?

"Is that an invitation to come up to the apartment that you did not want me to see earlier?"

"It might be, or it might just be I'm asking if you want a nightcap so we can decompress from our kind of crazy evening. But I mean, if you don't want to..." she says quickly as she slides toward the door.

"Oh, I do want to," I say. "Henry, I'm going to get out here. You can go home. I'll find my way back."

"Certainly, Mr. Spector," he says. "Have a good evening, Miss Haversham."

"Thanks. You too, Henry."

She jumps out of the car and I step out and slam the door shut. I watch as Henry drives off and Lila walks next to me.

"He's going to think I'm a slut, isn't he?"

I look down at her in surprise. "What are you talking about?"

"He's just dropped you off at my apartment and you told him to leave, so he knows you're not leaving anytime soon. He's going to think I'm a slut."

"Why would he think you're a slut?"

"Because..." She bites on her lower lip. "Well, you know."

"No. Why don't you tell me."

"Because, you *know*."

I chuckle slightly. "Come on, let's see your apartment."

"Don't expect anything fancy," she says as we head toward the main door.

I look around, and I don't want to be rude, but the street is not exactly lending itself to be compared to Park Avenue or Fifth Avenue.

"Come on, we got a little bit of a walk," she says.

"No elevator?"

"There is an elevator, but it doesn't work all the time." She giggles. "You think I'd be in better shape from having to go up so many flights of stairs so often."

"I can help you get into better shape if you want me to."

"Max." She turns back to look at me. There's a glitter in her eyes. "You are incorrigible."

"Well, I like to think that I turn incorrigible into encourage-able."

She groans at my bad joke. "Come on."

We walk up a flight of stairs for what feels like hours until we finally get off at a landing and walk toward a door. The corridor we walk down is dark and dingy and there may or may not be wet spots on the ground. I try not to think about where they may have come from.

"Remember, don't expect much," she says, turning to me with a small smile.

"I'm not."

She opens the door and we step inside. My jaw drops as I look around. The apartment is empty save for a blow-up mattress pressed against one wall, a black bag full of clothes that's sitting on the ground, and two paper plates on a countertop.

"Have you been robbed? Do we need to call the police? Is this what..."

"No, silly. I haven't been robbed."

"But where's your furniture and—"

"I don't have any," she says. "You're judging me, aren't you?"

Don't Quit The Day Job

"No," I say, but I am worried for her. "Why do you live in an apartment with no furniture?"

"I was living with my best friend and her sister and her niece and nephew, and we all kind of just decided to go our own ways. Oh, that sounds way worse than it is," she says. "My best friend ended up dating this amazing guy and moved in with him and then her sister and niece and nephew moved back to Florida to live with her parents. So we gave up the place and well, here I am."

"Here you are with no furniture."

"I have a blow-up mattress," she says, her hands on her hips. "And it's my own place. Do you know how much it cost for me to get this?"

"It's a studio in a not great part of town, but a lot?"

She giggles slightly and I'm glad she hasn't taken offense at my words. "It might not be a great part of town to you, but I love it and it's my own studio. The only place I've ever lived by myself, so yeah, I don't have furniture, but I'm going to get some as soon as I have the money."

I lean against the countertop for a couple of seconds and strum my fingers across the laminate and try not to flinch as I see some black drops in the corner. Does she have mice? I hope she doesn't have mice. I'm not going to say anything.

"What is it? Why do you look like that?" she asks.

"Nothing." And then, suddenly, it hits me. "That's why you didn't go to the audition that day, isn't it?"

"What are you talking about?" she says as she heads over to the fridge and opens it. "So, about that nightcap?"

"Yeah," I say.

"I have water, apple juice, milk, and two beers. I'm guessing you want one of the beers?"

"That would be nice, if you don't mind."

"I don't mind," she says. "Do you want a glass or..."

"That's okay," I say, shaking my head as I step forward.

She hands me the Corona and takes the other one out for herself.

"Cheers to being my first guest," she says.

"Well, I like the sound of that."

I look down at her lips. I just want to pull her into my arms. Instead, I open the beer and take a chug. It's cold, but it's not my favorite.

"So, like I was saying before you tried to distract me, you did it because you need furniture. You did it because you need a paycheck."

She blinks for a couple of seconds and shrugs.

"I mean, am I being responsible? Yes, but that's not the only reason why I didn't go to the audition. I just didn't think that I would get it and I couldn't cry on cue and well, I've just been a little bit stressed out, you know?"

"Why have you been stressed out?" I ask her. "Is it money?" I sigh. "That's why you took the job, isn't it? Because I offered you a shit ton of money and you couldn't walk away from it."

"You do remember that I decided to go for a job before I even met you. You do remember that, right? I had already decided not to take the audition before we met in the lobby."

"We met before you got to the lobby," I say, chuckling. "Or do you not remember that?"

"Oh yeah, we met outside." She shrugs. "Why?"

"I was just thinking about it." I run my finger down the side of her face and tug on her hair. "You never know. You may have gotten the role."

"It was unlikely. Anyway, I have a question for you."

"Go ahead. What is it?"

"Why did you hire me?"

"Huh?" I say, surprised at her question.

"Why?" she says, slowly. "Did you hire me?"

"Because I needed an assistant. What sort of question is that?"

"You are a named partner at a top law firm. You work on million-dollar cases and you hired *me*. I mean, I know I'm great, but you didn't really know I was great. So I want to know why you hired me." She grins. "And if you tell me that it was because you wanted me to sign a contract to be your sex slave for a billion dollars, you will owe me a million."

"Unfortunately, Lila," I say as I pull her toward me and kiss her forehead. "I did not hire you for a contract, no matter what your romantic brain may want you to believe. I hired you because of a bet."

"A bet?" She blinks as she looks up at me.

I kiss the tip of her nose.

"Yes, a bet."

"But—" she starts.

But before she can continue, I press my lips against hers and run my fingers down her back. She moans against me as she presses herself into me and I feel her arms around my neck, on my shoulders, squeezing. I run my finger down and up under her shirt until I reach the side of her bra. I go to pull her top up, but she pushes me away, blushing slightly.

"You need to tell me more about this bet. Is it something that I should be offended by?"

"No. Kingston just bet me that my next assistant wouldn't last a month."

"But that doesn't explain why you hired *me*."

"Well, I told him that I could make *any* assistant last for longer than a month. He challenged me, I pushed back, then he said I had to hire the first person that applied for the job, threw some money in the mix, and well, there you were."

"But I didn't go in specifically to work for you."

"I know," I say. "But maybe, just maybe when I saw you with your big blue eyes and your beautiful blonde hair in that very short skirt, my mind was a little bit captivated."

"So you did want me," she says, grinning.

"I think we can both admit that we wanted each other, right?" I say as I pull her top off and stare at her in her bra.

She looks up at me and nods slowly before she reaches over and tugs on my shirt. I lift it off.

"Shall we christen that mattress of yours?" I ask her.

She licks her lips, grabs my arms, and jumps up slightly. I don't hesitate to grab her under her ass and hold her to me as I walk toward the mattress.

"You're a little spitfire, aren't you?"

"I mean, I'm not that little and I'm not really a spitfire, but if you want me to be, I can be," she says, grinning.

"I like that you're not afraid to let me know what you want."

"Oh, like you want me to tell you vocally what I want?"

"If you're willing to," I say.

"What? You want me to say 'fuck me, big daddy'?"

I stare at her in shock and she bursts out laughing.

"Okay. Sorry I couldn't help myself, but you are kind of big."

"I'm glad that you like what you saw."

"I hope I'm going to like how it feels too."

"Oh, I have no doubt that you will," I say, as I lower her onto the mattress.

Her body sinks to the ground and I just stare at her in shock. She bursts out laughing.

"It's kind of a cheap air mattress. I think we might have to blow it up before we do the dirty."

"We can always do *the dirty* at my place if you want," I

say as I grab her hand and pull her up again. I can't believe I'm calling it the dirty, who am I right now?

"No, we're already here and I kind of like that you're in my space," she says, reaching up and running her hands down my chest, her fingernails digging into my skin, and I just love the way that she makes me feel.

"Okay then, where's the pump?" I ask, looking around.

I spot it plugged into the wall so I go over and turn the switch. We watch as the air mattress takes about ten minutes to inflate and I decide then and there that I'm going to buy her a bed because this is not going to work out for either one of us, and this sure as shit is not going to be the only time that I fuck my beautiful Lila.

When the mattress is done blowing up, I pick her up again and lower her onto the mattress. This time, I don't let go. Instead, I lower my body next to hers.

"Are we really doing this?" she asks as she runs her fingers down the side of my face.

"I think we are," I say. "So, Lucinda wanted us to have her orgy with us, did she?" I say as I unclip her bra and bury my nose between the valley of her breasts.

I kiss her soft, delicate skin and move my lips over to her nipple, where I suck and tug gently.

"She did," she moans. "In fact, she wanted a foursome. She told me that Jack would be 'very attracted to me'."

I growl as I look up at her and move my lips over to her other nipple, which I tug a little bit harder than the other.

"Ooh," she cries out in a moan. "I wanted to tell her that I already knew that he wanted me, but obviously I couldn't blow the secret plan."

"Obviously," I say, winking at her. "So shall we call her?" I ask with a grin.

"You're awful," she says, pushing me back slightly.

Without giving an inch, I grab her and roll onto my back so that she's on top of me.

"That's not funny, Max."

"I was just joking," I say as I roll her back over onto her back.

I then reach down and pull down her pants and underwear before spreading her legs. Her entire body is shaking as she stares up at me.

"You are absolutely gorgeous," I say as I plant my nose in her belly button and kiss my way down until I'm nestled between her legs. She's not completely bald, which I like. She's clean shaven with a trail of hair down the middle. I don't know if it was a design done on purpose or what, but I find it attractive.

I spread her legs open as wide as I can, then lower my tongue and lick up her slit. She moans, her cry of pleasure ringing around us making me feel harder and hotter as I slip my tongue inside of her.

"Oh, shit," she says as she clasps my head with her thighs.

I eat Lila like she's my last meal. She tastes absolutely delicious. I've never known pleasure and excitement like this before. As she cums hard and fast, I groan and kiss my way up to her mouth and kiss her lips. I position my cock between her legs and look down into her eyes.

"Fuck me, big daddy," she says, and she doesn't have to ask twice before I slowly slide into her.

She wraps her legs around my waist as I settle her around the base of my cock, then I fuck her hard and fast. All I can think about is coming, and just as I feel that I'm about to erupt, I pull out and explode all over her stomach.

I grin down at her sleepy face.

"Wow," she says.

I laugh as I reach over, grab my T-shirt, and wipe my cum off of her. I kiss her and pull her into my arms.

"So have you ever heard of cock warming?" I ask her.

She looks confused and shakes her head. "No. What's that?"

"It's actually just something I heard about recently."

"What? Do you want me to get a towel and warm your cock or something?" she asks.

"No, that's not exactly what it is. I can show you if you want."

"Okay." She nods sweetly and I roll her onto her side and lift her top leg. She stares at me in confusion as I slip my cock inside of her and still my body.

"Are we about to fuck again?" she asks.

I shake my head as I pull her into me and kiss her. I can feel her vagina wall tightening on my cock and I want to thrust again so badly, but I love the feeling of just being inside of her.

"What exactly is going on?" she asks in surprise as we just lay there while I stroke her arm.

"Supposedly, cock warming is when your vagina keeps my cock warm all night long," I explain. "Without any sexual activity."

"Oh," she says, looking surprised. "Wow."

"I think I kind of want to see what it feels like, don't you?" I ask her.

I'm not sure if I'm crossing a line that I shouldn't be crossing. We're not in a relationship. We've never even been intimate before this evening, but somehow I just need to feel her, be inside of her, remember everything about this moment.

"No," she laughs. "I think it's kind of romantic in a weird way."

"Are you calling me weird?"

"I'm sure I'm not the first person to call you weird."

"Maybe not," I say, kissing her again.

She reaches up idly and plays with my hair. "I'm tired," she says.

"Me too. We should sleep," I say. "We're going to be so warm. I think it'll be okay," I say as I hold her to me.

My right arm is already feeling stiff from the weight of her body lying on me, but I don't care. I don't care what aches and pains I'll have in the morning, I'm just enjoying this moment too much. I don't want to even think about what it means, but it feels like something special. Lila came into my life for a reason and I don't think it was to be my assistant, because as much as I enjoy being around her, I can tell from the way she reacted to the Whittington case that she is *not* cut out for this job.

Chapter Twenty-Two

Lila

My body feels extremely hot and there's something hard pushing into my hip. My eyes flutter open and I startle as I realize I'm in bed with Max Spector. And his entire body is against me.

"Oh my gosh. Oh my gosh," I whisper to myself, remembering erotic images from the previous evening.

Max Spector and I had the hottest sex of my life and I want to scream in excitement and tell the world.

I shift slightly, and that's when I realize that he's still inside of me. Are we making love and I didn't know it? I look down at his face, but he looks like he's sound asleep. Then I remember the night before and his asking me about cock warming.

Every image from the moment we'd entered my apartment crashes through my mind. I remember us teasing each other and drinking the Corona, him carrying me to the mattress and sinking to the ground, and us making love. Fuck, that had been hot. He was the best sex I'd ever had in my life. And then, he'd asked me if I'd ever heard of cock warming.

I bite down on my lower lip. I'd never heard of it before, but now that I have, I'm incredibly turned on, and the fact that he's still inside of me is absolutely crazy.

I shift and feel him move against my inner vagina wall. Fuck, it feels good. And if I'm not mistaken, he's at least semi-hard.

Holy shit. Wait till I tell Zara and Skye what's happened. Though, I'm not sure that I should tell Skye. I don't want her thinking poorly of me.

Who am I? I think to myself.

My breasts feel tender as I shift. I need to take a shower. I still think about how he'd come on my stomach, and while I'm not normally someone that likes men to come on me, I hadn't minded. And even though I'm on birth control, it makes me feel a little bit better that he hadn't cum inside of me, just in case.

I shift again, wondering if I can get out of the bed without him noticing, but his eyes fly open. He stares at me for a couple of seconds before they brighten.

"Good morning, Lila."

"Good morning to you too, Max."

"How did you sleep?" he asks, as he brushes some tresses of hair away from my eyes.

"Pretty good, but I have a little problem."

"Oh?"

"I woke up with some morning wood inside of me." I grin and he chuckles.

"Oh, yes," he says, shifting. "Huh?" He licks his lips, then moves slightly so that he thrusts inside of me. "Oops."

"Oh my," I moan. "Fuck."

"What?"

"So this is cock warming, is it?"

"I guess so."

"You do this with every woman that you sleep with, or...?"

"In fact, I've never done it before," he says, shaking his head. "I only heard about it recently."

"From someone you were—"

"Not from anyone I was dating or sleeping with. From someone who wishes she had been dating me."

"Uh-huh," I say, as I feel his fingers run down the side of my breasts.

"So," he says, licking his lips.

"Yes?"

"Are you thinking what I'm thinking?"

I giggle slightly, because I know exactly what he's thinking.

"I think so," I say as I shift slightly and push him back.

"Oh..." He grunts as I roll my body over so that I'm now on top of him with him still inside of me. "So you want to take charge, do you?"

"Well, I mean, I wouldn't want you to think you're my boss or anything," I tease, as I run my fingernails down his chest and start bouncing up and down.

"Fuck. Can I wake up like this every morning, please?"

"I don't know. Can you?" I giggle and close my eyes as I continue bouncing up and down on his cock.

He reaches up and grabs my breasts, causing me to cry out as his fingers flick my nipples. They're still sensitive from the night before.

"Oh, shit," I say out loud.

"I didn't hurt you, did I?" he asks quickly, and I shake my head.

"No, far from it. I just don't think I've felt this much pleasure in a really long time."

"Ah. Well, I'm glad to hear that," he says as he pulls me down and kisses me hard.

He grabs my hips, then my ass, and moves his body up so that he's thrusting inside of me from beneath. I moan, as I can feel myself already close to orgasm.

"Fuck," he curses. "I'm not going to last long."

And before I know what's happening, he's going faster and faster and I'm screaming his name out as I come.

"Oh, yeah, baby, say my name," he says, his fingers digging into my hips, hard, as he slams into me one last time and I feel him erupt inside of me.

I lean down and kiss him hard, losing myself in the feeling of his hands tangled in my hair, tugging.

"Oh, yeah," he says on a long, low groan.

We just stare at each other for a couple of seconds until he finally pulls his cock out.

"I think I'm going to go and shower," I say quickly.

"You need anything?"

I nod toward the kitchen. "I have some instant coffee. Haven't had enough money to buy an espresso machine or anything. And I don't have the exact bagel that you like, and I have no lox or cream cheese, but I do have some bread if you want to make some toast?"

"You have a toaster?" he asks in surprise.

"No, but there's an oven, and you can put it on broil and it will kind of toast the bread."

"You need a toaster."

"When I get my first paycheck, I guess I'll be buying a lot of stuff."

"Okay. Very smart, Lila," he says as he gives my bottom a little slap. "Go and enjoy your shower."

"Thank you, sir."

"I would join you, but we do need to get to work sometime today."

He looks at his watch, and I see that it's already nine AM.

"I know," I say, laughing as I head toward the shower. I make sure to grab my phone so that I can text Zara as soon as I get in there.

I close the door and turn on the water, then sit on the toilet. That had actually been the real reason I'd rushed out of there. I needed the restroom a lot more than I needed a shower.

"**Oh my gosh, Zara. You're not going to believe what happened last night.**"

"**What?**" She texts back immediately.

"**I had sex.**"

The phone rings within seconds.

I answer it and whisper, "I can't talk right now."

"You cannot text me and tell me you just had sex, then tell me you can't talk."

"He's still here."

"What?" she screams. "Who did you have sex with? Tell me right now."

"My boss."

"Holy shit!" she says "You did it. You fucked your boss. Oh my gosh. Lila, you're kidding me!"

"No. And have you ever heard of cock warming?"

"No. What's that? Please don't tell me it has something to do with fire. Please tell me you did not burn his cock."

"No, of course not, stupid. Anyway, I can't talk, I'm sorry. I'll call you later. But look up cock warming, because we did it last night, and it was fabulous."

"You need to—"

"I've got to go, sorry." I hang up quickly and giggle as I head into the shower.

I want to tell Zara everything, but I know if we actually get into a conversation, it will take forever, and Max will start banging on the door and there will just be too many questions. I grab my shampoo and squeeze it, massaging it into my hair as I relax beneath the hot spray. My body feels spent and exhausted, but it's the best sort of exhausted ever. I don't know who I am or what I've done to the old Lila, but I hope she never comes back.

I grab my body wash and start washing my skin, and immediately, my thoughts fly back to the previous day and being in the gym shower with Max, teasing him with that soap as I touched myself. Fuck.

A part of me wants him to come into the shower so that we can go again, but I know I need to pace myself. I have to figure out what the fuck this is and if it's going to happen again.

So many questions swirl in my mind.

I don't want to come off as a crazy bitch. I don't want him to think I believe we're now going to be in a relationship or anything like that, but I do want to know what everything that happened means for my future.

I grab my towel and step out of the shower, opening the door to let the steam out.

"You can shower in a little bit if you want. I just got done," I call into the room.

He's sitting on the edge of my air mattress, looking super tall and super built and way out of place in my little dinky apartment. He holds up the coffee cup and makes a face.

"This coffee is shit, by the way."

"It's instant. What did you expect?" I ask, laughing.

"I don't know. Something better than this. I think we need to get you a coffee machine."

"When I get my first paycheck," I remind him.

"Uh-huh." He stands up and heads toward me. "Why do you look so adorable in that towel? Is it bad that I want to rip it off of you and take you right here, right now?"

"Yeah, well, you're not going to do that because we have to be at work."

"I know. Are you still going to get me my coffee and my bagel this morning?" I glare at him and he starts laughing. "I'm joking, I'm joking. I do not expect you to get them for me today. In fact, maybe I'll treat both of us to breakfast before we go in."

"Oh, you don't have to do that, that's—"

"No, I know if I expect some good work out of you today, you will need to eat," he says. "And if you expect me to not be a grouchy asshole all day, I'm going to need some food too."

He steps back for a couple of seconds and takes a deep breath while running his fingers through his hair.

"So there was something I wanted to say before we head out."

"Oh?" I ask him, curious.

The air has shifted slightly and I'm not sure what is going on.

"So, we haven't really known each other that long."

"No, we haven't."

"And you're my assistant."

"I'm the very best assistant in all the land," I say, and he chuckles.

"And, well...I just don't want this to get out of the office, so if we could keep it between ourselves..." He makes a face. "You know, I would appreciate it."

"Of course," I say quickly, feeling absolutely devastated, like some sort of hooker that he's hooked up with on the side and doesn't want anyone to know about. "I mean, it's not like I would tell anyone that I hooked up with you. I wouldn't want to get a bad reputation or anything."

"What does that mean?" he says, frowning.

"I mean I wouldn't want people to think I was sleeping with the boss to get ahead or anything."

"Well, you're not sleeping with me to get ahead. That's not the reason why I don't want to discuss it, I'm just—"

"It doesn't matter. I'm going to get changed now. I suggest that you have your shower so that we can get some breakfast. There's a lot of work to do today, and I'm sure you're going to want to work on the Jack Whittington case and figure that shit out."

"About that, Lila—"

"It's fine, you don't have to explain anything to me. I'm just your assistant, and you're the attorney that went to law school and knows the law and all that good stuff." I shrug. "I mean, hey, you've got to do what you've got to do, right?"

"Are you upset with me, Lila? Is it something I said?"

He steps forward and tries to grab my hands.

"No. I guess I just realized the time and I don't want us to miss any more of the workday or anything." I press my lips together. "You should shower." I give him a fake smile. "And I should get ready. I want to make sure that I look professional, and that no one thinks that I'm sleeping my way ahead at the firm."

"Lila, that's not what I meant. I was just saying that—"

"It doesn't matter, Max. We had some fun, I'm sure we can both agree to that, but we're adults. That's all it was. We had a fun night, and we don't ever have to talk about it again." I can hear the petulance in my voice and I know that

I should let him explain, but I'm too in my feelings to be rational about what he's said. I want to tell the world about our amazing night, but obviously he doesn't feel the same. I'm not going to allow him to see how much he's hurt me. I can play it cool as well. However, the look on his face tells me that he thinks I'm being a child and my stomach sinks even further to the ground.

Chapter Twenty-Three

Max

I leave Lila at her desk and head toward Kingston's office. I can tell that she's slightly annoyed with me, and I'm not really sure why. We'd had an absolutely fantastic evening and an even better morning, but maybe she was starting to wonder if I was going to think about her differently.

"Hey, morning," I say, as I walk into Kingston's office without knocking. "You left a note on my desk."

"Yeah, it's 11:30 AM," he says, frowning.

"Okay, and?"

"I'm just going to cut to the short of it. Max, did you have contact with Mrs. Whittington last night?"

"What?" I stare at him in shock. How could he possibly know?

"Did you or did you not have contact with Mrs. Whittington last night?" He shakes his head. "Close the door, dude."

"What's going on?"

"Jack called me this morning. He's been having her

followed. There's a private detective taking photos and videos of her twenty-four-seven and sending them to Jack. He saw you in some photos at some gym with her and then at a smoothie place." Kingston crosses his arms. "Jack is pissed, dude."

"He's having me followed as well?" I say. I'm fucking pissed.

"He's not having *you* followed, he's having—"

"Yeah, he's having his wife followed, fine, but when I get caught up in the mess, it's not okay. That is not acceptable, Kingston. I don't need him reporting my movements to other people. I understand why he's following his wife and I understand that he would find out that I had contact with her, But he's crossing the line reporting my actions to you. He either trusts me as his lawyer and comes to me with his findings or he doesn't."

"I know. Look, I'm just saying that because of the cheating, he's already upset."

"He's the fucking one that set it up, Kingston. She's not cheating on him because she wants to, he wanted to spice up the fucking relationship and he brought another man into it. He set this whole fucking thing up so he can take her down without having to pay her a penny."

Kingston stares at me for a couple of seconds.

"That's what you think?"

"That's what I know. Lila—"

"Lila?" Kingston growls. "How does Lila know any of this?"

"It doesn't matter. I'm just saying that I don't think I'm interested in representing Jack Whittington in his divorce case. I don't want his business."

"But—"

"But nothing."

"What the fuck is going on, Max?"

"Who do we want to be, Kingston? Do we want to be a firm that's going to represent any scum for money, or do we want to stand on principle?"

"Ah, fuck." He looks at me. "You sound like you did on the first day of law school. I thought the law got into your thick head. The law is not about principle, it's about upholding the black letter of the law. It's about ensuring that—"

"You're not going to play professor to me, Kingston. I don't want to be the guy who takes on any client with pockets deep enough to afford me. What are we going to do, take on the mafia and drug lords next?"

Kingston presses his lips together.

"Obviously, I don't want us to take on any and everyone, but is this about Jack Whittington, who you didn't even really know of until a couple of days ago, or is this about that girl?"

"What girl?" I say, folding my arms, pretending that Lila hadn't gotten into my head.

"Your new assistant. Look, Max, forget the bet, okay? You don't have to turn her into the best assistant. You don't even have to have her as your assistant anymore. Fire her, get yourself someone good, and let's move on."

"I'm not going to fire her. She may not have the most experience in the world, but she's not that bad and she really cares about upholding—"

"Upholding what? Is she a judge?" Kingston barks, looking pissed. "Come on now, Max."

"Look, I don't think that you are—"

"Do you think I didn't notice that you both walked in this morning at eleven AM, looking at each other like the cat that got the fucking cream?"

I just stare at him.

"I saw the smile you gave her, and how you whispered in her ear. Is some pussy worth—"

"Max?"

There's a knock on the door a moment before Remy walks in.

"Oh."

"Hey, Kingston, Max. I was just coming to see...is everything okay?"

"I was just telling Max that he needs to figure out his life, because he's hired some chick that doesn't know shit about the law, and somehow she's put it in his head that we should not represent Jack Whittington, who owns freaking Jack's Shacks. This is a company that could make us a shitload of money."

"And I'm telling you," I growl. "I don't want to be a firm that only cares about the money. I want to be a firm that also cares about the people. I'm not going to screw Mrs. Whittington out of alimony and a settlement that she should receive from her husband. Yeah, she slept with another man. Yeah, technically, that is cheating. But it's *not* cheating if your husband can't fucking get it up and says that it turns him on. It's not cool that he then goes behind her back and takes photographs of her with these other men. Come on, Kingston. Come on, Remy. Does that sound right to you?" I slam my fists down on the table and they both look at me.

"Okay," Kingston says, holding his hands up. "I admit, it's not exactly above board. We don't know Jack's side, but—"

"I met the man, okay? He's not a good guy. And I met the wife. We don't want to screw her just to get his business. I don't want to do it."

"Wow." Kingston looks at me in surprise. "I don't know if

that blonde has cast a spell on you or something, but this is not the business partner who had a quarterly meeting with me last month talking about profit over everything else."

"Well, maybe that's not the right motivation. Maybe we've been approaching everything the wrong way. We've got money. We've got enough money to live more than comfortably for the rest of our lives. We've got enough money that if we have kids, *they'd* be set for life. We are some of the best attorneys in the country. Do we want to be the sort of people that just do this to make more money, or do we want to make a difference in people's lives?"

"I didn't get into public interest law," Remy says, shaking his head. "I mean, granted, I could take a few more pro bono cases, but—"

I chuckle slightly. "That's not what I'm saying. Look, I don't know what I'm saying. I'm just saying that I don't want to take the Jack Whittington case, and I do not want to ever hear you talking about Lila again." I level a glare at Kingston.

"Lila?" Remy says. "Your assistant?" He looks at me. "Wait, is that why you were late this morning?" He looks over at Kingston. "Holy shit, did they—"

"We're not discussing this right now." I say. "It's none of your guys' business."

Kingston lets out a long sigh. "I should have known. I should have known from the first time I saw that woman that she was going to be trouble."

"She's the right kind of trouble though," I say with a chuckle, and he just grins.

"Remy, what have we done?"

"I don't know, but obviously there must be something special about her if Max is giving her the time of day. I mean, remember that hottie in the barn? He didn't even blink at her."

"Guys, I have work to do. I also need to get my place ready, because my sister Marie is actually getting into town earlier than I thought, so if you will excuse me, I will dismiss myself, okay?"

Kingston nods and I head out of the room, practically sprinting toward my office. I see Lila sitting there, scribbling something on a legal pad, and all I can think is that I want to take her into one of the storage rooms and fuck the living daylights out of her.

"Get your act together, Max," I say to myself.

"Hey," I say, as I stop by her desk.

She looks up with a happy little smile, but then her expression changes.

"Yes, Mr. Spector?"

"You don't have to call me Mr. Spector." I say, leaning down. "You can call me Max."

"I think we should be professional in the office, don't you?"

I stare at her for a couple of seconds before I realize why she's upset.

"Lila, when I said that I didn't want us to discuss it, it wasn't because I regretted doing it. I just didn't want to make life complicated for us in the office. But if it's going to make you mad, then—"

"I'm not mad. Is there anything you'd like me to do? Shall I get Mrs. Whittington on the line so that you can offer her the measly ten grand or whatever it is?"

"I'm not taking the case," I say.

"You're not?" Her eyes widen. "But—"

"But nothing. He's not the sort of man I want to represent."

"Really?" she says, her eyes lighting up. "So you agree with me, he was a dog?"

"I want to make one thing clear, Lila. It's not for me to make any judgment calls about my clients, potential or otherwise. But that's not why I'm refusing the case. However, I have dreams and goals. I've always thought that I'd like to be a judge or a Supreme Court Justice, and, well, it matters to me the sort of cases that I'm taking."

"A Supreme Court Justice?" she asks. "Wow."

"Anyway, I need to go and take care of some business. I'm going to send you a couple of emails, I just need some paperwork sent off to the courthouse and some copies made, okay?"

"Sure. Anything else?"

"No. You have a great day, Lila."

"You too, Max," she says softly. "Thank you for last night."

"No, my darling, thank you. And thank you for this morning as well. It was..." I pinch the fingers on my right hand together and kiss the tips in the universal formation for a chef's kiss.

Chapter Twenty-Four

Lila

"He was gone all day," I say to Zara as we eat our Caesar salads in a cute little restaurant in Hell's Kitchen. "It made me feel like perhaps he regretted it."

"But didn't you say he stopped by your desk before he left the office?" Zara, ever the voice of reason, says as she reaches for a breadstick and dunks it into marinara sauce.

"Yeah...am I just overthinking this?" I ask her as I dunk my own breadstick and take a bite of the buttery goodness.

"I mean, you did hook up with him and you said it was kind of kinky."

"I mean, it was kinkier than I'm used to, but I don't know if it was kinky to him. I mean, what if he regrets it? What if he wishes I would just quit because he doesn't want to see me again, and..."

"Lila, you are really in your head way too much," she says. "I'm sure that he had work to do. Isn't he an attorney?"

"Yeah."

"And he's a partner, right?"

"Yeah."

"So he has a lot to do."

"But I just feel bad."

"Really? You feel bad, or you feel nervous that he doesn't want to do it again?" she asks, teasing me.

"I mean, of course I want to do it again, and I hope he does too."

"Girl, you're glowing," Zara says. "You look really happy."

"I mean, surprisingly, even though he annoys me and we banter and go back and forth a lot, he's fun. And maybe it's just because he's really good looking, but he makes me laugh, and I don't know, I just enjoy being around him."

"So why don't you text him and ask him if he wants to come over tonight?"

"What? I can't do that."

"Sure you can. And his response will tell you how you should feel."

"What do you mean?"

"I mean, if he says what time, you know he's totally into you."

"Yeah, that's true."

"And wouldn't you like to see him tonight?"

"I mean, if I'm being honest, yeah, but..."

"But what?"

"I don't want to seem too eager."

"Girl, don't play those games. Those games are from the seventies."

"Fine. I mean, I can text him. What should I say?"

"Just be like, 'Hey, what you up to? Want to come over tonight?'"

"Okay, should I do it now?" I look at her and she nods.

"Sure."

I grab my phone and quickly text Max. "**Hey, hope your day went well. Do you want to come over this evening?**" I hit send and the bubbles showing me that he's typing pop up almost immediately, sending my heartrate into a gallop. "Oh my God, he's responding already," I say. "I can't look." I grab my margarita and take a long gulp. "If he says he's coming over, I am going to need a couple more drinks because—"

"No, you're not," Zara says. "So what did he say?"

I look back down at my phone. There's no response and the bubbles have stopped. "He didn't send anything," I say. "I saw him typing and I guess he's second guessing what he was going to say." My heart deflates. "Oh my gosh, now I feel absolutely embarrassed."

"Girl, you shouldn't. You have nothing to feel embarrassed about. If you want to see him, you want to see him."

"I should have waited for him to message me. I should have waited for—" My phone pings and Zara's eyes light up.

"I bet you it's him."

"Let me see," I say as I eagerly open the message. "Hey, thanks for the invite. I can't tonight. Sorry. See you tomorrow." I stare at Zara. "Well, I guess I have my answer."

"That's not so bad. It sounds like he's busy. Plus, if he really wanted you to quit or he wasn't interested, he wouldn't have said he'd see you tomorrow."

"You think so?" I ask, shaking my head. I let out a long, deep sigh. "Oh my gosh, how am I in this position? How am I in this position, Zara? I just don't even understand it. My brain can only think about this man and what happened between us. He's most probably not even thinking about me at all."

"I very much doubt he's not thinking about you at all."

She leans forward. "The man's cock was inside of you all of last night, that sounds like he likes me to you."

"Or he's just a weirdo."

She giggles. "I don't think so. I mean, you haven't noticed baggies of people's skin or hair follicles, have you?"

"What?"

"Sorry, I was watching a serial killer show on Netflix the other day, and—"

"I don't want to hear about it." I take a deep breath. "So, I know I shouldn't keep talking about him, but..."

"But nothing. I'm here for you. I love you Lila."

"I know. Do you think he used me? Do you think he just wanted to have sex and—"

"No," she says. "I really don't think that. And you know I'm not the sort of person to lie about that because I know there are plenty of men out here who will fuck you and never talk to you again. I just don't get that vibe from him."

"But you've never even met him."

"But from what you've said to me, and based on the fact that he's responding so quickly, I think he is just focused on his work stuff and other stuff right now. Men aren't like us, Lila. Men don't have sex one time and become completely obsessed with their partner."

"I'm not completely obsessed with him."

"I know you're not obsessed with him, but you did just tell me that he's from South Carolina and that his family raised horses and that—"

"Okay, fine, so I Googled him and I know a little bit of information about him. That doesn't mean I'm obsessed with him. I mean, I couldn't find any information about any of the women he's dated."

"But I bet you spent a long time looking."

"Only half the afternoon," I say, laughing. "I mean, it

wasn't like I had much work to do." I grin. "Fine, okay. Maybe I'm getting close to stalker status, but I just kind of want to know where this is going. I mean, not that I think it's going anywhere, but—"

"Lila, take a deep breath. You're fine."

"I know. So what else should we talk about?"

"Do you have any other auditions coming up?" she asks. "How's the acting going?"

"I haven't even been looking, to be honest. I've been so focused on trying to do a good job and thinking about Mrs. Whittington and her divorce, which her husband hasn't even told her about, by the way, I guess I just haven't really—"

"Lila," Zara interrupts, shaking her head. "You cannot forget about your acting dream because of this job. You need to still keep going on auditions. You need to keep looking. Remember what your true goal in life is. This is why I want you to come and live with me. This is why—"

"No," I say. "I have to be Ms. Independent now. I have to take care of myself and if I'm going to make it—"

"Then make it."

"But it will have to be on my own timeline, and right now, I need to focus. I need to focus on paying my bills and buying some furniture. And well, yeah, I kind of like working with Max and I kind of want to see where this thing between us goes."

"Girl, just five seconds ago you were saying you felt like he used you."

"Okay, so maybe I don't think that exactly. Maybe I'm just a little bit overwhelmed by how quickly everything has been moving and by just how strongly I feel about him."

"Are you falling for him, Lila?"

"No," I say, and finish my margarita quickly.

"That's a lie," she says. "I can tell."

"I'm not falling for him, Zara, I've already fallen. I think of his silky blonde hair and the way it felt on my fingertips. I think about the way that he looks at me and makes me wetter than a water park. I think about the way his lips have sucked and touched me. I think about waking up with him inside of me." How could a woman not be obsessed with a man who had integrated himself so fully into her life so quickly? How could I not be obsessed with him? He's far from perfect, but he's perfect for me. As soon as the thought crosses my mind, I want to groan. Everything about this situation is cringe worthy, and yet, I love it. "I think I'm falling in love with him." I stare at her and she finishes her margarita without saying anything. "Tell me the truth, do you think I'm crazy?"

"Do I think you're crazy because you're falling in love with a man you barely know? Do you even know his middle name?"

"He doesn't have one. Well, at least Google says he doesn't."

"See? All the information you really know about him is from Google. You can't be falling in love with a man you haven't even gone on a date with."

"Well, we slept together."

"I know, and I know you must probably feel like you have this soul-tying connection with him, but you have to get to know him better."

"I know," I admit. "I just hope that he wants to get to know me better too."

"He'd be a fool if he didn't," she assures me, squeezing my hands. "You're beautiful, Lila, and I love that you have this connection, but I don't want you to give up on your dream. I don't want you to forget about acting. It's been your whole life up until now, and I'm just nervous that you're going to focus on this job and him and forget about what you really want to do."

"I will never forget about my dreams and goals to be an A-list actress," I say, shaking my head. "Of course I'm going to go to auditions, and of course I'm going to do everything I can to land as many roles as possible, but it doesn't hurt that I work for the most gorgeous man in the city and I can't seem to keep my mind off of him." My phone pings and I look down. It's Max. He sent me a picture of himself brushing his teeth and my heart races. I hold up the phone and show Zara and she smiles and shakes her head.

"He's attractive, I'll give you that, but why is he sending you that picture?"

"It's probably to let me know he's thinking of me." I say softly, and my heart melts. I know I'm being absolutely crazy, but maybe, just maybe, Max cares for me as well.

Chapter Twenty-Five

Max

"Hey, you're not sleeping, are you?" I whisper into the phone when Lila answers. It's one o'clock in the morning and I haven't been able to get her out of my mind.

"I was kind of asleep," she says.

I chuckle. "What do you mean you were *kind of* asleep?"

"Well, I was watching a TV show and I guess I must've fallen asleep."

"You were watching TV?" I ask. "I don't remember seeing a TV in your apartment."

"I was watching a show on my laptop, goofy."

"Oh, okay. What show?"

"It's called *Death in Paradise*. It's a British murder mystery. Have you ever seen it?" she asks.

"No," I say. "I don't really watch that much TV. So what are you up to?" I ask her as I lay in bed.

"Well, I basically just told you I was watching a show and falling asleep. What are *you* up to?"

"I am just in bed thinking about you."

"Oh, really?" she says. "Is that your way of telling me you want a booty call?"

"No. I would never expect a booty call from you, sweet pea."

"Uh huh...sure you wouldn't."

"I wish I would've been able to come over this evening. Thank you for the invite," I say, smiling into the phone.

"So then why didn't you come?" she asks.

"Because I was busy with a couple of things." For some reason, I don't want to tell her about Marie and the craziness that is my family. I mean, I don't want her feeling sorry for me. It's a little early to drop on her the fact that my father is a serial cheater and that my eighteen-year-old sister is coming to live with me because she's devastated that both her parents are cheating on each other. Definitely not something that Lila needs to be made aware of at this point in time, if ever. "So, are you wanting to get off the phone?" I ask, not really sure what to say.

"I know you didn't call and wake me up to ask me if I want to get off the phone. What's going on, Max?"

"Nothing. I was just here lying in bed thinking about last night and how much fun I had with you and how I hope we get to do it again soon."

"You mean the cock warming part or the smoothie part? And do not say you mean the spinning part because I'm never taking another spin class again in my life."

"Oh, darn it," I say, joking. "I was hoping you'd take a spin class with me again."

"No, you weren't," she giggles.

"No, I wasn't, but I'd love to take you out, maybe to dinner or something."

"Are you sure about that? We wouldn't want people in the office to see us together or something."

"Oh my gosh. You're never going to let me live that down, are you?"

"I'm just saying...*you're* the one who doesn't want anyone to know. I just wanted to protect you from talk in the office."

"I don't give a shit who knows. Which, by the way, Kingston and Remy already know."

"What? You told them?"

"No, but they guessed. They saw us walking in together late this morning."

"But how would they know that?"

"I never arrive late to work." I say. "Not once in all the years we've been together."

"Oh my gosh. So you were late because of me?"

"No, I was late because I was having a life for once, and hey, I'd do it all over again if you let me."

"So I want to ask you a question, Max."

"Okay, go ahead."

"Do you have a middle name?"

"What sort of question is that? Are you trying to steal my password or something?"

"Is your password your middle name?

"I shouldn't be telling you this, but, no."

"So then tell me. Do you have a middle name?"

"I do."

"And what is it?"

"It's Theodore."

"Oh my gosh, that is so cute. Max Theodore Spector."

"It's actually Maxwell Theodore Spector. What about you? Do you have one?"

"Yeah, it's Elizabeth."

"Lila Elizabeth Havisham. It suits you."

"Really? I think it makes me sound like I'm from the olden days."

"Yeah, it's an old-fashioned name, but you're far from an old-fashioned woman."

"Oh yeah? Why do you say that?"

"Because I don't know if an old-fashioned woman would have phone sex with me."

"Are you asking me what I think you're asking me?"

"I would never ask you such a thing."

"Good, because I'm not doing that with you right now," she says, giggling.

I feel disappointed. "But why not? You're supposed to be wooing me and getting to know me better."

"I think I know you pretty well already, Lila. My cock was inside of you all of last night. I think it could describe every inch of your vagina walls if it had to."

"Max!" she squeals.

"What? I'm just saying. It was very warm and loving. Thank you for keeping my cock safe."

"You're stupid. You know that?"

"I do," I laugh. "And I should let you go."

"Really? You woke me up for like a five-minute conversation?"

"Well, we can chat if you want."

"I'd love to chat. What do you want to chat about?"

"Let's chat about our favorite books."

"Okay, but I don't want you to fall asleep. I don't know that I read anything that you would find interesting."

"I don't mind falling asleep on the phone with you," she says softly. "I mean, if you fell asleep with your cock inside of me, I think we can fall asleep on the phone together."

"That sounds good to me," I say, and she starts telling me

about her favorite book. I smile as I listen to her, my eyes closing. She has a beautiful, melodious voice, and I know that I'm falling for her. I also know that this is probably the very worst timing.

* * *

"There you are, Marie," I say as I pick my sister up from the airport. She's standing there with two big suitcases and looks just as innocent and beautiful as I remember. She runs into my arms and gives me a big hug.

"Oh my gosh, Max, I've missed you so much."

"I've missed you too," I say. "Is everything okay?" I look at her face. "You have to tell me what's going on, okay? You've had me very nervous and I'm sure Dad and your mom are freaking out."

"I don't ever want to go back. I'm not going back. Promise me I don't have to go back."

"You're making me very nervous. What is going on?"

"I don't want you to judge me."

"Marie?"

"Please don't judge me." She starts crying and my heart immediately breaks.

"What is going on?" I press. I grab her hand and pull her to the side.

"Max?"

"Yes?"

"I'm pregnant."

"What?" I stare at her in shock and let go of her hand. "You're what?" I stare at my little baby sister who is looking more and more like a woman than I've ever remembered. "Is this a joke? Is it April and I didn't realize?"

"It's not a joke. I'm pregnant." She looks at me nervously. "Are you disappointed?"

I let out a deep sigh? "Does my dad know? Does your mom know?"

"No. I didn't tell them. I don't know what they would do."

"And the father?"

"He wanted me to have an abortion, but I'm not having an abortion. I'm not doing that to my kid. Please, Max. Please help me."

"Oh my gosh. I just don't even know what to say right now, Marie. How could you have had unprotected sex? How could you have let this happen?"

"Don't tell me you've never had sex without a rubber, brother." She sounds as much like an adult as she looks, and as I stare at her, I realize what she's saying is true. I had not used a condom either time I'd been with Lila. I quickly grabbed my phone and text her.

"You're on birth control, right?"

Marie stares at me, a slight frown on her face. "Please tell me you're not texting Dad that I'm pregnant."

"No," I say, glaring at her. "It's not my place to tell him, but you're going to have to tell him eventually, especially if you want to stay here. Oh my gosh. We've got so much to figure out. I cannot believe this."

"You're not mad at me, are you? You don't think I'm a slut?"

"Marie, I love you. You're my sister. I will always be here for you. And if you're going to have a baby and you decide that that's what you want to do and you want to keep it, we'll figure something out. You're only eighteen though, and you still have to go to college and you—"

"I don't want to talk about it right now," she says. "Can we just go back to your place and get pizza?"

"Yeah," I say, as I look down at my phone. Lila still hasn't responded. I realize now that maybe I should have prefaced my text with something else, but I'll explain it to her later. "Come on, Marie," I say, grabbing her suitcases. "Let's go home."

"Thank you, Max. I knew I could count on you."

"I'll always be here for you, Marie. I love you. You know that."

Chapter Twenty-Six

Lila

It's been two and a half weeks since I started working at the law firm, and while I can't say that it's the best job I've ever had, I'm actually really enjoying getting to work on small cases. The sad part is, I haven't seen Max in over a week and a half. Sure, we usually text every night, but it's not the same.

I open my refrigerator and stare at the empty contents. I really need to go and get groceries now that I've received my first paycheck, which had been the largest paycheck I'd ever seen in my life.

I have a frozen pizza in the freezer and some taquitos that I can put in the oven.

I look at my inflatable mattress and think about how much fun I'd had that night with Max. I want to know where he is, why he hasn't been to work, but he hasn't volunteered the information to me and I don't want to be nosy. A part of me thinks that the reason he hasn't come in is because he doesn't want to see me and he doesn't want me to get the wrong idea, but I ignore that possibility because why would he still be texting me if he had absolutely no interest? I know I want to have a conversation with him, but I'm scared. I don't even know what to say. "Hey, Max, you know that night that we pretended to be boyfriend and girlfriend and we had mad crazy sex and you kept your cock in me all night? Well, that was kind of fun. We should do it again, if you don't mind sleeping on my air mattress that isn't the most comfortable."

"He could invite you over," I whisper to myself. He has a nice place with plenty of bedrooms. My phone starts ringing and I pick it up, thinking it's going to be Zara. I stare at Max's name on the screen and my heart races as I answer. He doesn't normally call me. "Hi. Long time no speak, stranger," I say into the phone.

"I thought I'd check on my new assistant to see how she's doing," he responds.

"I'm doing well. I've been helping Remington out with some work because you didn't really leave me much to do."

"I know. I'm sorry about that. Some stuff came up, and well, it's just been a pretty hectic week."

"Oh, so will you be in next week?"

"Most likely. Why? Have you been missing me?"

"I mean, I don't know if I would say *missing*, but I *do* work for you, and I just thought—"

"Max, can you come here a second?" I hear a female voice in the background and freeze. Who was that?

"Just give me a moment, Marie," he says, and my mind races. Haven't I heard him talking to a Marie before? Who the hell is Marie?

"Do you have to go?"

"Yeah, in a little bit," he says, lowering his voice. "I just wanted to see how everything's going."

"I mean, it seems like you're busy right now, like you have been all week, doing other things, huh?"

"I mean, it has been crazy," he says.

"Max, the doctor sent me an email," the girl says, and my jaw drops open. What doctor, and why would Max care? What is going on?

"Hey, I am so sorry, Lila. I actually have to go."

"Okay, so—" But before I can even finish my sentence, he's hung up. I'm not happy. I'm not happy at all, and I don't even know what to do. Is Marie his girlfriend? An ex come back into his life? I hate that I still don't have the answers to these questions. Whoever she is, it sounds like he cares about her. I hate being an over thinker. I hate not being brave enough to ask him all the questions rambling in my brain. I just don't understand it, and I don't know if I have any reason to question him about any of it because who am I to him, really?

I pull out the frozen pizza from the freezer and turn the oven up to 400 degrees. I don't really want frozen pizza, but I nixed the idea of ordering Chinese takeout, as I don't know how much longer I'll be able to work for Max if he does have a woman in his life. I feel like the jealousy that is vacationing in my stomach would never leave if I stayed with him. I call Skye to distract myself from thinking about Max, and I'm happy when she answers on the second ring. "Hey, I was just about to call you!" she answers.

"Oh, you were?"

"Yeah. So I know you said you weren't sure about doing the dancing thing, but there is a party coming up on Saturday and we need another girl. I was wondering if you might be free."

"I don't know." I say, but then I think about Max and Marie, whoever she is. "I mean, you enjoy it, right?"

"It's fun and it's great money," she assures me. "And it's not like the guys do anything. They can't touch you unless you want them to, and then they'll pay you loads of money."

"Okay, I guess."

"Oh, by the way, I was speaking to Kingston today."

"Yeah?" I probe. "Don't you speak to him every day?"

"Well, yeah, duh, but it's what I overheard him saying when I left the office."

"What did you overhear him saying?" I'm confused now. I have no idea what she's talking about.

"Well, anyway, he was giving me a list of tasks, which by the way, he sucks as a boss. Anyways, as I was leaving, Remington comes into the office..."

"Okay."

"...and they start talking about Max."

Suddenly, I'm all in on the conversation.

"What did they say?"

"Well, Remy lowered his voice and whispered something to Kingston, and Kingston was shocked."

"What did he whisper?"

"I don't know initially what was said, but then Kingston said something like, 'Marie's pregnant? Holy shit.' And then they both looked at me, and then I left the office, so I didn't get to hear anything else."

"Oh, wow." My heart drops into my stomach at the news. "So that's why she needed to go to the doctor, or why the doctor was emailing her."

"You know her? Who is she?"

"I have no idea who she is, but I think she might be his ex-girlfriend or something. A couple of weeks ago he had a call and he was just saying her name over and over and he's been out of the office and I was just on the phone with him and I heard her speaking to him."

I hear my voice cracking. I feel like I'm about to cry.

"Hey, are you okay?" Sky says, and there's real concern in her voice. "I'm sorry."

"You've got nothing to be sorry about. Why wouldn't I be okay?"

"You liked him, right?"

"What are you talking about?"

"I know we don't know each other super well, but I could tell that you thought he was cute and he thought you were cute, and I almost thought that you guys hooked up, but then he hasn't been in the office in so long I just figured I imagined it."

"We did hook up," I admit, my voice barely more than a whisper. I don't care who knows. He's a dog and he deserves to be treated as such by me and my friends.

"You hooked up with him? Holy shit. No way."

"It was pretty amazing," I say. "And I kind of thought he liked me and then he just disappeared, but maybe that's when he found out. Maybe that's why he hasn't been in the office. Shit, maybe that's why he messaged me that day asking if I was on birth control."

"You guys did it with no protection?" I blush at the gentle admonition in her tone.

"I was caught up in the moment, and I know it wasn't my smartest decision, but I am on birth control, so it doesn't matter that much."

"Wow. Do you think that he was nervous he might have two women pregnant at the same time? Holy bananas. Could you imagine? He'd be on Jerry Springer if Jerry Springer was still around.

"I don't even want to think about it." I groan. "Maybe he's just trying to be a standup guy, and that's why he's gone back to her," I ponder out loud. "Maybe he wants to be there for his kid." I bite down on my lower lip. "I don't even know what to think. Oh my gosh. I can't work for him if he's going to be getting married and having a kid with someone else. I'll just feel disgusting, but I need the money."

"Well, I hate to bring this up now, but you can make $1,500 on Saturday if you dance at this party with me."

"Fine, I'll do it," I say. "Just send me over the information."

"Are you sure?"

"Yeah. You said it was fun, and, well, I need more experience dancing anyway. What if I get an audition to play like a stripper or something?"

"Yeah, this way you'll ace that audition." She giggles. "I mean, not that you want to play a stripper."

"I mean, it's not like I have many options right now," I say and let out a deep sigh. "Oh, Skye, what am I going to do?"

"I don't know. I'm sorry. It sucks when they're so good looking but also so obnoxious."

"Wait a second..." I say.

"What do you mean? What?" she asks innocently.

"How's it going with you and Kingston?"

"Girl, I cannot stand his ass. He is one of the most annoying men I've ever met in my life."

"Oh, no. I didn't realize it was going that poorly."

"Yep," she says, sighing.

"If I could quit right now, I would."

"Oh shit. It's that bad?"

"Maybe even worse than that. He thinks he's God's gift to women. You won't even believe what he said to me the other day."

"Oh, what did he say to you?"

"Well, I was about to head to lunch—" My phone beeps and I see that it's Max.

"Hey, I hate to cut you off, Skye, but Max is calling me. Can I call you back in a little bit?"

"Of course. In fact, you want to grab a drink?"

"You mean now?"

"It's not that late," she says "Maybe we can grab a bite and a drink and I can tell you all about my Kingston story so that you don't have to think about that jackass?"

"Sounds perfect," I agree. "I'll talk to you later."

"Sounds good."

I click over to the other line.

"Yes?" I snap.

"Hey, it's me, Max."

"I know," I bite.

"Is everything okay, Lila?"

"Why wouldn't it be? Is everything okay with you?"

"Yeah. I just realized that you were still speaking when I hung up earlier and I just wanted to make sure that you didn't think that—"

"It's fine. I'm about to head out, so if there was nothing else..."

"Oh, where are you going?"

"I'm going to grab a drink with a friend."

"A male friend?" he asks, sounding suspiciously jealous.

"None of your business."

"What? Hey, is everything okay, Lila?"

"I'm fine. Why wouldn't it be?"

"You just sound weird."

"I don't sound weird. You sound weird."

"You want to FaceTime later tonight?"

"Why?"

"I don't know. So we can see each other. It's been a little while."

"I don't know what time I'm going to be back, so I'll talk to you later."

"Are you mad at me for some reason?"

"Why would I be mad at you, Max?"

"Because I didn't want people in the office to know."

"No, I totally understand why you didn't want people in the office to know. You didn't want to look like a dog when everyone found out the truth—"

"What are you talking about, Lila?"

"—in eight or nine months. Yeah, you wouldn't look so good then once the real story came out."

"Lila, I don't—"

"I have to go. Bye," I say and hang up. I stare at the phone in my hand as it starts ringing again, but I don't want to talk to Max again right now. I power off the phone and rub my thudding head. My eyes feel heavy and all of a sudden I feel nauseous.

Turn your phone on and call him out on everything, Lila. The little voice in my head shouts at me. *Grow up and ask him straight out if he's having a baby.*

I know I should just ask him straight out. But I'm scared to hear his answer. I'm scared he's going to tell me that he's having a baby and can't do whatever we've been doing. Jealousy swims in my stomach and my skin feels warm. I'm annoyed with myself that I'm acting like a baby. I'm annoyed that I don't have the courage to learn the truth. But even more than anything else, I'm annoyed by how hurt I am by the whole thing.

Chapter Twenty-Seven

Max

It's been two nights since I last spoke to Lila. She hasn't even responded to any of my text messages. I have no idea what I said or did to upset her, but I can barely focus during the day, wondering what she's doing.

"Hey, Max," Marie says as she hands me a slice of pizza.

"Yeah?"

"Thank you so much for everything you've done this week, booking all those doctor's appointments, going with me to them, helping me to break the news to Dad and my mom. I really appreciate it."

"I know. You've really got yourself into a bad position here, Marie, but like I told you, you're my sister and I love you."

"I know, and I know that Dad is mad at me, and probably you too now. I just want to say thank you. I know he wants me to give the baby up for adoption."

"And you're sure you don't want to do that?" I ask her. "I'm fully supportive of whatever decision you make."

"I want the baby. I know I'm young and I know it's not really the best option to be a single mom, but I have so much love to give and..."

"I know," I say. "So we'll figure it out. I just...I'm going to have to go back to work next week."

"I know. And we're going to go shopping for baby stuff tomorrow, right?"

"No, I have a bachelor party tomorrow to go to and I'll be hanging out with some friends. But maybe on Sunday?"

"Okay," she says. "Fine. I can figure some stuff out to do."

"Good," I say. "And we're going to see if we can't get you into a university here in The City. I've already spoken to a couple of friends who have kids and they've put me in contact with several different nanny agencies. So when the time comes, we'll have help."

"You really don't have to do that, Max. And you really don't have to buy me an apartment in this building. I really—"

"Marie." I give her a look. "I love you, but we're both going to need our independence. But you *are* my little sister, so I'm going to have you close."

"But next door?"

"Let's just say they liked the offer that I made."

"You really are the best big brother."

"Well, I'm glad you think so. Now, if you don't mind, I need to make a call."

"Of course," she says. "Thanks again."

"You're welcome." I grab my phone and decide to call Lila instead of texting her. The phone rings but goes to voicemail and I let out a deep sigh. I decide to try again. She answers this time.

"Yes? Can I help you?"

"What's with the attitude, Lila?"

"Nothing. What's going on? Is this business related? Do you need me to get you a bagel and coffee? What do you want from me, Max?"

"I just wanted to see how you were doing and possibly have a nice conversation with you and—"

"And what? You want phone sex? Is that it? You want me to come over or you want to come over to my place? You want to stick your cock in me again all night? What is it, Max?"

"Whoa, where is this coming from?"

"I'm just saying that I'm just not another warm hole for you to fill up."

"I never thought that you were. And I apologize if you did not enjoy the cock warming. I'm sorry. You could've let me know at any time."

"That's not it. I just wish you had told me about Marie."

"What?" I blink in surprise. How does she know about my sister?

"I said I wish you would've told me that Marie was pregnant."

"I don't know that I knew that Marie was pregnant when we made love."

"Oh, so then is that your excuse for it being okay and still calling me?"

"What are you talking about Lila? My excuse for what?"

"For being a two-timing, low down son of a bitch," she says. "How can you call me when your girlfriend is pregnant with your baby?"

"What? What are you talking about?"

"Marie. She's pregnant, right?"

"Yes, and I don't know how you know that but—" There's a knock on my door and I sigh. "Yeah?"

"Hey, can I order some Greek food?"

"Not right now, Marie. I'm on the phone."

"Oh my gosh. She's there right now?"

"Yeah, she's here right now. She's staying with me," I say.

"So she's staying with you and you thought it was a good idea to call me. What, she can't have sex now that she's pregnant?"

"Are you disgusting? I would never sleep with my sister. Lila, are you out of your mind?"

"Your sister?" She sounds shocked.

"Yes. Marie is my sister. What were you thinking?"

"Oh shit," she says. "This is awkward."

"Lila, please tell me what's going on."

"So, I heard Marie in the background the other day, and then I found out that she's pregnant and you haven't been at work and you kind of went all quiet and I just thought that maybe your life got complicated and maybe your ex got pregnant."

"You thought that Marie was my ex-girlfriend?" I don't know whether to be amused or angry. "You thought I got my ex-girlfriend pregnant and I decided to step up to the plate and take care of the baby, but still have you as a side piece? Really? And you thought I'd be calling you while she's here in my home?"

"I mean, we don't know each other that well, but..."

"No, we don't, but I thought you would sense that I'm not the sort of guy to do something like that. You're the one that told me you had this great read on people."

"And I guess my initial read was more accurate than my latest one. I'm so sorry, Max. Oh my gosh. Please forgive me. I feel like a fool."

"Is that why you've been so cold and standoffish?"

"Yes."

"So it's not because you regret me coming over and us making love and everything moving so quickly?"

"No. I thought you regretted it."

"I don't regret a second of it. Do you want to go out tomorrow? I had plans, but I can blow them off. I—"

"I can't. I already have plans. I'm sorry."

"With a guy?"

"No, no. Not at all. Just with some friends. And, well, if I could blow it off, I would, but my friend's counting on me and I can't. You know?"

"What about afterwards?"

"I don't really know how long the plans are going to last or where it's going to be. And, well, I'm sorry, Max. But maybe Sunday?"

"I can't on Sunday. I'm taking my sister to go look for baby toys and clothes, even though I think it's way too soon. But I want to show her that I'm supportive."

"How old is your sister? Can I ask?"

"She's eighteen." I sigh. "Way too young to be a mom, but she wants to keep the baby and I respect that. I'll be the best uncle there is."

"Wow. You're so kind and loving. And is that why you haven't been in the office this week?"

"Exactly. I've been taking her to doctor's appointments and we went to get her New York driver's license."

"Her New York driver's license? I thought she was just visiting you."

"Well, it turns out that she's moving to New York now, and that is definitely going to complicate my life a little bit."

"Yeah, you can say that again."

"But I hope it's not going to complicate what we have going between us..." I say as I walk over to my door, close it, and lock it. I get back onto my bed and pull my shirt and jeans off. I lean back against the headboard. "Can we FaceTime?"

"I guess so," she says. "But why?"

"Because you owe me, don't you think?"

"I mean, maybe a little bit. How can I make it up to you, Mr. Spector?"

"Show me your boobs," I say, and she bursts out laughing.

"You're such a guy."

"I am, and I won't dispute it." I press the button to FaceTime her, and she answers almost immediately. I'm happy to see that she's sitting on her mattress wearing a tight tank top. It appears that she doesn't have a bra on. "Take it off," I say.

"Excuse me, Max. You may be my boss, but you cannot tell me to just take off my top."

"I can't?" I ask, laughing. "But mine is off."

"That's like me saying, 'Pull down your boxers and show me your cock.'"

"Fine," I say, pulling them off and pointing the phone down. She squeals and bursts out laughing.

"Max, you can't do that!"

"Why not? I'll do whatever you ask. Like, if you asked me to play with myself, I would."

"So we're really going to do this?" she says.

"I mean, I've been missing you like a motherfucker. So if you're down, I am."

"You really want to have phone sex?"

"No. What I really want is to fuck you hard and fast and have you screaming my name like you did when I was at your apartment. But unfortunately, that's not a possibility right now."

"I guess," she says, biting down on her lower lip. "So show me again."

"What do you want to see?" I say.

"I want to see your face and your chest and your cock."

"I'll show you my cock again if you show me those breasts," I say.

"Fine." She pulls up her top and holds the camera above her.

I stare at her juicy, luscious breasts. "Fuck, I want to suck on those nipples so badly right now," I say. "Play with them for me."

"What?" She giggles nervously.

"Touch them. Pretend they're my fingers."

"Max, I don't know. I've never done anything like this before."

"Close your eyes and just listen to me. Do as I say."

"Um..."

"Just do it, Lila."

"Fine. I guess you *are* my boss."

"Exactly." I grin as I settle back into the bed. "Run your fingers down your chest, slowly."

"Okay," she whispers.

"Now, move your right thumb against your nipple and flick it gently. Imagine it's my thumb. Now, use your index finger and pinch slowly. Imagine it's my fingers. If I was there right now, I'd lower my mouth onto your nipple and my teeth would sink into your areola and I'd tug and pull and suck."

"Oh, yeah?" she whispers. "And then what would you do?"

"And then I'd run my tongue all the way down your stomach and I'd pull your panties off with my teeth, and you'd moan." She moans loudly then, and I grunt. "Yeah, just like that. And then I'd flick the tip of my tongue against your clit one, two, three, four times until you were wet for

255

me. Put your fingers on your clit. Tell me, how wet are you?"

"As wet as Niagara Falls," she says, moaning.

"Slide your fingers back and forth."

"Only if you slide your fingers up and down your hard cock," she says. "Imagine they're my fingers. Imagine I'm there next to you and I'm lowering my mouth and swallowing you whole. I'm bobbing my head one, two, three."

"And then I'll twist you around," I say, getting into it. "And I'd put your butt on my face and suck your asshole and lick it clean. Then I'd switch to your clit and fuck you with my tongue as you go down on my cock."

"And I'd bounce on your face," she says. "In time with your cock sliding down my throat."

"And I'd thrust into your mouth," I say. "Fuck." My hands move up and down and I can feel myself close to coming. "Are you as turned on as I am?"

"Yes," she says. "Don't stop."

"Oh baby, I'll never stop. And then I'll pull you down and I'll center you right over my cock, and I'll bounce you and thrust into you hard and fast, just like you like it. And your breasts will bounce against my chest and then against my face, and then..."

"Oh yes," she screams. "Yes, yes."

"Fuck, yes. Say my name, Lila. Say my name."

"Please, Max. Oh, please. Fuck me hard. Fuck me good."

"Anytime you want it, baby." And then I feel myself coming hard and fast. "Fuck, yes. Fuck." I groan as I lean back and spurt all over my sheet. "Wow," I say a couple of seconds later. "Let me see your face." She points the camera at her face. Her lips are parted and her face is flushed red.

"That was so hot," she says. "I didn't realize it could be that hot."

"Neither did I. Are you sure I can't take you out tomorrow? Are you sure I can't fuck you just like we talked about?"

"I wish, Max, but I can't."

"Fine," I say. "But I'll see you on Monday."

"Yeah? You'll be back in the office?"

"Yes. I'll be back. I'll be looking forward to seeing you."

"I'll be looking forward to seeing you as well," she says.

"Goodnight, darling."

"Night, Max."

Chapter Twenty-Eight

Lila

I hurry into the party and follow behind Skye as she leads me into a small room. She gives me a quick hug.

"You look pretty."

"Thanks." I'm a little bit nervous as I look around the small room at all the different costumes. "How many different women are there going to be here today?"

"It's just the three of us. It's just a bachelor party for some guy that's marrying like a cousin of the Kennedys or something. I don't think it's going to be crazy."

"Oh, wow. Cool. So what exactly am I expected to do?"

I feel a little bit guilty about being here, especially as I haven't told Max. In actuality, I really had wanted to call Skye and tell her that I changed my mind, but I knew she was depending on me and I didn't want to let her down.

"So you'll be in the cake and then you'll pop out and be like, 'Surprise, happy bachelor party!' and then we'll all do a couple of little dances around and then we see where it goes from there. You'll be fine." She picks up a bikini top that has two half coconuts. "You're going to put this on."

"A coconut bra?" I stare at her in shock. "You're kidding, right?"

"I'm sorry, but this is the costume. I'm thinking the guy had something for Hawaiian girls or Tahitian girls or something."

"But I don't look Hawaiian or Tahitian."

"But you'll look close enough with the coconut bra," she says hopefully, and I just laugh.

"And please tell me I'm not wearing a thong."

"Well, you are wearing a thong, but..." She holds up a grass skirt. "This will be covering it, so it's not like you're just shaking your butt cheeks for the world to see."

"Why does this feel so wrong?" I ask as I stare at the attire I'm expected to wear.

I cannot believe I'm going through with this.

"1,500 reasons why," she says. "Besides, it'll be good music. I chose the playlist and it'll be fun and you don't have to do anything you don't want to do. These men can't touch you and they're not going to be expecting anything crazy. We're not like strippers, you know?"

"I guess not."

I think back to the previous evening and the phone sex I'd had with Max and how I'd stripped my top off. I blush slightly.

"Hey, you okay? You totally zoned out there."

"Yeah, I was just thinking about something else."

"Oh no, not about Max and his pregnant ex-girlfriend, Marie."

"Oh my gosh. I didn't tell you. That's not his girlfriend or his ex or anything."

"Do not tell me it's his wife. If it's his wife, you should sue."

"No, it's not his wife. It's his sister."

"His sister?" She looks at me for a couple of seconds. "So he doesn't have a pregnant anybody?"

"No. He's just helping his eighteen-year-old sister out."

"Oh, now I like him. Dang it. I didn't want to like him. I wanted to hate him as much as I hate Kingston."

"I know. Kingston does sound like a bit of a jerk."

"Girl, he's more than a bit of a jerk. Anyway, so you and he are back on or...?"

"I mean, I wouldn't say we're back on. It's not like we were anything, but we're at least talking again."

"Are you sure it's just talking? Did you fuck him again?"

"No, but we did have phone sex yesterday and it was amazing."

"Phone sex?" she says. "How amazing can phone sex be?"

"When you're doing it with Max Spector, oh my gosh. It's definitely better than real sex I've had with some guys." I laugh. "Though, I don't know if I would ever say that to their faces."

"Oh my gosh. If I had phone sex that was better than real sex, I would tell all of my jerk-off ex-boyfriends exactly how much better it was. Anyway, we should talk about it later. You want to hang out after the event?"

"Yeah, that sounds great. I'm so glad that I met you that day."

"Me too. To think, before that audition we didn't even know each other and now we're the best of friends."

"We really are. How's Juniper by the way? I haven't spoken to her in a while."

"I think she's busy writing her book and her boss is a

jackass too. In fact, we should probably start a club like The Horrible Bosses Club or something."

"We started that already. Remember?"

"I know, but we never had an official meeting and this was my way of reminding you of that."

"Oh, my bad. Sorry."

"It's okay. I suppose you don't think Max is so bad anymore."

"He's still a little bit of a jerk. I mean, I like him, but he's not the best man I've ever worked for. Not that I've ever worked for anyone that I loved. I mean, not that I ever worked for anyone I was sleeping with, but anyway, let's chat later."

"Yeah." She hands me the clothes. "Change into these, and when you're done, let me know. I'm going to put you into that box over there."

"Oh, is that the cake?"

"Yeah. When you hear me tap on it four times, that is my signal to you to jump out and do a little dance. Okay? I'll point out the bachelor to you when you get out."

"Okay. That sounds easy enough. I hope I don't mess up."

"You'll be fine," she says. "You're a natural. You're an actress. Pretend you're on Broadway."

"I suppose," I say. "The case of The Billionaire Bachelor."

"Or you could pretend that you're in a murder mystery a la Agatha Christie."

I giggle. "I've been watching this British TV show called *Death in Paradise*, and I guess I'm just thinking about different cases from that show."

"Oh my gosh. I love *Death in Paradise*. Have you seen *Beyond Paradise* as well?"

"No, not yet. Is it good?"

"It's so good. I just love Humphrey. It's a little bit more depressing than *Death in Paradise*, but it picks up. I'm so excited for more episodes."

"Oh, I can't wait to watch it." I smile at her. "Maybe we can have a murder mystery marathon one day."

"Oh, definitely. I love British murder mysteries. The cozy ones though. Not the dark ones. Have you seen *McDonald & Dodds*?"

"Oh, yeah. *McDonald & Dodds* is cool. Sometimes I just think to myself, what is she thinking? But then I'm like, I'm not British and I'm not a detective solving murder mysteries, so maybe I just don't get it. She's a great actress though," I say.

"Yeah, she is." Skye gives me another quick hug. "Okay, change. Get into the cake, and then the party will get started."

"Sounds good."

I quickly take off my clothes and put on the coconut bra and the black thong and straw skirt. Nothing feels comfortable, but I suppose that's how life goes. I get into the box and I'm glad I'm not claustrophobic because it smells weird and it's dark and it's very warm. I hope I'm not going to be in here for too long.

After about five minutes, I feel the box being moved into another room, which is much louder. I can hear music and conversations, but I can't quite decipher what anyone's saying. I wait for the taps and think about what I'm going to do when I get out of the box. What sort of dance will I do? Should I sing?

My mind drifts to Max. I feel happy. It's weird how happy. I shouldn't feel this ecstatic, but knowing that Maria's his sister has just taken a burden off of my shoulders. Not that he's my boyfriend, or that we're going anywhere, but the fact that he's been texting and calling me has to mean something.

I hear the four bangs on the side of the box and take a deep breath before I push up and jump out. The room is full of eligible, good-looking bachelors and I just start dancing around. I hear the Sabrina Carpenter song *Please, Please, Please* playing, and I move my hands to the beat of the rhythm. My blonde hair bounces up and down and I feel the coconuts shifting back and forth. They're barely holding my breasts in. I hope to God they don't slip off.

I move to the right and dance around the room singing along to the song. I spot Skye pointing at one guy and I head over to him. He has a huge grin and red lipstick all over his face. I'm wondering who gave it to him. He certainly won't be getting any of *my* lipstick on his face.

"Are you the bachelor?" I ask as I stand in front of him. I speak in my best Marilyn Monroe tone and he grins.

"The one and only. I'm Jeremiah Crestview."

Jeremiah Crestview. I try not to giggle. What a name. He definitely came from money with a name like that.

"Well, Jeremiah, why don't you have a seat and I'll give you a treat."

Skye looks at me with wide, happy eyes, and I shrug, happy at the little rhyme I've come up with.

"Oh yeah, baby, take those coconuts off," he says as he sits down.

Another guy sits down next to him and I'm guessing it's his best friend. I start moving back and forth in front of them, shaking my ass and the coconuts without getting too close. The song changes to an Adele hit that I don't really think is appropriate for a bachelor party, but I'm not going to tell Skye that as she chose the music.

"Baby, shake those coconuts like your mama wanted you to," the bachelor says, and I try not to raise an eyebrow at him. He's a little bit of a jackass.

I decide to step away from him when he reaches out to pull and tug on my straw grass skirt. I see that there's a small little table and decide to get on top of it and dance. At least then they'd be getting a good view, but I wouldn't have to worry about them trying to touch me.

I move over to the table and start dancing around, happy when the music changes yet again to an Usher song. I close my eyes as I swing my hips to the beat, dancing around. I can feel lots of eyes on me.

"Oh, hey, we have some new guests."

Someone jumps up and I turn toward the door to see who's come in. My jaw drops as I see a shocked looking Max standing there in a suit. He looks devastatingly handsome as always. His eyes narrow as he walks toward me and I can feel myself feeling faint.

"Lila?" He glares up at me.

"Hi," I say, offering him a small little wave.

"What the fuck are you doing here?" he demands, and before I know what's happening, he's grabbing my waist and lifting me up and carrying me in his arms.

"What are you doing?" I cry, slapping at his chest. "I'm dancing."

"I don't think so." He carries me out of the room and into the corridor. "What is going on here? Is this the plan you said you had with your friend that you didn't know what was going on?"

"It's just like an acting gig. She wanted to help me out because she knows I want to be an—"

"Dancing on a tabletop in a coconut bra is not an acting gig, Lila." He glares at me then pushes on a door, steps inside, and closes it behind us. We're in a small bedroom. He puts me down unceremoniously and glares at me. "What is going on?"

"So I promised my friend that I'd be a dancer for the day because they really needed someone and I thought it would be good practice for my acting and..."

He crosses his arms. "Really? And just how far were you willing to go for your acting?"

"I wasn't going to go far at all. I didn't want them to touch me. That's why I got on the table."

"You do realize they could see up your skirt and see your ass you were shaking it around."

"I mean, I'd rather them see my ass than them touch my ass."

"Who touched you?" he says. "Let me go out there and speak to them."

"No one touched me. It's fine." I pause for a second. "Hold on. You didn't tell me you were going to a bachelor party today."

"You never asked me if I was going to a bachelor party today."

"But you asked me to hang out."

"I did."

"But you had this event."

"And I was going to drop this event for you." He smirks at me. "However, it seems like you were not going to drop this event for me."

"I mean, I promised my friend and they needed another dancer and I didn't know you were going to be here."

"I didn't know you were going to be here looking so fine and sexy in two coconuts." He leans forward and gives me a kiss on the lips. "You look beautiful, by the way."

"You are just saying that because you want to get my coconuts off."

"Oh, I do want to get your coconuts off, but I'm not just saying that," he says, smiling as he touches the side of my face. "I've missed you."

"I've kind of missed you too. Just a little bit. Even though—"

"Shut up while you're ahead, Lila," he says, smirking. "Sometimes we don't have to say everything we're thinking."

"So what are you thinking?"

"I'm thinking that I would love a lap dance from a sexy dancer in a straw skirt and a coconut bra."

"Really? But I just told you I don't allow any touching."

"But wouldn't you make an exception for me?" he says in a growl. "I'll pay you well."

"How well?" I say, winking at him.

"I'm not going to give you a million dollars to take those coconuts off, Lila."

"I wasn't going to ask for a million, though it would've been nice if you offered."

"Fine. I'll give you a million dollars to take those coconuts off," he says, laughing.

I just shake my head and push him back down onto the mattress.

"So what's next?" he asks.

"You'll see."

I jump on top of him and start gyrating against his pants. I'm pleased to feel a hardness between my legs. He's already horny.

"Someone feels like they've been a big bad boy."

"You want to call me a dirty daddy?"

"No, I want to call you a bad boy," I say as I pull off my coconut bra.

Don't Quit The Day Job

He licks his lips and immediately leans forward and takes one of my nipples in his mouth. "I've been waiting a long time to do this," he says.

"Fuck. You taste just as I remembered."

"I don't know that we should be doing this here," I say. "I'm supposed to be working."

"You do have a nine to five, you know..."

"I know I have a nine to five, but this is my second job."

"So now this is your second job?" He raises an eyebrow in challenge.

I continue gyrating my hips on his lap. "Yeah."

"Well, I'm going to offer you some advice, my dear."

"And what is that?" I say as he flicks his fingers against my nipples.

"I'm going to say don't quit the day job, because if your acting is as good as your dancing, you're not going to make it."

"You're such a jerk," I say. "You don't think I'm a good dancer?"

"I think you're okay. But don't make me report you to HR."

"Oh, yeah? I dare you to report me to HR."

I lean down and unzip him and pull out his cock.

"Oh, yeah? I can."

I pull my panties to the side and rub his cock against my clit, moaning loudly.

"Fuck, that feels good."

"How far were you going to go, Lila?"

He glares at me.

"Excuse me?" I say, lifting myself up, then lowering myself down on him.

He grunts as he grabs my ass and brings me closer to him.

"Fuck," I say as he slides completely inside of me.

"How far were you going to go with those other men?"

"All the way," I moan and then glance at him. "Oh wait. I mean, I want to go all the way with you." I giggle at his look. "What? You've just got me so confused right now."

"I've got you confused, huh?"

"Yes," I mumble as I bounce up and down on his lap, my breasts pushed against his chest.

"Oh, fuck yeah. That's so good. Oh, fuck yeah. Don't stop, Lila," he begs.

The door opens and the music comes flooding in around us. I still against him.

"What's going on, guys?" Max shouts over the ruckus.

"Hey, is that one of the strippers?"

I'm not sure who's there, and I don't want to turn around and look.

"Get out of here!" Max shouts.

"Hey, will you let us know when it's our turn?"

"Get the fuck out!" Max shouts, and his entire body shudders with the force of his yell. I find that I quite like primal Max.

"Okay, you don't have to hog the stripper all to yourself."

The door closes and Max pulls me off of him. "You're not working this job again. Do you hear me, Lila?"

"Says who?" I challenge, glaring at him.

I'm still horny and now I'm pissed off that I'm not even going to be able to come.

"Says me," he says. "I don't know what you thought you were doing, but this was not a good idea."

"I mean, I didn't know what I was doing either, so there's that."

"You didn't know the guys would be hot and horny and want to rip your clothes off?"

"Well, Skye told me it'd be low-key."

"Not Skye from the office."

I bite down on my lower lip. "No."

"You're a terrible liar. We're leaving Lila."

"No, I—"

"We're leaving, Lila."

"Fine," I say. "But before we do..."

"Yes?" I say as he lifts me up.

"I need to fucking finish what we just started or I'm not even going to be able to think straight."

He bangs my back against the wall and I hold on to his shoulders as he thrusts up inside of me.

"Oh yeah, this is where I belong. Deep inside of you."

"Don't stop," I whisper as he starts to fuck me hard and fast.

"Oh, I won't," he whispers back.

And as we bang against that door, I know that this is the second best fuck of my life.

* * *

"You really don't have to take me home, Max," I say. "I'm fine."

I stare at him with big beguiling eyes, trying to read his mind, because I certainly want to know what he's thinking after everything that's just happened.

"I want to make sure that you get home okay. Plus, I'm still mad at you."

"What do you mean you're mad at me? Why are you mad at me?"

"For putting yourself in a situation like that." He shakes his head.

"A situation like what? You weren't complaining when you were banging me up against the wall."

He shakes his head slightly. "It's not about that. It's about the fact that you were in a room full of guys, wearing a coconut bra and a thong, shaking your ass on a table."

"Nothing was going to happen. Skye—"

"Well, I'm going to speak to Skye." He frowns. "Actually, I'm going to speak to Kingston, who's going to speak to Skye, because that's just not a good look for the firm."

"What do you mean it's not a good look for the firm?" I glare at him. "It's got nothing to do with the firm."

"She represents the firm, and—"

"She doesn't represent the firm. She's barely worked there for a couple of weeks, just like me. And she makes good money from this. And I will absolutely hate you if you speak to Kingston and she gets in trouble when he's already not nice to her."

He stares at me for a couple of seconds. "What are you talking about he's not nice to her?"

"I don't know the full story, but he's kind of mean to her and I think she wants to..." I pause.

I can hardly tell him that she wants to quit. He does still own the firm.

"What were you going to say, Lila?"

"Nothing. Can we talk about something else?"

He pauses for a couple of seconds and strokes my hand. "I don't know what I'm going to do with you."

"I mean, you could always fuck me again," I say, grinning at him, and he chuckles slightly.

"You are going to get me into trouble."

"Only if you don't get me into trouble first," I say. The cab stops and we hop out. "Oh, so you're coming up?"

"Yes," he says, nodding.

"I still don't have much furniture," I laugh. "So it's not going to be super comfortable."

"It's fine," he says as we walk into the building and make our way up the stairs. "The elevator's out again?"

"Yeah," I say. "I guess I should be grateful because it's given me more definition in my glutes and my calves, but..."

"But you don't really want that definition, do you?"

I look back at him and laugh.

"Yeah, well, I mean...not because I have to walk up a bunch of stairs. I'd rather have it because I was going to the gym, and—"

"You go to the gym?" he asks with a raised eyebrow.

"I don't know what that look is about. Are you saying that I don't look like I go to the gym?"

"No, I'm just saying that when we were at the spin class, it didn't indicate to me that you worked out frequently." His lips tremble.

"You're so mean, Max." I say, slapping him on the shoulder. "You're totally saying I'm out of shape."

"I'm not saying that you're out of shape. I'm just saying that you didn't seem to have a lot of breath when doing the sixty-minute cardio class."

"So you noticed that I was breathing hard?"

"I think the entire room noticed you were breathing hard." He starts laughing.

I can't stop myself from laughing as well. "You're making fun of me."

"Hey, I like to be honest with you, right?"

"Yeah, I guess I appreciate that," I say as I open the front door. "Come on in. Would you like a drink?"

He stares at me for a couple of seconds and shakes his head. "No. What I want you to do is grab your bag and pack some of your stuff."

I turn to him with a frown. "What are you talking about? Grab what bag and what stuff?"

"You're not staying here," he says, looking around.

My air mattress is flat on the ground.

"You deflated it this morning?"

"No, I didn't deflate it, but I told you before, it's kind of cheap so you have to keep blowing it up and—"

"You're not staying here, Lila. This is a shithole."

I stare at him, feeling quite offended by his words. "It's not a shithole, it's my place, and—"

"I know you love it, and I know it's the first place you've had by yourself and it means a lot to you, but this can't be comfortable. You have no chair, you have no couch, you have no bed. I'm not going to let you stay here."

"You cannot tell me what to do. I may be your assistant, but—"

"I don't want you to stay here because I care about you, Lila." He grabs my hands and pulls me to him. He kisses my nose. "I care about you and your comfort and I want to spend the rest of the weekend with you."

"But I thought you said you had plans with your sister tomorrow..."

"I do, but that doesn't mean you can't join us."

"What?" I say, my eyes widening.

"I want to spend the rest of the weekend with you, and I'd like for you to meet Marie. I'm sure she'd love to meet you." He shakes his head in an exasperated fashion. "I mean, she might be a little bit mouthy and over the top when she does meet you, so just be prepared."

"What do you mean? Is she going to hate me?"

"Oh, no. I think she's going to love you. But she is going to go on and on and on about how I've been single forever, and how she never thought I'd meet a nice girl like you."

"What?"

"I'm just predicting that's what she's going to say." He laughs. "So grab a bag and some stuff and spend the weekend with me. I would spend the weekend here, but I really wouldn't be comfortable."

"Fine," I say. "You do know that when I get a couple more paychecks under my belt, I'm going to decorate and furnish this place, and you'll never want to leave, right?"

"We'll see," he says.

My heart soars at the words, because I realize that I've just talked about him coming here in the future, and he didn't get red or stammer. Maybe he does kind of like me. Maybe it isn't just about the sex. Though, I don't want to get ahead of myself. The sex is pretty fucking amazing.

"I'll just bring some clothes and some underwear," I say. "I don't really have much else to bring. Oh, maybe my laptop."

"Why are you bringing your laptop?" He tilts his head to the side.

"Because I have a crazy boss who likes to send me emails in the middle of the night asking me to do different projects, and just in case."

"I have a feeling your boss won't do that."

"But just in case," I say, grinning at him as I grab my laptop.

"Come on, let's go back to my place," he says, smirking as we walk back out the door. "Are you sure you're ready for my sister?"

"Are you sure you're ready for your sister to meet me?"

"Yeah."

"But then she'll know about us and it will really be out there, and—"

"I don't care. I'm sorry that I told you previously that I

didn't want people in the office to know, but I don't care. I want you to get to know my sister. I want you to be a part of my life."

I stare at him wide-eyed.

"What is it now, Lila?" he asks.

"I'm just surprised by your words."

"Why?"

"I don't know. Maybe because you don't seem like the sort of guy that would want a relationship."

I stammer over my words, because I've just put the R word into the universe, and I don't know how he's going to react.

"Who says I want a relationship?" he asks, and I feel my heart sinking.

Why had I mentioned it? Oh my gosh.

"So this is just about sex for you?" I ask.

He grins then, his eyes sparkling. "Are you telling me it's not about sex for you as well?"

"Oh, of course. It's all about sex," I say. "In fact, I'm trying to get you to impregnate me so I can be set for life, child support and all that."

He stares at me for a couple of seconds, and for a few dreadful moments, I think he thinks that I'm being serious.

"I'm just joking, Max, don't worry."

"I know that you're joking." He bursts out laughing. "I just didn't realize you had such a black sense of humor."

"Hey, I can be sarcastic and funny and comedic and scare the living daylights out of you all in one."

"Who says that you scare me?"

"You're telling me that me telling you that I was hoping you would impregnate me and make me set for life didn't scare you for even one second?"

"No," he says. "Maybe the thought of impregnating you doesn't scare me as much as you think."

"What?" My jaw drops and he bursts out laughing.

"I mean, not anytime soon. I just want to enjoy the practice."

"You are crazy." I shake my head, though my entire body is glowing. "Do you think we're..."

"Do I think we're what?" he asks as we walk to the side of the road and he holds his hand out for another cab.

"Do you think this is all moving way too fast?"

"Yes," he confirms, nodding. "Do I think that we're absolutely crazy?" He turns to me as a Yellow Cab pulls over. "Yes."

"Why thank you, Max. I'm glad to hear you think that."

He opens the door for me. "You can get in. I'll put the bag in the back."

"Okay." I say, as I slide into the back of the cab.

I wait a couple of seconds, then he gets in beside me and tells the driver where we're headed to.

"I just can't believe this is my life right now," I admit, as I stare at him. "Are we just two crazies?"

"Maybe." He shrugs. "But maybe you were right."

"Maybe I was right about what?" I ask.

"Maybe life is just one big romance movie and we're the main characters in this part."

"So I'm the heroine and you're the hero?"

"I'd like to think that is true. Why? Do you think I'm the villain?"

"No," I say. "I very much think that you're the hero. You're so handsome and hot."

I touch his thigh and lean over to give him a kiss on the lips. His eyes widen as he looks at me.

"And I very much think that you're the main part of my story," he says. "Ironically."

"Why is that ironic?" I frown slightly as I pull away, but he grabs my face and holds me close to him and kisses me hard.

"Because I never thought romance would be a central theme in my life," he says. "I always thought my book was more of a thriller, and now it's starting to become more of a romantic comedy."

"Oh. And you don't like that?"

"It's just something different," he says. "I thought I was more of a John Grisham, but it turns out I might be more of a Nora Roberts."

"No, darling, I think you're more of an E. L. James." I laugh.

He nods and kisses me again. "You might be right about that. So, shall I get a red room?"

Chapter Twenty-Nine

Max

"Marie, I would like to introduce you to Lila. And Lila, I would like to introduce you to my sister, Marie."

My sister looks up from the couch and stares at Lila. Her eyes widen as she jumps up, and there's a huge smile on her face.

"Lila? Who is Lila exactly?"

Marie looks at me and I glare at her. I look over at Lila and hope she's not upset.

"It's okay, Max. I don't expect you to have told your sister about me with everything that's going on."

"Is this your girlfriend?" Marie gushes. "Oh my gosh, you have a girlfriend and you didn't tell me? And she's so pretty!"

"Oh my gosh, you're so sweet," Lila says, stepping forward. "You're absolutely gorgeous. You must have got your looks from your mom, because you're way better looking than Max."

"I love you already," Marie says, giggling as she leans

over and gives Lila a hug. "What are you doing with my doofus of a big brother?"

"Oh, just making his life the best it's ever been," Lila says in response as she looks over at me.

My heart races as I stare at them. I love both of these women. The thought hits me, and all of a sudden, I feel stiff. Do I love Lila? How on Earth have I fallen in love with her already? But then it strikes me that maybe my spirit had known who she was from the very moment it had seen her walking in the street. I dismiss the thoughts of love from my mind, because I'm not a believer in love at first sight, and I certainly don't believe in true love, and I certainly don't want to turn Lila's already too-romantic brain into a whirlwind.

"Max, are you ignoring me?" Marie says, swatting me on the shoulder.

"Sorry, I was just thinking about something. What's going on?"

"I was saying that we should all go to dinner, and then maybe we could watch a movie, and—"

I stare at Marie and shake my head. "Darling, I love you, but I want to spend some alone time with Lila."

"It's okay," Lila says quickly. "I'd love to get to know Marie, especially because you're going to be moving to The City, right?"

"Yeah," Marie says, nodding slowly. "Did Max tell you he bought me the apartment next door?"

"He did?" Lila's eyes are wide as she shakes her head. "No. Wow, you've certainly been busy."

"Well, if Marie's going to be going to college and having a baby and staying in The City, she needs to have someone to look after her. And while I love her, I certainly don't want to live in the same apartment as her forever."

"Thank you, big bro. That makes me feel great." Marie giggles.

"I mean, you know that I love you, and if you really want to stay here, if it makes you safer, you can, but—"

"I'm joking. Of course I want my own place. Plus, he said he's going to give me an unlimited budget to furnish. How awesome is that?"

"I want an unlimited budget to furnish something," Lila says.

I stare at her for a couple of seconds, at her laughing blue eyes, and I want to tell her that I would give her an unlimited budget for anything she wanted. She's joking, and I know that she wouldn't accept a penny from me, but I want to make her life easier, I want to make her life more comfortable, and I'm going to have to figure out a way to do that without making her upset. I know that she won't move in with me, not right away, and that's probably for the best because we really don't know each other that well, and even though I would love for her to move in, I understand how much she is enjoying her independence, even if she is living in an unfurnished shithole.

"Hey, Marie, do you mind if I take Lila to the bedroom for a second?"

"Are you about to make my baby a cousin already?"

"No." I glare at her. "I just want to talk to her about something."

"Fine," she says. "I was just about to watch 27 *Dresses* anyway." She grins at Lila. "I'm so glad you're dating my brother. He is already a better person for knowing you."

"What are you talking about, Marie?"

"Don't think I haven't noticed how different you've been," she says, laughing. "Normally, you don't have that much time for me, and you certainly wouldn't have taken a week off of work. You're much more chill and cool, and I've noticed that you just seem happier."

I stare at her for a couple of seconds.

"What are you trying to say, that I wasn't happy before?"

"No, but I feel like you're really enjoying life now." She looks over at Lila. "And I see the way you look at her, I see the way she looks at you, she's your lobster."

I stare at her for a couple of seconds.

"What?"

"It's a term...oh my gosh, are you too old to understand what that means?"

"She's saying that I'm your person," Lila giggles. "You're so sweet, Marie, but I don't want you to scare Max. I don't know if he—"

"You *are* my lobster," I say softly. "Maybe I've waited my entire life for this moment, or maybe not. Maybe this is absolutely ridiculous and there's way too much estrogen in this house and it's making me go crazy."

"Tell yourself whatever you want." Marie says as she heads back over to the couch. "See you later, Lila."

"Sounds good." Lila turns to me. "So what did you want to discuss with me?"

"Come, I'll tell you in the bedroom."

We head down to my room, and I close the door.

"Is this your way of trying to make love to me again?"

I growl as I pick her up and carry her over to the bed and drop her down onto the mattress. She giggles as I get down beside her and kiss her, my fingers running over her breasts.

"Max, you shouldn't," she says, laughing as she reaches up and grabs my crotch.

"Actually, that's not why I brought you in here." I kiss the side of her face. "But maybe later."

Don't Quit The Day Job

"Are you telling me no to sex right now?"

"I'm telling you that there's something I want to talk about with you."

"Okay." She rolls onto her side. "What is it?"

I look into her eyes.

"So I have a proposition for you."

"Yeah, what is it?"

"You have no furniture."

"Yeah, I have no furniture, we've already established that."

"You need furniture."

"And I told you, once I get a couple of paychecks—"

"You need furniture now," I say, staring at her.

"Well, I don't have the money, and I'm not taking the money from you." She glares at me and pokes me in the chest. "Don't even think about buying me furniture and having it shipped to my place. I will kill you. I will literally pull your heart out and eat it if you do that."

"That sounds kind of disgusting," I say, wrinkling my nose. "I know I'm sweet, but am I that sweet?"

She just stares at me.

"That's not the proposition I had for you."

"Okay. Well then, what is?"

"I was thinking, what about if..." I pause slightly.

"What?" she says.

I grab her waist and pull her closer to me, then wrap my leg around her hip.

"Max, what are you saying?"

"What if you want to have a little contract with me?"

"Huh?" she says, as I reach my hand up under her shirt.

"What if we have a deal?"

"What deal?" she asks.

"I don't know. Maybe that you're my sex slave for the next month and I give you $25,000."

"Are you freaking kidding me?" she says, pushing me away. "I am so offended. I cannot believe that you think I will sell my body for twenty-five grand."

"Fifty grand then?"

"No, Max," she says, glaring at me. "I'm not going to sleep with you for money. That's absolutely ridiculous. That's not romantic."

"What? You're the one that said that—"

"Max," she says. "If we're getting into a relationship, and you like me and I like you, I'm not accepting money for sex. I don't want there to ever be a time in our relationship where you question me."

"Okay. Well, I was just joking."

"No, you weren't."

"Okay, maybe I wasn't, but it was just for fun."

"What do you mean for fun?"

"I don't know, like role-playing. Come on, let's be real, we both know I wouldn't have to pay you one cent for sex."

"Haha, very funny, Max."

"I just don't want you to be in that place with nothing. It's not comfortable, and when you..." I pause. I was about to say when you love someone, you want them to be comfortable. "Well, when you care about someone," I say quickly instead. "You want them to be comfortable, and I have plenty of money."

"I know you have money, and I'm very appreciative of you offering it to me, but I'm not going to accept your money to buy me furniture. I have to do this myself."

"You are so stubborn, Lila Haversham."

"And that's why you like me, Max Spector." She grins, and I just shake my head.

"Maybe," I say. "So you're not willing to take this proposition?"

"No, I'm not. But thank you very much for offering."

"Well then, I'll just have to speak to HR on Monday.

She frowns slightly. "About what?"

"About the fact that you've been given a pay raise to $300,000 a year." I grin.

"Max!" She shakes her head. "you cannot pay me $300,000 just to be your assistant."

"Oh, yeah? You wanna bet? I am a named partner at the firm. I think my assistant deserves to make $300,000, especially seeing as I text her and email her at all hours of the night and day, and she wakes up extra early to get me my coffee and bagel."

"You're really going to do that, aren't you..." She groans.

"Yes. Now, come closer to me."

She shifts so that she's up against me. I run my fingers down her back and touch her lips lightly.

"You're so beautiful. Maybe even the most beautiful woman in the world."

"Maybe because you haven't seen many women in the world?"

"No. I could see every single woman in the world, and none of them would shine any brighter than you."

I know just as surely as there is a sun in the sky that she's much more than my lobster; she is my soulmate. She is the woman that I've been waiting for my entire life and I didn't even know it. Maybe, just maybe, she and I have known each other in another life and we've come back together. My heart and my soul feels attached to her. I grab her hands and clasp them. There's an energy that's buzzing between us.

"Do you feel that?" I ask, and she nods slightly.

"It's like electricity," she says.

"We've got this connection." I stare at her like I'm seeing her for the first and last time. I could be blind and I would still know it was her. She has imprinted on my very soul. "I'm not crazy for feeling it, right?"

"No," she says, shaking her head. "I feel it as well."

"This is really special, Lila."

"You think so, Max?"

"I think so." I kiss her knuckles. "It's about more than the hot, crazy sex that we have."

"I know," she says. "You know what I was reading?"

I shake my head.

"What?"

"Did you know that cock warming is actually part of the dom-sub relationship?"

"Maybe when I first learned about what it was. Why?"

"Well, you know that cock warming is not just in the vagina?"

"What do you mean?"

"Well, some women just warm their man's cock in their mouth for hours. They just lie there like it's a lollipop."

"Are you telling me you want to suck my cock for hours?" I ask, grinning at her.

"I think we both know that if I were to suck your cock for hours, you would come multiple times, and the point of cock warming is not to cum, it's just to..."

"To what?" I say, growling as I press my lips against her. "You know I'm fucking hard right now. I don't even want to talk about this anymore."

"Why? What do you want to do instead?" she asks, grinning as she rolls on top of me and sways her hips back and forth.

I close my eyes as I feel her moist panties against my fingers.

"You know exactly what I want to do, sweetheart," I say, and I reach up and bring her down toward me and kiss her hard.

We both know that we're meant for each other, and now I'm going to show her just how much.

Chapter Thirty

Lila

I have never felt as happy as I have in the last month. It seems to me that my life can't be any better. I spend most evenings at Max's place, and when he's not home, Maria and I watch a movie or make dinner together. I feel like everything is finally falling into place in my life. Making love to Max has just gotten better and better, and we seem to have gotten into an easy relationship that makes me question how I've ever thought relationships could be hard. I suppose once you meet the one, you just know. My phone rings as I'm getting ready for bed and I see that it's Zara. "Hey," I answer. "What's up?"

"I was just checking to see how you're doing, stranger."

"I'm good. I've just been really busy between hanging out with Max and doing stuff with Marie. It's just been a lot."

"Yeah, I figured," she says. "You said you're going to have a dinner party next week, right?"

"Yeah. I'm really looking forward to it. I can check with

Max if it's going to be Friday or Saturday if you want. I can't wait for you to meet him."

"Me either. How's the acting stuff going?"

"Oh, fine," I say, though a little bird in my head whispers that it's not really fine.

"Have you been to any auditions lately?"

"No, not really. I've been so focused on Max and I've been focused on working and trying to ensure that—"

"But this wasn't supposed to be a job for the rest of your life, right? You were just doing it to make money so that—"

"Yeah, but things in life change. It's not like I'm Angelina Jolie or Julia Roberts. I was probably never going to make it as an A-list star."

"But what about the fact that you wanted to get an Oscar and you wanted to write a play and produce your own show and—"

"One day, Zara. You know how it is. What's that saying? A dream deferred is—"

"Why are you deferring your dreams, Lila?"

"I'm not deferring my dreams. I'm really happy."

"I'm glad you've met Max, even though I don't even know him, and I'm glad that you're happy, but this all seems to be moving really quickly."

"I know you think that, but when you know, you know. It's not like he and I just met last night. We...sorry." I sigh deeply.

"I'm just concerned. It's not even about the relationship. I fell in love quickly as well. I just want to ensure that you're not giving up your dreams for love, because at one point you will come to resent him."

"I know, and I'm not giving up anything, okay?" I look up and I see Marie standing there, question on her face. "Hey, I'm just talking to Zara."

"Oh, I can't wait to meet her."

"Yeah, you'll meet her at the dinner party that we have. Hey, Zara, can I call you back? I'll speak to Max and see what day works."

"Okay," she says.

"I'll talk to you later."

"Sounds good."

I hang up the phone and look at Marie.

"Is everything okay? You sounded a little agitated."

"I'm fine. Zara is just concerned that I'm giving up my dreams of being an actress for the relationship, and I'm really not. I just..."

"Oh, I didn't even know that you were into acting," Marie says, and I frown slightly.

"What? What do you mean?"

"I didn't even know that you were an actress. I thought you were just Max's assistant and girlfriend."

I stare at her in surprise. My identity for most of my life has been that of Lila: wannabe Thespian. It's weird to me that I have a new friend that doesn't even know that. I guess maybe I haven't talked about it, really. Marie grabs my hand and pulls me to the kitchen.

"Hey," she says. "You look upset. You want a drink?"

"I'm okay. Actually, maybe I'll have a strawberry milkshake if you are making them."

"Sure," she grins. "I will make one special Marie milkshake for you."

She opens the freezer and pulls out a tub of ice cream and turns back to me.

"So your best friend is concerned that you've given up your dreams of acting. You tell her you haven't given up your dreams of acting, but I didn't even know that you wanted to be an actress or were an actress and I've never heard you and Max talking about it." She lets out a long sigh. "And as much as I love you and I love my brother and I'm so happy you guys have found each other, I don't want you to give up your dreams for this relationship, Lila."

"I haven't given up my dreams. I'm just so happy right now that I haven't thought about acting and I don't have that much time and—"

Marie raises her eyebrow. "Because you're working as an assistant to my brother."

"Yeah, but—"

"Come on, be honest with me. Do you really love working as a legal assistant?"

I stare at her for a couple of moments. "I love working with Max."

"Yeah, because you guys are in the beginning of a relationship. You always want to be close to the one that you love. But if you could talk about your dream job, would this be it?"

"No." I wrinkle my nose. "But I just don't know how to balance everything. I still need an income and—"

"Why don't you give up your apartment? You're here most of the time anyway."

"I am, but I just don't think it's a good idea to give up my apartment. I don't know where this is going. And like you said, it's all new and—"

"I've never seen my brother like this with anyone," she says. "Trust me, you guys are the real deal."

"Thank you for saying that, but..."

"But what?"

"But it's still new, and as much as it's been absolutely amazing, I just don't know what's going to happen and I don't want to get carried away, you know?"

"I get it," she says, nodding.

"So what'd you want to do this weekend?"

"I'm not sure. I think that...oh, hold on. Sorry. My friend Skye from work is calling me. Hey Skye, what's going on?"

"Hey, I'm just calling you because I sent you an email and I wasn't sure if you got it because I haven't heard back from you."

"No. What's the email?"

"It's about an audition for a part I think you would be perfect for."

"Oh, really?"

"Yeah, I would go, but Kingston is a jackass and he says I can't take any time off right now, so I thought it would be perfect for you, and I know Max would give you the time off."

"Time off for an audition?"

"Yeah, the role's in L.A., but—"

"Oh, I can't go to L.A. right now, Skye."

"What do you mean you can't? You don't think Max would give you the time off?"

"It's not that. It's just that...I just don't want to go right now. L.A. is so far." I press my lips together. "The fact of the matter is, I don't want to leave New York. I don't want to be away from Max. I love spending as much time with him as I can, and I know deep inside that I'm postponing my dream, but it doesn't feel like a dream anymore. It's not what I live for. I don't wake up in the morning picturing myself winning an Oscar or Golden Globe anymore. I don't wake up in the morning reciting monologues from Shakespeare. I don't wake up in the morning thinking about anything other than how happy I am to be with Max, and I don't know if that's a good thing or a bad thing, but right now I don't care. I don't even want to think about it. Thanks for letting me know Skye, but I don't think I'm going to try for it."

"Okay," she says. "Well, that sucks because I really think that you might've got the role. And while it's not a huge part, I think the film director has plans to submit it to Sundance and—"

"Hey, I got to go, okay?" I hang up because I don't want to hear about all the opportunities that could come from this potential role. I'm grateful that she thought about me, but hearing about the role is stirring something in me that resembles want and right now I don't want to want anything else. "So what were you saying about this weekend," I ask Marie.

"Did you just get an audition that you turned down?" Marie's eyes are narrowed and she's scowling at me.

"I mean, I didn't get the audition. My friend just thought there was a role I might be interested in auditioning for, but I'm not going to. So what were you saying?"

"Oh, I was going to ask you what you wanted to do this weekend."

"I'm not sure. I can ask Max what—"

"Max isn't going to be in town," Marie says, shaking her head. "I think he's going to D.C., right?"

I stare at her blankly. This was the first I'd heard about it. "What do you mean he's going to D.C.?"

"I think he's going to interview for a job. You know that his goal in life is to become a Supreme Court Justice eventually, and I think there's a job in D.C. that has opened up that would help him to start achieving some of those goals to become closer to a nomination."

"What?" I stare at her, realizing that I hadn't taken the conversation I'd had with Max about him becoming a Supreme Court Justice seriously. The conversation had gone in one ear and out the other. I'd assumed he was just talking about dreams he didn't actually think would come true; much like me telling people I wanted to win an Oscar. "He's moving to D.C.?" I stare at her and she looks nervously at me. My heart sinks as she twitches. How had I not realized how serious he'd been about his career goals?

"I mean, he didn't tell me that he's moving to D.C. I just assumed that because he's going to D.C. about a job that if he got the job, he would move there." She looks at me nervously. I mean, it's a long ways away, and I mean, I know he wouldn't just want to leave me in New York by myself. So maybe he has other plans, but...

"Oh, I'm sorry. You look devastated."

"I'm just confused. He and I have been together...I mean, we haven't been together for a super long time, but we've been together for a while and I thought we were in this really close, loving relationship, and I didn't know he had any interest in moving to D.C. I didn't know he was going for a job interview. I didn't know he was going to be away this weekend. Does that mean he's not even serious about our relationship? Am I just a placeholder in his life?" I press my lips together and Marie looks panicked. "Please don't blame yourself. I needed to know this."

"No, it's not anything. Please, Lila. I'm sorry. I shouldn't have brought anything up."

"No, it's okay. Maybe I just realized that I'm giving up dreams and aspirations for Max, but he's not doing that for me, and he's not even thinking about me and what I want and my goals and dreams and our lives together. How could he not even tell me?"

"Maybe he's planning on telling you tonight?"

"Maybe," I say.

The door opens then and Max walks in, a wide grin on his face.

"How are my two favorite girls?"

"Good," Marie says quickly. "I'm just making strawberry milkshakes. Do you want one?"

"No, thanks," he says, shaking his head as he walks over to me. He pulls me into his arms and gives me a long deep kiss. "Hey, you."

"Hi," I say, kissing him back passionately. I love the feel and the smell of him. He smells like home on a warm summer night; familiar and relaxing.

"So what do you guys want to do for dinner?" he asks.

"I think that I am going to go to a meetup tonight," Marie says. "So you guys can do dinner without me."

"Okay," he says. "If you're sure."

"I'm sure."

"What about you, darling? What would you like?"

"I was thinking maybe we could do Korean barbecue," I say softly.

"Ooh, sounds great," he says. "I love some galbi."

"Yeah, me too." I play with my hair idly and peer at him from under my lashes. "Hey, I was thinking that maybe this weekend we could go to Chinatown and..." He stares at me for a couple of seconds and shakes his head slowly.

"This weekend?"

"Yeah. Is there a problem?"

"Oh, actually, I'm going to be out of town this weekend, but maybe the following weekend."

"Oh, okay, sure. I didn't know you were going out of town."

"Oh, it was just a last minute thing," he says, clearing his throat.

"Where are you going," I ask softly, smiling as if I don't know.

"Oh, just..." he rubs his stomach suddenly. "Hey, Marie, I think I will have a strawberry milkshake after all, that looks so good." He walks into the kitchen and grabs a glass. "Do you mind making me one?"

"Sure, big bro." Marie nods slowly. Her eyes are on me and she wrinkles her nose. She noticed, just like I have, that he changed the subject.

Why would he do that? I think to myself. He doesn't want me to know that he's going to D.C. He doesn't want me to know that he's hoping to get another job. Doesn't he trust me? Doesn't he care about me enough? Maybe this relationship wasn't as serious as I thought. Am I a fool to be giving up my dreams for Max and he's not doing anything for me? The money is great, but I want more from life than money. I want more from him. And if I can't get that then I need to remember what my dreams have always been. I grab my phone and open my email and check to see the link that Skye has sent me.

I click on it and decide that I'm going to submit my name for an audition, even if it means going to L.A. If Max is looking for other jobs and doesn't care about staying in the same city as me, then I'm going to do the same thing. I'm not going to be the woman that gives up everything in my life for a man and for love when he doesn't even care about it.

My heart breaks slightly as I stare at him, dancing around the kitchen, acting goofy. He looks over at me and gives me a big, wide smile, his blue eyes light and happy. I love this man. I love him more than I thought I could ever love anyone. But I'm not going to put myself in a position where he can break my heart and leave me with nothing. I'm not going to put myself in a position where he can leave and I've got nothing to fall back upon. If he wants to have his secrets, he can, but then I'm going to have mine as well.

Chapter Thirty-One

Max

"Thanks for the ride, Henry." I say as I get out of the car and head into the office.

It's Monday morning and I've been gone all weekend and I'm missing Lila. I can't wait to see her. It's been the longest amount of time we've spent apart since we decided to start seeing each other.

I head inside and walk toward my office, but I frown when I see that she's not at her desk. It's already eleven o'clock. I grab my phone and call her, but it goes to voicemail.

"That's weird," I mumble out loud, then I decide to call Marie.

"Hey, big bro. How's it going?" She answers on the second ring, sounding her usual cheery self.

"Hey, I'm good. I was just wondering if you know what Lila's been up to."

"Um no. Why?"

"She's not at work."

"Oh, she's not back yet?" she says.

"Back from where?"

"Oh, I don't know," she says quickly, and I frown. What's she talking about? "So how was D.C.?"

"What are you talking about?" I say.

"You were in D.C., right?"

"Oh, yeah. Yeah, of course. It was fine."

I chuckle slightly. I hadn't been in D.C., but I had told Marie I was going to D.C. because I hadn't wanted her to know where I was really going and guess what I was really doing. Because I didn't want her to slip up and tell Lila anything.

"Why are you laughing?"

"I'm not laughing. I was just thinking about something," I say. "Is everything okay?"

"Yeah, everything's fine," she says. "Why didn't you tell Lila you were going to D.C.?"

"Um, she knew I was going away this weekend."

"Yeah, but she asked where you were going and you didn't tell her."

"Because I didn't want to lie to her."

"Why won't you tell her you're looking for a job on the Supreme Court? Why didn't you tell her you were going for a job interview?"

"What are you talking about, Marie? I never said I was going for a job interview."

"Then why did you go to D.C.?"

"I didn't go to D.C.," I admit, frowning. "I just told you I was going to D.C. because I didn't want you to know I was going back to South Carolina for the weekend."

"Oh," she says. "Wait, why did you go back home? Oh my gosh. It's not because of me, right? Is he angry?"

"I did go to see Dad, but it had nothing to do with you." I frown. "Why did you think I went for a job interview?"

"Because you said you were going to D.C. and I figured that was the reason why. Why else would you go?"

I sigh. "I have no idea where you got that from, but whatever."

"Lila thinks you went to D.C. for a job interview as well."

"What? Why would she think that? Wait, you told Lila I went to D.C,. for a job interview?"

"Because you didn't tell me that you were going to South Carolina and you didn't tell her either. If you were going back home, why wouldn't you tell her?"

"Because I didn't want her to know." I sigh. "Marie, sometimes you have to just keep your mouth shut. Okay?"

"I'm sorry. I just didn't know that you weren't still pursuing your dream of being a Supreme Court Justice."

"What are you talking about? You don't pursue a dream to become a Supreme Court Justice by moving to D.C. That's not how these things work." I sigh. "Anyway, you do or you don't know where Lila is?"

"I don't know. She told me she was going away this weekend and I haven't heard from her. But I know she was upset that you didn't tell her about your trip and yeah, maybe that's my fault because I kind of told her that you wanted to become a Supreme Court Justice and you might be moving."

"Marie, why would you do that? You know that..." I pause. "Anyway. I'll talk to you later. I gotta go. Okay?"

"Okay," she says. "Sorry."

"I know you didn't mean to make any trouble. I love you. I'll talk to you later."

I hang up and shake my head. *Fuck* I think to myself. I try calling Lila again, but it goes to voicemail. I decide to leave a message.

"Hey, it's me, Max. I really need to talk to you. Can you call me when you get a second?"

I hang up and pace back and forth. There's no way I'm going to be able to think about work while I'm wondering where she is. I decide to go and speak to Skye and see if she has any idea. I drop by Kingston's office and see her standing there talking to Juniper.

"Hey, you two."

"Oh, hi Mr. Spector," they say in unison.

"Can I ask you a question, Skye? Maybe you as well Juniper."

"Sure," Skye says, nodding. "What is it?"

"You don't happen to know where Lila is, do you?"

Skye looks at Juniper and Juniper looks down at the ground. I frown.

"So, I'm taking it that you *do* know where she is. Can you tell me? I really need to speak to her."

"She is not in New York right now," Skye says, looking nervous.

"Will you tell me where she is?"

"I don't really know if I should." She looks down at the ground as well.

"Please. I don't really know what's going on here and I really would like to know."

"Lila's in L.A.," Skye blurts.

"What?" I blink. "What are you talking about? Why is she in L.A.?"

"She had an audition." Sky shrugs. "And she's made it to the last round and it seems like she might get the part."

"An audition for an acting gig?"

"Yeah." Skye nods. "This could be really big for her career. You know it's always been her dream to be an actress."

"I know," I say, nodding slowly. "Thanks for the information."

I head out of the room and back to my own office, where I close the door and sit down. It's true. When I met Lila, she told me she wanted to be an actress. That had been her dream and goal and we haven't talked about it once since we'd started dating and all of a sudden I feel guilty. All of a sudden I feel like I haven't really allowed her to be herself. I've been so happy with the relationship as it was going that I hadn't thought about her other dreams. But it was also true I hadn't thought about my own dreams of becoming a judge. My life is going perfectly now that she's in it. I realize that maybe I've been selfish.

I call her again, but she doesn't answer. This time I send a photo of myself with a wry smile and then I text her.

"Hey, we need to talk."

Just as I finish sending the text, my phone rings and my heart leaps into my chest hoping it's her, but it's my dad.

"Hey, Dad. What's up?" I say.

"Just checking you made it back to New York okay."

"I did. Thank you for checking."

"I just want you to know that I'm proud of you, son."

"What?" I say, frowning slightly.

"Taking on Marie and the baby, looking after her, I know it's not your responsibility, but I know it's most likely what she needs. Her mom and I are a big mess."

"It's okay. You know I love her. I'll always be here for her."

"And you coming and asking for grandma's ring...that was a lot and I'm proud of you. I want to say that I'm excited for you as well."

"I just wanted to get the ring, Dad."

"But it's for an engagement, right?"

"It was," I say, staggering. "But..."

"But what?"

"Maybe now's not the right time. I wanted grandma's ring because I did want to propose to Lila. I think she's the love of my life, but..."

"But what?"

"She thinks I was in D.C. this weekend."

"Okay, and?"

"She ended up going to L.A. for an audition because she wants to be an actress."

"Okay, and?"

"She didn't tell me, but that's maybe because I didn't tell her where I was going. I didn't think she would mind, but I didn't want to have to lie to her. So I didn't want to say any place and I didn't want to tell her I was going to South Carolina to get the ring because I wanted to propose to her and I wanted it to be a surprise." I sigh. "But maybe everything's just happening too quickly. Maybe I am rushing her into something she's not ready for yet."

"She loves you though, doesn't she?"

"I'm pretty sure that she does, and I know I love her. I know she's the love of my life. I know I want to make her my wife, but when I met her, she wanted to be an actress. In fact, she was on her way to an audition that day, but she didn't bother because she needed to make money. And I don't think working for me is her dream, and as much as I love having her by my side, I want her to achieve her dreams and I want her to go for what she really wants out of life and I don't want to stop that because she feels like she needs to stay here with me."

"So you're not going to propose to her?"

"Not yet," I say. "I need to speak to her in person. I need to see what she's thinking and feeling. I love her so much. I don't want to let her go, but I love her enough to want her to do what she wants to do without feeling any sort of guilt."

"This *is* the one, isn't it Max?" my dad says.

"Why do you say that?"

"Because you love her enough to let her go. That's true love," he says gruffly. "I'm proud of you."

"Thanks, Dad."

"I know you think that I didn't understand when you decided not to train horses. I know you think that I didn't respect your decision to become an attorney and you had something to prove to me, but I respect you more than you'll ever know, son."

"Thank you, Dad. That means a lot."

"You're welcome."

My phone beeps and I see that it's Lila.

"Hey, I have to go, Dad. That's her."

"Good luck, son."

"Thank you." I click over quickly.

"Hey, Max, it's me."

"Hey," I say. "I was wondering when I was going to hear from you."

"Sorry, I was busy."

"I know. It's okay. So how's everything going?"

"Max, I think I have to quit," she says abruptly.

"What?" I frown into the phone.

"I know that I'm your assistant and I know that we're dating and all that, but I've always wanted to be an actress and I just got a role for a movie and I want to take it. You understand, right?"

I take a deep breath. "Yes, I understand."

"This is not how I expected everything to go. Plus, I know you want to follow your dreams, right?"

"Sorry, what?"

301

"You know, in D.C., becoming a Supreme Court Justice and everything."

I know I should tell her that I wasn't in D.C. I know I should tell her that *she's* my dream, not becoming a Supreme Court Justice, but I don't want to hold that over her head. I don't want that to be a determining factor in whether or not she takes this role. I want her to succeed. I want her to make it as an actress.

"Are you going to come back?" I ask.

"Yeah. I mean, I'll be back, but I'll have to practice my lines and get ready for this role and I just don't know if I can do that and work for you at the same time."

"That's okay," I say. "When are you back?"

"Tomorrow evening."

"Send me the flight information and I'll pick you up."

"Oh, no, you don't have to do that. I don't want you to have to keep going back and forth to the airport."

"Lila, send me the flight information and I'll pick you up."

"Okay," she says softly. "Thanks."

"Congratulations, by the way. I'm really proud of you. You're really going to be a big star one day, Lila."

"You don't have to say that, Max." Her voice cracks slightly.

"I'm not saying it just to say it, Lila. You're special, and if I've never said it before, I want you to achieve every single one of your dreams. I will always be your biggest supporter."

I want to tell her that I love her. I want to tell her that I'll always be by her side. I want to tell her that I'll wait forever for her, but that's a conversation I need to have in person. That's a conversation where I have to touch her and look into her eyes so that she can see how true and real my feelings are.

So instead, I just hang up and sit in my chair and stare at the door because I don't know what I'm going to do if she tells me that she doesn't want to be with me. I don't know what I'm going to do if she tells me that she wants to focus solely on making it as a star. I don't know what I'm going to do if she tells me she doesn't want me in her life anymore.

My heart breaks for a few moments. Everything I thought I knew about life and destiny, about dreams and goals and making it was wrong. My job doesn't matter. The amount of money I have in my bank account doesn't matter. The only thing that matters is being with the woman that I love. The only thing that matters is getting to hold her in my arms and kiss her and tell her how much she means to me. And I hope, I pray that I'm not losing her. I look at the ring that I've gotten for her, and I hope and I pray that one day it will be on her finger.

Chapter Thirty-Two

Lila

My flight arrives thirty minutes early and I decide to walk to a coffee shop and get myself an espresso while I wait on Max. I'm giddy with happiness that I landed the role of possibly my lifetime, but a part of me feels nervous and sad. I don't want to leave New York. I don't want to move to L.A. and I don't want to end things with Max like this. But when I'd received his text message saying that we had to talk, I had a feeling that he was going to tell me it was over. I had a feeling that he'd been offered the job in D.C. and was going to tell me he was going to move.

It broke my heart. I just didn't know how to think or to feel. I didn't know how my life could be upended by someone I hadn't even known for six months.

I drink my espresso and think about calling Zara or a Skye or Juniper, but I don't even want to talk to anyone. I just want to sit in my feelings. I can feel tears starting to roll down my cheeks as I sit here. I'm sad. I shouldn't feel so sad. I should feel happy. I'm about to achieve a milestone that

I've been thinking about since I was a little girl. I finally landed a role in a movie. I was going to be the star of a film with a producer that had actually worked for big studios and they wanted to submit to Sundance and to Cannes. If everything goes well, I could become a real name in the industry. It could lead to real roles that pay a lot of money and could very well set me up for stardom.

But as I sit here holding my cup, I realize I don't care about any of that. I didn't get into acting to become famous. I went into acting because I love the creative ability to be different people and live different lives and soar into different worlds. And maybe part of that was because I didn't have my own life. I didn't have my own love. I didn't have my own dreams other than acting, but now I do.

My phone beeps and I see that Max is five minutes away. I smile as I look at his name on my screen. Max has grown into the most important person in my life and it's scary. I finish my espresso, fold up the little paper cup, and put it into the trash. I grab my suitcase and roll it toward the front so I can jump into whatever car Max is arriving in.

I wonder if Henry is surprised about our relationship. He's always very polite and nice to me, but I wonder if he feels like everything has moved so quickly.

My phone rings and I answer. "Hey."

"I'm pulling up right now."

"Okay. I'm standing outside," I say. I look to the left and I see a bright red Mercedes pulling up. "Nice car," I say as I stare at the G Wagon.

"Hey, that's me," Max says, grinning.

"You're in a Mercedes?"

"Yeah, I rented one to pick you up."

"You're picking me up without Henry?"

"Yes, I do know how to drive, you know."

"I know, but you always have the driver."

"I wanted to pick you up myself," he sounds emotional and I'm not sure why. I've never heard his voice this deep before.

I watch as the Mercedes pulls over, stops, and Max jumps out of the car. He comes running to me, and because I'm stupid and girlish, I run to him too. He lifts me up and swings me around and kisses me as if he hasn't seen me in years. And I kiss him back, holding on to him like this is the last time we will ever be in each other's company. I kiss him as if he's going away to war. I kiss him as if I don't know if I'll ever see him again, and then he sets me back down.

"I like what you've done with your hair," he says, grinning.

"It's just a ponytail. I've had it in a ponytail many times."

"I know," he says, grabbing my hand and squeezing. "How was the flight?"

"Not bad. Long, but I guess not as long as an international fight."

"True." He walks over to the car and opens the passenger door. "In you go, my dear."

"Thank you. You're such a gentleman."

"I try. It's the southern man in me."

"I guess I should have dated more southern men in my life."

"Well, you won't be doing that anytime soon, I hope," he says, though, there's a concerned look in his eyes.

I just grin and he slams the door shut. I watch as he grabs my bag and puts it into the back of the car, then slides into the driver's seat.

"So congratulations again. You're going to have to tell me all about this role. What's the movie about?"

Don't Quit The Day Job

"It's called *Animals Behaving Badly*," I say, staring at him.

"What?" He raises an eyebrow as he starts the car and pulls out. "*Animals Behaving Badly?*"

"Yeah." I laugh. "It's not really about animals. It's about men and women, because at our base we're all animals."

"Okay, and what's your role?"

"I'll be playing the role of Lisa. She's just graduated from college and she is dating a middle-aged man who's married."

"Ouch," he says.

"Yeah, but it's even more complicated than that. He's actually the husband of her lifelong friend."

"What?" he says. "Her lifelong friend who's also graduated from college?"

"No. So when she was younger, she worked in a bakery for money for college, and the owner of the bakery is her friend Simone, and the guy she's having an affair with is Simone's husband."

"Oh, that sounds horrible."

"Exactly. She feels super conflicted. She loves him because she thinks he's the love of her life. Yet, she feels incredibly guilty because she's betraying Simone who's always been there for her."

"Well, yeah, she should."

"And well, basically Simone ends up dying."

"Oh, this sounds a little depressing."

"It is kind of sad. But then when Simone dies, Lisa is left a bunch of letters."

"Letters from Simone?"

"Exactly. And she reads the letters and basically, she finds out that Simone knew that she was having an affair with her husband and that Simone didn't blame her. And that Simone just wished for her the strength to leave him and to actually have her own life."

"Wow. That's dreadfully nice of Simone."

"Well, it turns out that Simone had also been the other woman and that the husband was actually her best friend's baby daddy. And that Simone had stolen him from her best friend, and that's why she knew that she couldn't judge my character because the saying is as you get them is how you lose them. Anyway, there's this scene where she goes down to the ocean and she realizes that she doesn't like who she's become, and that even though she's been blaming him, she also isn't any better." I stare at him. "Sorry, I've just been going on and on."

"No, it sounds really interesting. It sounds like a role you can really sink your teeth into."

"Yeah. I thought that it was nuanced enough to really push me to my limits because obviously, I think my character's a dog and a bitch, and I would never be friends with someone who slept with a married man. But I guess that's part of being an actress."

"I guess so," he says. "I'm excited to see the movie. When do you have to go back to L.A. to start filming?"

"I'm not sure," I say. "We might be going to Canada and a small town in Croatia."

"Oh." He looks at me. "So you won't even be in the States."

"I'm not a hundred percent sure yet. I think they're still figuring out the shooting locations." I lick my lips nervously. "So how was D.C.?"

"I wasn't in D.C., Lila," he says after a couple of moments.

"What? What do you mean you weren't in D.C.? Where were you?"

"I went to South Carolina," he says as he merges onto the freeway.

"But you were in D.C. looking for a job. Were you in South Carolina looking for a job?"

"I don't know where Marie got that from, but I wasn't looking for a job. I'm a partner at a law firm, Lila. You know that."

"I know, but your aspiration is to become a Supreme Court Justice. I thought there was some job that..."

"Oh, you and Marie really do not know much about the law and the pathway to becoming a judge." He starts laughing. "There's no job that is going to make it easier for me to become a Supreme Court Justice in D.C." He shakes his head. "I told Marie I was going to D.C. because I didn't want her to know I was going to South Carolina."

"Oh, was it about her and the baby?"

My head starts pounding.

"No," he says. "It was about something else."

"Are you going to tell me?" I ask him, wondering if he trusts me enough to tell me what was going on in his life.

"Lila, of course I'm going to tell you. I didn't want to tell you beforehand because I didn't want to ruin the surprise, but perhaps that was a mistake."

"What surprise?" I wrinkle my nose. "It's not my birthday. You're not throwing me a surprise party or something, are you?"

"No," he says. He takes a deep breath and pulls over to the right and gets off.

"What are you doing?"

"I need to have this conversation with you face to face. I think there's a little park around here," he says.

We drive for about five more minutes in silence before

he pulls over and we get out of the car. He grabs my hands and pulls me toward him.

"So Lila, there's something I have to tell you."

My heart races. *He's going to dump me* I think to myself. Tears rush to my eyes.

"I love you."

"What?" I say, and I can't stop the smile from spreading across my face.

"I love you. Like stupidly love you. Crazy, stupid, intoxicating love."

"You love me? What? That's why you pulled over? Are you just going to keep saying that or..."

"Or what?" he says teasingly.

"What do you want me to say?" I pause, pretending I'm stupid.

"Really Lila?"

"I love you too, Max. Obviously."

I reach up and put my arms around his neck. He leans down and kisses me long and hard.

"I love you more than there are stars in the sky," I say.

"Good," he says.

"Good? That's it?"

"No, I just wanted to make sure that we were on the same page before I tell you why I was in South Carolina."

"Um...you're making me nervous."

"Lila, I went to South Carolina to get my grandma's ring."

He reaches into his back pocket and pulls out a little black box and opens it. I stare down at a beautiful diamond ring. My jaw drops.

"Wow, that's amazing."

"Not as amazing as you," he says. "I wanted my grandma's ring because I wanted to use it to propose to you, but I realized that I've been selfish. I've been rushing this relationship because I love you and we've just connected so well and I think you're the funniest, most brilliant woman I've ever come into contact with. But I've realized that we still don't know each other well enough to make that step."

"What do you mean?"

"I met you and I knew you wanted to be an actress, but in the last month we haven't once talked about your acting. And to be honest, I haven't even thought about it and that's not right. I need to prove that I support you in every which way and..."

"I didn't realize how serious you were about the fact that you wanted to become a Supreme Court Justice," I say, nodding. "And I feel like I should have asked you more about those goals when we first spoke about it." I feel guilty for not having asked him more about his aspirations in life.

"I don't even want that anymore," he says. "I realized that I wanted to go down that route because I wanted to prove to my dad that I was the best I could be, because I had issues with him about his dreams for me. But I don't want to become a Supreme Court Justice. I don't need to prove anything to my dad. I love being an attorney. I love my partners and I love the work that I do, even when I sometimes represent those who do not stand on the same moral ground as myself."

I laugh slightly.

"I love you, Lila. I want to spend the rest of my life with you. I want you to be my wife. I want to have kids with you, but I also want you to achieve your goals and dreams and I can wait."

"Are you not going to propose to me anymore?" I say, staring at him and then at the ring in his hand.

"I didn't want you to have to..."

"Are you not going to propose to me anymore, Max Spector? You went all the way to South Carolina to get a ring and now you're not going to propose to me?"

"I don't want to stop you from..."

"Proposing to me is not going to stop me from going for my dreams." I glare at him.

"So you're saying you would say yes?"

"Ask me and see."

He looks down at me with so much love in his eyes that I feel like my own heart is going to burst out of my chest. He drops down onto one knee and grabs my hand and looks up at me.

"Now, this is not what I had planned or the romantic proposal that I was going to create for you, but I suppose sometimes spontaneity in life means more. I love you Lila Haversham. I have loved you since the first moment I saw you. I think we are soulmates that have been searching for each other for our entire lives. I believe that if we were here before, we were together. I believe that our souls are tethered to each other. Our spirits know that they're home. I want to marry you and I want to make you my wife. I want you to be the mother of my children and I'm willing to wait however long it takes for those children to come. I will follow you around the world. Whatever you want. I just want to be by your side. Will you marry me?"

"I feel like I have no words," I whisper.

And as I stare down at him, I realize that he's everything I ever could have wanted and dreamed of. The tears spring to my eyes and I jump up and down.

"Yes, Max. Yes! I love you so much. I love you so much. I will marry you. I will follow you around the world as well. You are definitely the other part of me. Your heart is my heart."

He slips the ring onto my finger and hugs me close to him. I reach up and touch the side of his face and kiss him.

"You know something, Max Spector?"

"What?" he says.

"When I was on the train that day and I was trying to practice my lines, I couldn't cry because I wasn't connected to the emotions. I wasn't connected to the character because I'd never had my heart broken in such a way that it meant anything to me. I'd never been that distraught by a relationship, and now here I am crying with happiness and tears that will never stop because I love you so much and I realize that's something I never had before. That's why I hadn't yet made it as an actress, and I think that's why this audition went so well for me. Because I feel the words as I say them now. I'm not just acting a part. When I say you're my heart, you're my soul, you're my everything, I feel it in every fiber of my being because you, Max Spector, you are all those things and more to me. I love you so much and I know this has gone incredibly quickly, but when you know, you know."

"I love you Lila, and before you even offer, do not even think about giving up that job. We will make it work."

My jaw drops as I stare at him. "How did you know that I..."

"Because I know you. I know how selfless you are. I know how much you love me as well, and I know you'd give up that role just to be with me. Well, now it's time for me to give up something for you. If we have to go to Croatia, to Canada, to freaking Timbuktu, I will go. I want you to make it as an actress. I want you to become a star and I will do whatever I can to make it happen."

"You know what I realized, Max?" I say softly.

"No. What?"

"I realized that my dream isn't necessarily to be an A-list actress and star in movies. It's to create. I've always wanted to write and star in my own show and I love New York way more than I love L.A."

"Thank you for saying that," he says. "Even though I would've moved to L.A. with you, I prefer New York as well. And you know what, Lila?"

"What?" I say.

"If you are my fianceé, then I think you should be okay with letting me fund a play that you put on and—"

"Max, I'm not going to have you—"

"Hold on," he says. "I haven't finished."

"What?" I say.

"I was going to make a joke about you signing a sex contract with me, but maybe this is not the time nor the place."

"Max, you're too much."

"I know, but maybe not too much that you'll still want to marry me?"

"Of course," I say. "I want to marry you and love you and have your babies and oh my gosh, what is Marie going to say?" I look at him. "She's going to be absolutely flabbergasted."

"I don't think so," he says. "You know that first day that she met you?"

"Yeah."

"She told me that she knew you were the one for me." He grins. "Marie knows me like I know the back of my hand."

"She really loves you," I say, nodding.

"And I love her and I'm so glad the two of you get along because I just feel like the luckiest man in the world."

"And I'm the luckiest woman in the world. Oh, and by the way, Max?"

"Yeah?"

"You know what you said to me that one time?"

"What?"

"You know when you said don't quit your day job?"

"Yeah," he says with a chuckle.

"Well, I'm about to tell you that I'm going to hand in my official notice because as much as I love you and as much as I love working for you, that day job is not what I want to do with my life."

"I know," he says. "And if I'm honest, as much as I love working with you as well, it would probably be a little bit better for my financial status to have an assistant that knew what she was doing and didn't throw her two cents in on every case I took."

"What? I'm still going to throw my two cents in. It's important that you represent people that..." I pause. "Okay, I'll let you do your job if you let me do mine."

"Always," he says, kissing me again. "Now, can I take you somewhere special?"

"What do you mean?"

"I mean, I haven't seen you in days and I have a cock that needs to be warm."

"Max!"

"I'm just joking," he laughs. "Unless you want to."

I reach down and slide my fingers inside the front of his pants. I'm surprised to feel that he's already hard.

"Ooh, someone's waiting for me."

"Always," he says, licking his lips. "I love you so much, and as much as I want to keep talking to you, I just need to be inside of you right now, Lila."

"Well then what are we waiting for?" I giggle. "Because I

think I've been a very bad girl and I'm going to need you to teach me a lesson."

"Oh, so you want to role play?"

"Of course, big daddy."

"Big Max, you mean."

"Super Max."

"Super Max sounds good." He runs his fingers through my hair. "When we get married, can I tell the officiant that you want to be legally wed to Super Max."

"No." I run my fingers down his arms and then wrap them around his waist. I press my head against his chest and listen to his heart beating. He reaches down and lightly squeezes my ass and then rests his head on top of mine. "When we get married, I will be saying yes to Max 'Big Daddy' Spector."

"And I will be saying yes to Maria Conchita Violeta Estella Diaz." I can feel his chest vibrating as he laughs and then kisses the top of my head.

"You remember her name?"

"I remember everything you've ever told me. It's burned into my brain." He pulls back slightly and I look up at him. "You would have gotten the role if you went for the audition."

"Unlikely." I smile and touch the side of his face. "But thank you for saying that."

"You're welcome, my sexy mamacita."

"I'm glad I didn't go to the audition."

"So am I." He presses his hardness against my stomach and growls. "I just have one request for you."

"You want me to give you a blowjob now?"

"No, silly." His face turns serious. "I just want you to know you can ask me anything. At any time. If you are nervous, worried, jealous, whatever. I'd rather you come to me then jump to conclusions about something. I don't want us to have silly misunderstandings."

"I can do that." I nod slowly and then reach up and pull his face down to mine. "I love you, Max. And I trust you. I promise to come to you when my overactive brain starts going crazy."

"Good." He says before he kisses me. "Now, let's go home before we get a citation for public lewdness because I don't know how much longer I can keep my hands off of you."

"You love me. You want to marry me. You want to sex me up all night long." I sing as he leads me back to the car. He presses me up against the door, runs his fingers up my top and then kisses my neck. I reach up under his shirt and touch his warm skin and tremble as he growls against my ear.

"I love you more than you'll ever know, Lila," he whispers in my ear. "Don't you ever forget that."

Chapter Thirty-Three

Max

Three Weeks Later

If any of my friends or family had told me that I'd be madly in love by the middle of the following year, I would have bet my life savings that they were wrong. I had never wanted to fall in love, never dreamed about having a family, never even considered falling for a bubbly blonde who was quick to jump to conclusions and even quicker to laugh. Lila was the sunshine that I'd never known I'd needed in my life. The oxygen to my lungs.

I stare at the case files on my desk and know that I'm not going to be able to concentrate for the next few moments because my mind is still on Lila and the morning surprise she'd given me. Lila never ceased to amaze me and when I woke up to her wearing nothing but my new red silk tie, I hadn't been able to stop grinning. Especially when she danced around my bedroom singing showtunes before doing her final performance on my face. I can still taste her on my lips.

Don't Quit The Day Job

I open up my laptop and click on the mail icon on the bottom of the screen so that I can email her.

From: MaxSpector@Chaseparkerspector.com
To: Lilathethespian@gmail.com
Re: The 26 ways I love you!

Good morning, I wanted to tell you that I'm grateful you are my fianceé. I also wanted to say that A is for All the ways you make me happy. I was thinking that maybe I should buy some more ties. What color would you like to wear tomorrow?

From: Lilathethespian@gmail.com
To: MaxSpector@Chaseparkerspector.com
Re: The 26 ways I love you!

Firstly, it's afternoon now, my love. Secondly, I hope you buy a blue tie to match your eyes. And I expect my own private dance tonight or tomorrow.

I want my very own Magic Max.

From: MaxSpector@Chaseparkerspector.com
To: Lilathethespian@gmail.com
Re: The 26 ways I love you!

I don't think you want to see me dancing. I'm no Channing Tatum and I don't think I ever will be. :)

But I can buy a blue tie if that's what you want to see me in.

From: Lilathethespian@gmail.com
To: MaxSpector@Chaseparkerspector.com
Re: The 26 ways I love you!

Magic Max, I want a special dance. I want to see those hips gyrating and that cock bouncing.

From: MaxSpector@Chaseparkerspector.com
To: Lilathethespian@gmail.com
Re: The 26 ways I love you!

Does thrusting count as bouncing? Is this your way of telling me you want us to record ourselves?

From: Lilathethespian@gmail.com

To: MaxSpector@Chaseparkerspector.com

Re: The 26 ways I love you!

No and no way.

I do not need to watch my boobs and belly bouncing all over the place.

From: MaxSpector@Chaseparkerspector.com

To: Lilathethespian@gmail.com

Re: The 26 ways I love you!

I love watching your boobs bouncing, preferably in my face. I miss you. How are the lines going?

From: Lilathethespian@gmail.com

To: MaxSpector@Chaseparkerspector.com

Re: The 26 ways I love you!

I love you too. I'm getting there. I can't believe we fly to Vancouver next week. I'm so grateful you're coming with me for the first two weeks. You're the best boyfriend ever.

From: MaxSpector@Chaseparkerspector.com

To: Lilathethespian@gmail.com

Re: The 26 ways I love you!

I am printing this email out to remind you of those words.

I can't wait to go to Canada with you. I may or may not have planned a couple of weekend trips for us.

From: Lilathethespian@gmail.com

To: MaxSpector@Chaseparkerspector.com

Re: The 26 ways I love you!

Where?? TELL ME!

From: MaxSpector@Chaseparkerspector.com

To: Lilathethespian@gmail.com

Re: The 26 ways I love you!

It's a secret, Lila. I have to be able to surprise you every now and then.

I laugh as my phone immediately starts ringing. Lila does not like to be kept out of the dark for any reason. I press answer and lean back in my leather chair.

"Yes, my darling?"

"Where are we going?" she demands, and I burst out laughing as she squeals. "Are you taking me to go look at bears?"

"Why would you think that?" I can't help but smile at how excited she sounds. Lila had told me recently that she always wanted to see a bear in the wild and I'd told her I'd always wanted to see a lion. So after one passion-fueled evening, we'd decided that our first trips together would be a safari in Kenya and Uganda and a camping trip to Banff...because Lila had never been and wanted to see if she'd enjoy roughing it.

"Max, tell me now. Where are we going?"

"It wouldn't be a surprise if I told you." A warm feeling spreads through me as she growls into the phone. There's something about how emotive she is that always makes me happy. "And don't bother asking Marie either. She doesn't know."

"Whatever." She laughs. "How's the search for the new assistant going, by the way?"

"Oh, I didn't tell you? Mrs. Ramsay, a retired legal secretary that worked with Kingston when he was a summer associate, applied for a job. Turns out she doesn't like being retired as much as she thought. She wanted to work with Kingston, but he has Skye, so she will work for me instead."

"Oh..." Lila lowered her voice. "So how's it going with

Kingston and Skye, by the way?" she asks casually, but I know how invested she is in my answer. I'd overheard Kingston and Skye shouting at each other the evening before, but I wasn't sure about what. When I'd asked Kingston how it was going with Skye, he'd changed the subject, but I could tell that she had gotten under his skin.

"Great," I say slowly. "I think they're a perfect match."

"That's a lie, Max Spector, we both know that they are not a perfect match. If I had a dollar for every time Skye had complained about Kingston to me, I'd be a millionaire." She giggles.

"She complained about him?"

"Honey, didn't I tell you about the hot annoying boss club that me, Skye, and Juniper created?" Her voice is bubbly. "You guys suck."

"So you're telling me I should tell my partners that their assistants are talking smack about them?"

"You better not. Or I will never let your cock see my mouth or sweet spot again."

"Oh not, not the sweet spot." I stand up and head to the door. "Are you at home?"

"Maybe, why?"

"Because I'm coming to see you."

"Max, it's the middle of the day. You need to work and I need to rehearse."

"I'm hungry."

"Order some food in."

"What I want to eat can't be ordered." I growl into the phone. "I'm hard just thinking about you."

"Hard or hungry?"

"Both." I step into the hallway and stifle a groan as I spot Kingston headed my way with a huge scowl on his face. Skye is walking behind him, her long red hair piled on top of her head and she's mumbling something under her breath. "Hey, I'll see you in twenty minutes, Lila. Love you."

"Love you more." She hangs up and I put my phone into my pocket. "Hey Kingston." I walk over to my partner and he nods without stopping. "You got a second?" I press and he nods again before turning to Skye.

"Let me speak to Max and then I will meet you in the office. Please ensure you have all the correct files on my desk and be prepared to discuss what just happened." He's almost scolding her and I watch as Skye just rolls her eyes and continues walking.

"Have a great day, Skye." I smile at her. "Lila said you're coming to dinner on Friday night, right? Look forward to seeing you then."

"Thanks, Max." She beams at me, her green eyes crinkling in the corner. "I'm looking forward to it."

"You're having her over?" Kingston raises an eyebrow as he gestures me back into my office. He watches her walk away and then turns back to me. "Good luck with that." His words may sound polite, but his tone indicates that he thinks it's going to be horrible. Interesting.

"With what?" I ask him as he closes the door behind me. "New assistant not going well?"

"Not as well as yours went." He grins and clucks his tongue. "You're welcome, by the way."

"For?"

"You wouldn't be knocking boots with Lila if I hadn't told you to hire her."

"Kingston..." I shake my head. "You're so classy."

"I know." He grins. "Gabe is back tomorrow by the way so we're going to have a morning meeting to go over the books and the status of some of our top cases."

"Sounds good to me." I nod. "It will be good to see him."

"We're going out for drinks in the evening as well, if you want to join. Not sure if the new ball and chain will stop you."

"I have the balls." I pat him on the shoulder and smirk. "And maybe I'll get some chains as well. Lila likes to experiment just as much as I do. Maybe you should get a girlfriend as well; stop you from being such a grouch lately."

"I'm not a grouch." He clears his throat and then shakes his head. "Okay, maybe I've been a bit annoyed lately, but Skye is driving me insane."

"Oh?" I hide a grin. "Why is that?"

"Let's just say she is testing my last nerves."

"So I take it you don't want to come to dinner Friday night?" I ask as he just stares at me. "I don't suppose you want to see her outside of the office, do you?"

"She thinks I never leave the office. She thinks my life is this job." He grunts. "Like I have no life. I could have ten dates tonight if I wanted. In fact, I could have one hundred dates tomorrow night. In fact, I should come on Friday with a date. Show Skye who the real workaholic is."

"Uhm?" I stare at him for a few seconds processing everything he has just said. "Is this your way of saying you're coming and bringing a date?"

"Yes." He grins suddenly. "And don't tell Skye. I want it to be a secret."

"Okay then. I hope you know what you're doing."

"Oh, trust me, I know exactly what I'm doing." He nods and heads back to the door. "Anyway, I'll see you later. I have work to do."

"Sounds good to me." I watch as he leaves my office, then I pull out my phone and text Lila. **"Make sure to get food for two more on Friday and maybe some**

fire extinguishers as well because I have a feeling there are going to be many explosions at dinner."

I smile to myself as I send the text and wonder if love might come to another member of the law firm soon.

Epilogue

Lila
Two Weeks Later

Max: Where are you right now?

Lila: A coffee shop stuffing my face with a chocolate croissant and the best coffee I've ever had in my life. I went to Le Louvre and saw the Mona Lisa and it was so much smaller than I thought it would be. The room was packed as well. I decided I deserved a treat.

Max: I'm sorry I had to work this afternoon. Wish I could have gone with you.

Lila: Max, I'm in Paris. On a surprise trip that you booked. Staring at the Eiffel Tower in the distance. You do not have to be sorry.

Max: I just thought I'd be able to spend all my time with you, but this stupid case...

Don't Quit The Day Job

> Lila: It's fine. You're a lawyer. You work hard. I understand. Plus, the nights are always ours. If I can't have all the days, that is fine as well.

> Max: I spoke to Marie and she sends her love. She wants you to find her an Hermes scarf and a Cartier watch.

> Lila: She has such cheap taste, hahaha.

> Max: Use my black card, of course.

> Lila: Of course. I do not have Cartier money. LOL.

> Max: Treat yourself to whatever you want as well.

> Lila: Max, no. I'm not with you for your money.

> Max: I know. You're with me for my big dick.

> Lila: MAX! I am blushing RED right now.

> Max: Wish I could see you.

> Lila: I'm glad you can't. By the way, it's not that big.

> Max: That's not what you were saying last night. Quite literally, in fact.

> Lila: I do not recall.

> Max: "Oh Max, don't stop, oh my, please, don't stop, fuck, you're so big, I think it's going to split my insides."

> Lila: You're an idiot. I didn't say that.

I burst out laughing as I read the texts. I love Max. I love how silly he is. I love how much of a hard worker he is. How he focuses on his job, how he focuses on me. He's one of the good guys. He really does care about making a difference.

"Excuse me, beautiful lady, may I have this seat?" A smooth French accent interrupts me and I look up with a face of regret as I'm about to tell them no. My eyes widen when I see that it's Max standing there in a cornflower-blue shirt and black jeans. His hair is slicked back like he just had a shower and his blue eyes are laughing as my jaw drops.

"Max, what are you doing here?"

"I came to find the fairest maiden in all the land." He grins as he pulls out the chair next to me and sits down. "Have you been driving all the French men as crazy as you drive me?"

"No. But that's not what I'm asking." I smile as he leans over and gives me a kiss on the cheek and shifts his chair closer to mine. "How did you find me?"

"We shared our locations, remember?" His fingers run up my bare thigh and play with the material of my denim shorts.

"Oh yes," I giggle. "I thought you were having me followed like that psycho, Mr. Whittington."

"No, goof." He runs his fingers down the side of my face and gently brushes his thumb against my lower lip. "I haven't updated you on that case yet, though."

"There's an update?" I grab a hold of his thumb and nibble on it before I suck it for a few moments. His eyes darken as he bites down on his lip. My stomach flips as he lets out a low guttural sound and leans forward to kiss me properly. His hands grab my face as his lips press against mine and his tongue seeks entry. He slides into my mouth smoothly as he kisses me and I taste the sweetness of a mint on his breath. My fingers grip into his taut muscles and by the time he pulls away, I feel like I can barely breathe.

"Would you hate me if we went back to the hotel in five minutes?" He grips my thigh again and his gaze is so intense that I feel my panties growing wet.

"Could never hate you, but I want the update on Jack Whittington," I press eagerly as I reach down and grab the half-eaten chocolate croissant. I offer him a bite, which he takes willingly, and I yelp as he takes another big bite. "Max!"

"I'm a naughty boy, I know." He makes a sad face. "I'm sorry." He pouts and then grabs the last bite. "Forgive me?"

"Max!" I lean back and cross my arms and pretend to cry. "I was looking forward to that. I was savoring every last bite."

"You can savor every last bite of me in ten minutes." He grabs my hand and squeezes. "I promise to let you enjoy every piece of me."

"You wish." I laugh and blush as he blows in my ear.

"I savored every last inch of you last night." He whispers. "I have to admit that the reverse cowgirl is one of my favorite positions, but I did miss seeing your face."

"Really?" I giggle. "You almost pulled my hair out."

"You almost made my dick fall off," he says, with such a straight face that I can't help but laugh out loud.

"It better not," I say, snuggling up to him. "So tell me, what's the latest with the Whittingtons?"

"Lucinda Whittington threatened to sue Jack for the unlawful distribution of sexual images and recordings. And she was going to go to the tabloids with her story."

"Oh shit, he didn't want bad publicity, did he?"

"Nope." Max shakes his head as he strokes my shoulder. "So he made her a new offer."

"How do you know all of this?" I ask, frowning. "I thought you dropped the case."

"I did, but Kingston is now his attorney." He shrugs. "This is just between us, Lila."

"I know." I kiss his cheek. "So what's the new offer?"

"The new offer was twenty-five million dollars." Max laughs as I gasp loudly. "Only, she didn't take it."

"She didn't? What? She wants more?"

"She just wanted her husband." He makes a face.

"But he's an asshole." I shudder in distaste. "I would have taken the money and ran."

"Well, that's not all." Max grins. "Turns out Jack had been fucking around with several other women..."

"Oh?"

"And there are three new babies being born into the Whittington Clan soon."

"Triplets?"

"Can babies born to three different women be called triplets?"

"Omg, he's a dirty dog. So Lucinda still wants him back?"

"She changed her mind about wanting to be with him." Max grins. "Instead, she asked for a hundred million and got it."

"No way." My eyes are practically bulging out of their sockets now. "A hundred million dollars? DANG."

"And do you remember the friend of hers from the spin class?"

"Uhm, vaguely. The one that was on the phone outside when we went to get the smoothies?" I ask.

"Yes, I guess her name is Marta. And guess who is now in a relationship with Lucinda?"

"No way."

"Along with Marta's husband, Nils. Turns out they believe in ethical non-monogamy and are all in a throuple and moving to a commune in Arizona."

"You're joking, right? Because there is no way."

Max's eyes are bright as he shakes his head. "Every single word is the truth."

"Dang." I giggle. "Wow."

"But I haven't told you the best part yet."

"There's more?"

"Lucinda asked Kingston to ask me if we'd be interested in doing partner swaps."

"What?" My jaw drops. "I hope you told him no."

"I told him hell no. I don't share my fianceé with anyone and my body is all hers."

"It's all mine, baby." I giggle as I run my fingers down his chest and over his heart. I can feel his heart racing as I press my palm against him. "I love you, Max."

"I love you too, Lila. Also, just know I will never ask you to sign a prenup."

"You don't want to protect your fortune from me?" I press my lips to the side of his mouth. "What if I'm a golddigger?"

"I'll take my chances." He moves his mouth so that now we're kissing. "I wouldn't care about money if I was no longer with you. You're my everything."

"Spoken like a true romantic." I caress his face as I stare deep into his eyes. "I have a feeling we're forever."

"I have a feeling that we've been together forever for centuries," he whispers against my lips. "I think that if reincarnation is real, that we always find each other. If time travel ever becomes a thing, I will always find you."

"But how will I know it's you?" My heart is about to burst in happiness.

"I'll be the dipshit who can't stop looking at you." He grins as he lightly kisses me again. "And we'll have a code phrase."

"Oh?"

"I'll tell you, don't quit the day job, and then you'll know it's me."

"You're an idiot, Max Spector." I burst out laughing as he doles out a hundred kisses all over my face. "But I love you more than life itself."

"And I love you more than the stars in the sky." He brings my hand up to his heart again and holds it there. "This is yours, Lila. All yours. Only to be shared with our kids and grandkids when we have them. You are my world. Now let's get back to the hotel before the entire city of Paris tells us to get a room."

Thank you for reading Don't Quit The Day Job. If you would like to read a bonus chapter from the book, you can get it here!

If that link doesn't work, you can get the bonus chapter here: https://dl.bookfunnel.com/4rxacqoubv.

The next book in the series is Not The Boss of The Year, starring Kingston and Skye. You can GET it here!

Dear Sir/Madam,

I would like to nominate my jerkface of a boss, Kingston Chase for the worst boss of the year award. I don't know if that's a category at your esteemed paper as yet, but if not, it should be.

Yours Sincerely,

Skye Redding

Skye,

You do realize you sent this to me, your boss, right?

Not Amused,

Kingston Chase

Kingston,

Maybe if you cracked a smile some days, you wouldn't be the monster that you are.

Skye

P.S. And of course I realized. I was just giving you a heads up before I actually submit something.

Skye,

Just so you know, you never have to let me know before you want to give me head...a heads up.

Kingston

This was the email exchange after one week at my new job. Not even I could have predicted where this was going. I had no idea just how much Kingston Chase would change my life.

GET YOUR COPY HERE!

Acknowledgments

I'm going to be honest here, I've never had a hot boss. I've had plenty of annoying bosses though...PLENTY! And a hot professor in college that made me act like a FOOLIO! But that's a story for another time.

Thank you to everyone who picked up this book and got to the end and thought to themselves, I want to read more from this author because I don't want this journey to end.

I assume that's why you're reading this. If you hated the book and you got to the end and still continued to read, you're a masochist...and I have an ex-boss to hook you up with. :)

I hope this book made you laugh as you read it. It definitely made me laugh writing it. I was laughing so hard that I thought maybe I should have a go as a standup comedian, but then realized that I'm not good on a stage. And I don't like tomatoes. Especially not in my face.

Thank you to the wonderful members of my ARC team! Thank you to my Facebook and Instagram followers who leave me comments and tell me how excited you are to read my books. When I'm feeling low and thinking my writing is awful, it is your comments that keep me going.

It has been a crazy couple of years, but I am so thankful to get to write books that I love for a living. I hope you enjoy them.

If you enjoyed this one, I'd love to hear from you.

You can email me at jaimie@jscooperauthor.com!
Here's to romance that makes us laugh and swoon!
Jaimie
XOXO

Also by J. S. Cooper

Mid Thirties Slightly Hot Mess Female Seeking Billionaire

Never Been Tamed

Worst Boss Ever